PRAISE FOR M. B. WOOD

Stranger: ... *a well-told* ... *superior second installment of an intriguing dystopian saga.*

—*Kirkus Reviews*

STRANGER

Clash of the Aliens

M. B. WOOD

WFP
WordFire Press

STRANGER

Copyright © 2018 Faucett Publishing LLC

EBook ISBN: 978-1-68057-049-6
Trade Paperback ISBN: 978-1-68057-048-9

Cover artwork by Michael J. Canales
Kevin J. Anderson, Art Director
Published by
WordFire Press, LLC
PO Box 1840
Monument CO 80132
Kevin J. Anderson & Rebecca Moesta, Publishers
WordFire Press eBook Edition 2019
WordFire Press Trade Paperback Edition 2019

Printed in the USA
Join our WordFire Press Readers Group for
sneak previews, updates, new projects, and giveaways.
Sign up at wordfirepress.com

🏵 Created with Vellum

THE STORY SO FAR ...

A brushfire war in the Middle East—fueled by ancient hatreds and fought with modern weapons—spreads globally. Islamic fanatics paralyze the industrialized nations with massive electromagnetic pulses, then follow up with decapitating missile attacks.

Chaos rules as the US financial system fails. Credit cards, checks, order entry systems—everything stops working. Food, medicine, fuel ... everything necessary for human survival becomes scarce. Soon enough, the people with guns are the ones who make the rules.

Taylor MacPherson loses his wife, Vivian, in a nuclear attack on Washington, DC. Taylor's troubles mount when thugs murder his neighbor and attack him in his home. Conditions deteriorate, and Taylor, fearing for his life, flees to the Cleveland Metropark to take refuge until order returns. Chris, a teenage refugee, tells him how her father was killed and her mother, Franny, was raped by Knuckles, a motorcycle gang member who loves classical music. Taylor, realizing that others are suffering, takes in Franny and her children. More refugees arrive and their group grows.

Even though grief-stricken by his own loss, Taylor organizes the refugees, building shelter and defenses. They settle on a hill in the Rocky River gorge in the Metropark and turn it into a stronghold.

Meanwhile, the alien Qu'uda learn that their exploratory ship, the Star Seeker, had a disastrous encounter with an alien species they call "Hoo-Lii." The Qu'uda are a long-lived, hermaphroditic species. Gender change is a survival characteristic brought on by living on a planet subject to periodic catastrophes. In response to the Star Seeker incident, the Qu'uda set up a space observatory to warn against any approaching aliens and receive a faint television broadcast—Nixon's resignation speech, from far-off Earth. Using a small asteroid, the Qu'uda build a huge interstellar spacecraft to travel to the solar system.

On Earth, during the long, hot summer, Taylor and his companions fend off a major assault by a gang. Such difficult times forge these refugees into an extended family, the Clan, whose name reflects Taylor's Scottish heritage. Franny comes out of her shell and uses her accounting skills to become Taylor's right hand in managing their scarce resources on the road to self-sufficiency. Over time, Franny learns of Taylor's loss. She consoles him and realizes he is more than a friend. During their first Christmas together, a pale imitation of seasons past, they become lovers.

More refugees arrive at the compound as starvation tightens its grip on the land. Gangs coalesce under Skid Vukovitch, who appoints himself mayor of Cleveland. Taylor rebuffs Skid's demand for tribute. Using an army of conscripts, Skid besieges the Clan's stronghold. In the battle, a sniper shoots Franny, who dies in Taylor's arms. He continues to fight and is wounded.

Franny's daughter Chris recognizes Skid as the man who killed her father and raped her sister. She leads a band of horsemen after Skid and kills him. With the gang's stranglehold loosened, trade begins once more and a measure of prosperity returns.

Taylor, heartbroken and suffering from his wounds, begins to deteriorate. Concerned about his health, his friends recruit an attractive young widow, Noelle, to be his housekeeper and take care of him in every way possible. Recovering, Taylor resumes leadership of the Clan and sets out to rebuild civilization from the wreckage of the Collapse.

ॐ

Meanwhile, the Qu'uda asteroid ship is halfway to Earth when they detect the electromagnetic pulses from the nuclear bombs. Even though their race regards those who use such weapons to be insane, they cannot turn back. The Qu'uda must continue on to the world of madness.

CHAPTER ONE

A dot of light in the cold, moonless sky brightened, stretched, and expanded into a line of white fire.

Taylor McPherson stopped, transfixed, as the line slowly crept east across a black sea of stars.

What the hell is that? Taylor shivered.

It was moving far too slowly to be a meteorite. For just an instant, he thought of the space craft his world had once launched. *Could it be a rocket climbing into orbit?* The harsh reality of life after civilization's collapse extinguished all hope of that. It had to be something else.

Moments later, the line faded away. The night sky again became a black veil sprinkled with multi-colored stars.

A worn but still functioning rail gun platform orbiting near the North Pole, a solitary leftover from before the Collapse. Heat from the fusion engine of the enormous alien spaceship aroused the platform's infrared sensors.

The rail gun platform's gyros spun into life. The platform rotated slowly and lined up on the infrared flare of the alien ship's engine.

When aligned, the solid-state relays discharged a massive current flow into the electromagnetic coils of the rail gun.

A depleted uranium slug, jacketed in a tough tungsten-steel alloy, accelerated along a hundred and fifty feet of rail to a velocity of twenty-five miles per second.

The gyros had rotated the platform too far. The slug struck the alien ship's iron-nickel hull, producing a brief flash of blue-white light.

The platform's gyros re-oriented the rail gun and its pitted solar cells recharged the capacitor banks. It was ready and the sensors locked onto the fierce fire of the ship's fusion engine.

It fired.

ॐ

Taylor glanced at the bare trees and shadows that concealed the squat homes huddled on top of the hill. This fortified community, located within the Rocky River valley, was a refuge against the savagery of the society that had emerged.

For twenty years, chaos had ruled. Now warfare and worry made the world a primitive place, stuck at the level of a pre-industrial society.

Taylor was sure the strange light in the sky was an unknown cosmic event. He rubbed his eyes and looked again at the sky to find some trace of what he'd seen.

Maybe I just imagined it.

As he turned to resume his way home, the world brightened and his shadow grew sharp, distinct. He glanced back at the sky to see a glowing ball of white fire brighter than a full moon. It faded fast. It was where the strange line of fire had lingered.

What in God's name was that?

CHAPTER TWO

The Egg-that-Flies orbited above the bright blue planet with its abundant and fertile continents. It was truly rich with life and a prize worth the long trip. Now it was time to refuel before taking possession of the planet, eliminating its mammalian life, and establishing it as a new home for a colony of Qu'uda.

Something struck the side of the ship, the Egg-that-Flies, making a sound like a hammer striking a giant gong.

Cha KinLaat DoMar, the ship's navigator, swept scanners over the exterior of the hull.

Nothing. *Maybe it was a meteoroid.* He re-oriented four of the ship's particle beam defenses on the forward section to cover its fuel tank. They normally swept debris from the ship's path while underway.

Cha KinLaat ignited the Egg-that-Flies' fusion drive and the ship accelerated. He set the course through the planet's gravity well so the ship could take advantage of the planet's rotation.

The ship's course would head toward the outer part of the system. There they would get fuel from a gas planet for its fusion drive. Then they would return.

Cha KinLaat expanded the scanner's field of view to reveal a long, ungainly satellite. *More space debris,* he thought. *This planet is so rich that its inhabitants had metal to waste.* He saw a flicker of light on the satellite.

The ship's beam weapons stuttered, emitting multiple pulses. The defense system reacted to a fast-moving slug.

The beam weapons were too late.

Even as the satellite flared into incandescence, the slug reached its destination and ripped through the outer cooling coil on the ship's drive. Polycarbon containment exfoliated in a cloud of glittering black flakes, driven helter-skelter by jetting coolant.

The drive's cooling system's pressure drop initiated an automatic shutdown.

Gravity failed as the flaring fusion drive winked out.

Cursing, Cha KinLaat lost his grip and cartwheeled through the air. He caught a handhold and scanned the readouts. He saw a major pressure drop in the drive's cooling system.

In the zero gravity, Cha KinLaat floated, disoriented. Alone in the navigation station, he had total responsibility for running the computer operating the ship's drive system. He propelled himself back to his station and gave the command to replay what had happened.

On a monitor, a data set overlay a jerky image of a smooth projectile. It was small and moving very fast.

The monitor brightened as powerful beams flashed out. The projectile remained on its original trajectory.

Oh, so that's what hit us.... Cha KinLaat thought.

"Cha KinLaat." It was Mata ChaLik, leader of the Defenders of Qu'uda, the comm-net.

"Why did the drive shut down?"

"We have a superconductor coolant pressure warning."

Cha KinLaat queried the drive computer. "What caused the pressure drop?"

Drive failure this close to a planet demanded immediate action. The Egg-that-Flies had no capability of landing on a planet—deep space was its only home. A strong gravity field would tear it apart. The ship was a giant fuel tank with living quarters at one end and a fusion drive system at the other.

"Major gas breach, external line," the drive computer said. "High gas flow rate. Shutting down affected system."

A second, higher pitched chirp caught his attention. It was the navigation computer.

"Navigation, yes?" Cha KinLaat said.

"Gas leak causing course change. Ship will enter atmosphere in one-eighth of an orbit. Shutting down affected gas distribution system."

Cha KinLaat knew they needed a sustained burn from the engine. "System status, can fusion sequence be initiated?"

"Low coolant pressure mandates system lock out," the drive system biocomputer answered. "Repair required."

"What's going on?" Mata ChaLik said. "Well?"

"The drive shut down. We may enter the atmosphere."

"May?" Mata ChaLik's voice rose. "Find out, and now."

"I'm doing that." Cha KinLaat calculated the new course. The pulse of gas from the leak had turned the ship toward the planet. "It's going to ..." He rechecked the figures. They were headed toward the atmosphere.

Fear gripped him like a predator.

Cha KinLaat knew if the Egg-that-Flies crashed into the planet, the explosive impact would be like that of an asteroid.

"Atmospheric impact imminent."

The navigation image showed the Egg-that-Flies touching the outer edge of the atmosphere, a cool, green object changing to one of flashing white.

Cha KinLaat anticipated the searing heat of the impact dissolving him into his constituent atoms. *Is this is how I die?* he thought. *This should not be happening.*

The ship vibrated with a roar that turned into an insane shriek. It shuddered and banged like a giant cymbal. The deck creaked as though about to break. Gravity came back with a surge for an instant under the deceleration from hitting the top of the planet's atmosphere.

Cha KinLaat slammed headfirst into the forward bulkhead. Pain exploded in a red haze.

I'm still alive, Cha KinLaat thought, surprised.

Once again, he floated freely in zero gravity.

The navigation screen showed the Egg-that-Flies had touched the upper atmosphere at just the right angle and had bounced off. Free from the clutches of the atmosphere, the ship coasted high into the cold safety of empty space. As the ship cooled, it pinged and crackled.

"Display course and projected course," Cha KinLaat said.

I'm astonished the Egg-that-Flies didn't break up under those stresses.

The navigation display showed the ship had a highly elliptical orbit. The apogee reached far into space, but the perigee dipped back into the top of the planet's atmosphere.

"Mata ChaLik," he called on the comm-net.

"Yes?" His voice was faint and distant.

"We're in orbit around the planet."

"Are we safe?" Mata ChaLik sounded relieved.

Cha KinLaat hesitated. "No."

The image of the Egg-that-Flies being consumed in a fiery dive into the atmosphere still haunted him, for the navigation computer projected that lay ahead.

He cringed.

"What? You have something else to tell me?"

"We will enter the atmosphere on the next perigee pass. We must boost the ship's orbit."

"Do it."

"Options for emergency drive startup?" Cha KinLaat spoke to the drive biocomputer.

"Diversion of reserve fuel to increase cooling system capacity. Not known if coolant pressure can be raised to operate drive system. Leak cause and status unknown."

"Emergency override," Cha KinLaat said. "Blow down one-half of reserve fuel through the cooling system."

He-3 fueled the on-board power supply as well as the fusion drive.

"Initiated."

"Cooling system status?" Cha KinLaat asked.

"Pressure marginal and fluctuating, temperature stable."

It violates normal procedures, but I have no choice. We must have thrust, he thought. *This is a job for Bilik Pudjata, the builder of the drive system.* "Bilik, come to the navigation station and take control of the drive system. We must get it started. Only you know how to do that."

Bilik knew that something was very wrong, but he knew the drive system and its computer. "Start drive sequence."

Helium-3 entered the propulsion tube where lasers flared like a colony of stars. The fuel ignited. The fierce heat expanded the gas in the cooling system. Pressure rose, the leaking coil stretched and ruptured. Coolant spewed into space.

The superconductor coils overheated. Magnetic fields convulsed and collapsed violently. White-hot fusion plasma, pinched by the dying gasp of a powerful magnetic pulsation, cascaded into a fusion explosion. A globe of pure energy blossomed on the stern of the Egg-that-Flies.

The explosion slammed the ship forward.

Bilik collided with the rear bulkhead. There was no up or down. He spun freely in the zero gravity and absolute darkness, lost somewhere in nowhere.

Is this death? Distantly, words echoed.

Dizzy and sore, he focused on them.

"Bilik, answer me. What happened?" The harsh tonalities of Mata ChaLik's voice anchored him.

"The fusion drive ..." Bilik said, barely able to speak. He dug his claws into his sides. Their sharp bite helped him regain control. "I don't know." His head throbbed violently.

"We have no drive," Mata ChaLik's voice was lower in volume but even more difficult to ignore. "I see no data on my comm-net. What happened?"

Emergency lighting brightened into a dull orange. Alarms bleated throughout the ship. Dust and debris floated through the navigation station's air.

Bilik grabbed a claw-hold and stared at the status monitors: The hull was intact; the life support systems still functioned. *The ship is tougher than I thought.* Warning icons for the propulsion system flashed randomly. He activated the outside monitors. He could not see the propulsion system.

"I tried to start the drive system," Bilik said.

Nothing seemed to make sense. Pain filled him.

"Explain what happened," Mata ChaLik said.

"The propulsion system—" Bilik started to say.

"Get on with it."

"Egg-that-Flies, do you hear me?" a voice came from the external communication system.

"Who is that?" Mata ChaLik's voice resonated with anger.

"This is Dekah NahBu, scout-pilot on the third Bird-that-Soars. I was inbound to dock on the Egg-that-Flies when I saw an explosion. The back of the ship vanished. Everything aft of the fuel tank is gone. Nothing but ragged metal remains back there."

"Everything is gone?" Mata ChaLik asked. "Everything? Navigator Cha KinLaat, what is our new orbit?"

"It looks stable, but for how long, I don't know."

"Figure out how much time we do have," Mata ChaLik said. "And quickly."

"Yes, Mata ChaLik, leader of the Defenders of Qu'uda, I hear your command."

༇

Bilik's calculations revealed the explosion had raised their orbit but it would still lose velocity on each perigee pass. "The Egg-that-Flies has somewhere between 2,000 to 4,000 orbits before it drops into the atmosphere."

"I see. Send me a more precise estimate. This time, use a private channel," Mata ChaLik said. "Do you understand?"

Bilik replied using the formal title acknowledging the rebuke. "Yes, Mata ChaLik, leader of the Defenders of Qu'uda, I understand."

CHAPTER THREE

Taylor MacPherson stared at the fading after-image in the night sky. *Could someone have found a working ballistic missile?* The idea stirred memories. A flash of fear flooded his feelings.

Twenty years ago, a war in the Middle East fueled by ancient hatreds and fought with modern weapons became global. Fanatics resorted to nuclear weapons, first attacking with massive high-altitude EMP bursts that paralyzed the electronics of the industrialized nations. Supine and blind, the nations lay defenseless against the nuclear tipped missiles that came next.

A lump formed in Taylor's chest. His wife, Vivian, had been in Washington DC along with millions of others on the east coast and had been incinerated in the nuclear fire.

Ohio was untouched, for none of its cities had been targeted. Taylor still found it hard to believe how quickly—within days—the financial system had failed and anarchy had become the norm.

A breeze stirred the tall oaks and beech trees. The top of the mesa-like hill was almost surrounded by the river. Most of the horizon was visible from this lookout point eighty feet above the Rocky River. He turned onto the stone path that led into the familiar warren of houses on this mound called the Hill.

Taylor paused on the steps of his home—a blocky sandstone two-story house. How different it was from the early years, especially that first winter. That was when Franny had become his lover and found they were made for each other. During a siege of the hill, a sniper had killed Franny and his heart was broken again.

Taylor stared at the carpet of stars in the night sky—millions of them, and in all colors. *I wonder what was it that just flared so brilliantly? This is what it must have been like in the middle ages.* It reminded him of the cold clear nights of the first winter and the harsh conditions that had brought waves of refugees as starvation gripped on the land.

Civilization had collapsed to a medieval level.

It was Chris—Franny's daughter, now a battle-hardened fighter, who had recognized the man who'd killed her sister and raped her mother. She had gone after him and killed him without mercy.

Chris and her horse-mounted fighters had swept northern Ohio clean of the gangs; they were the ones who had restored peace to northern Ohio. After that, trade had begun and brought a measure of prosperity. *That was key to our survival.*

Over twenty years, Taylor had learned the lights of civilization around the world had gone out. During that period of time, there was constant warfare fought at a primitive level. Technology had disappeared. The more Taylor thought about the strange lights in the sky, he was sure they may not have been natural events.

They worried him.

CHAPTER FOUR

"How long to make the repairs?" Mata ChaLik's voice boomed from the comm-net.

"The explosion destroyed both the propulsion system and the spare propulsion tubes."

Bilik Pudjata had constructed the drive system and his duties included maintaining it. However, he had never expected the need to build a new system far away from the support of their home planet of Qu'uda.

"Then make a new one."

"We do not have metal forming equipment to make a new propulsion tube." Bilik chose his words carefully. "We brought spare parts instead of equipment, remember?"

He had fought a losing battle to install equipment to fabricate new parts. Mata ChaLik had insisted on bringing additional weapons, which took up valuable cargo space originally allotted for the metal fabricator and other tools.

"Surely you can make a propulsion tube. We have an abundance of iron, plenty of power, and skilled crew members." Mata ChaLik used a tone reserved for ignorant trainees. "So, when will you have the drive system restored?"

"Mata ChaLik." Bilik kept his voice low and neutral. "We cannot cast iron under zero gravity conditions and make a part with the required integrity. So, to make it within the gravity centrifuge, we must remove the food production and air regeneration system to get enough space to build a metal caster."

He referred to the complex agricultural system that was the heart of their life support system.

"Once uprooted, it will be impossible to restore, which means the ship will lose its capability to travel between the stars. We will be forever dependent upon supplies we carry, which would be insufficient for a long voyage. That would mean we could never return home."

"What?" Mata ChaLik's voice quavered with anger. "I do not want to hear what you cannot do. You must rebuild the Egg-that-Flies' propulsion system. And soon. Do you not understand?"

"I cannot do it on the Egg-that-Flies. It does not have the space or the equipment."

Silence descended on the comm-net. All had heard his words.

"Then, Bilik Pudjata, go to where you can make the parts for the propulsion system. Go to the surface of the planet below and make the parts." Mata ChaLik's voice had a deadly quality. "That is an order. Do you understand?"

"Yes, Mata ChaLik, leader of the Defenders of Qu'uda, I understand." Bilik acknowledged his authority.

If we abandon the ship, Bilik realized, *we'll be refugees on an alien world. Sooner or later the ship will crash into the planet below. That's sure to devastate its ecosystem.*

A mixture of fear and anger nibbled at Bilik's mind. *Right now, the only thing we have is limited time and that lies heavy upon our claws.*

He knew there was not even enough fuel left to send a message drone back to Qu'uda.

A wave of fear expanded from the corner of Bilik's mind.

༄

"Bilik Pudjata."

"Yes, DalChik DuJuga." Bilik recognized the familiar voice of the spokesperson for the Keepers-of-the-Egg. The Keepers had the responsibility to counterbalance the military authority of the defenders and maintain internal harmony.

"You must be surgically altered to resemble the aliens so you can move freely among them."

"Really? Is that necessary?"

Their society valued conformity, including appearance. To be non-conforming in either thought or appearance meant to be sidelined from the center, out of favor, without influence.

"Can you make a propulsion tube here?"

"No."

"Do you have metal forming equipment?"

"No."

"Then you must go among the aliens to find those items needed to make a replacement propulsion tube," DalChik said. "The change in your appearance is for your safety and benefit."

DalChik DuJuga told Bilik how the Keepers-of-the-Egg had come to their decision and how the ship's medical team would shape him and fit him with a mask to make him look like an alien. He did not tell Bilik their image of the planet's natives was based solely on the observations and images taken by a scout in a high-flying Bird-that-Soars.

It took the medical team several days to lengthen his arms, flatten his face, and give him a nose. During surgery, they removed his head crest, his stubby tail, and the webbing between his digits.

When he woke up, Bilik discovered they had removed the claws from his feet, which made him feel almost naked, defenseless. They dyed his skin and implanted fibers on his head and face to match the aliens' hair. They installed lenses to hide the vertical pupil slits and orange color of his eyes. They fitted him with a face mask made from a breathable polymer to complete his disguise.

Bilik became totally different, no longer recognizable as a Qu'uda.

Bilik found they had replaced his original biocomputer with two larger and more powerful personal biocomputers. He felt like he had lost a friend, for one of the new biocomputers was a vocal stranger that spoke many languages. The second biocomputer, economical with words, served as his personal defense system and provided communications via a satellite inserted into a geosynchronous orbit. It was the personification of a male warrior, which it urged Bilik to become.

The surgical team modified his hormonal system to increase his muscle growth and strength, which made him totally male. There was no "she" left in his psyche or body. Never again would he be an egg-bearer, for the flood of male hormones had destroyed his female aspect.

Bilik was bigger, stronger, and faster than any of the crew but still smaller than most of the aliens.

The crew's attitudes told Bilik they were now afraid of him. He no longer felt like he belonged—it was like he was an outsider, far from the center. He sought out the spokesperson for the Keepers-of-the-Egg.

"DalChik, my appearance repels my crewmates. What can be done about this?"

"When your mission is over," DalChik said. "We shall reverse your modifications and you'll be made to look like us again. The surgical team will look upon this as a great opportunity to practice their skills."

That gave Bilik scant comfort.

It was now time to take the last remaining Bird-that-Soars down to the surface of this strange planet for a closer look.

CHAPTER FIVE

Bilik piloted the Bird-that-Soars—a shuttlecraft—down through the atmosphere during the middle of the night. The bumpy ride took him to a section of land along the southern edge of an inland freshwater sea —it was the shallowest of the five freshwater seas, adjacent to rich, fertile land.

Remote surveys had shown it was the most likely area to have iron. It was the southern-most body of water of the five. Inland, the terrain was flat with widely scattered native dwellings and communities.

Bilik activated the craft's array of sensors and scanners, which detected traces of metal, much of it iron. *There has to be equipment to melt it*, he thought. He started scanning the individual buildings.

The sensors indicated a group of buildings that were especially rich in iron, the signature of a foundry. *This world was once highly developed*, he thought. *Iron is everywhere, much more than our home world of Qu'uda.*

The foundry was adjacent to the confluence of two rivers where there was a community of natives. It was time to take a closer look.

Bilik slowed his craft to a hover and descended in the large open area alongside the building. He worried the shuttle's size would make it difficult to conceal even under the cover of darkness. He scanned the area and detected no movement or warm bodies before climbing down from the craft. Earlier tests confirmed the atmosphere was breathable and free from pathogens.

Yet, he wasn't ready for the exotic aromas of this strange world—a mixture of fragrant and metallic scents, overlain with the stink of decay. Once on the ground, he found lush, soft vegetation underfoot. The smells both excited and worried him. The odor of decay suggested to him there had been much death and destruction here.

Inside the building, he found piles of metal fragments and slag, which confirmed it was an iron foundry. His hopes rose, but a close examination revealed the equipment was a mass of flaking rust. Water from a leaking roof had dripped on the equipment. It was corroded beyond repair.

Once back in the shuttlecraft, Bilik started its fusion engines and rose vertically before accelerating into an easterly flight. Bilik again flew the craft slowly, scanners and sensors recording data continuously.

After crossing a wide river, the sensors once again indicated the presence of iron concentrated in a small area. It was contained within a building that appeared undamaged.

Bilik put the craft down some distance from the building and activated the scanning equipment, again checking for signs of mammalian life. Detecting none, he left the shuttlecraft and went inside the building. The roof appeared sound and there was no water damage. Deeper into the cavernous building, he stopped in front of a tall, cylindrical structure surrounded by slag and iron fragments.

It looks like a metal melter, he thought, *but where's its power connection?* An abundance of slag and metal fragments convinced him it had been used to melt iron. He clambered up the adjacent metal stairway and peered into the huge cylinder. He accessed the memory section of his biocomputer to see if there were any technologies his civilization had used that were similar to this device. It wasn't long before he got his answer.

Great Egg! It's a primitive iron-melter. It uses combustion for energy. Bilik realized it was technology his civilization had abandoned many generations ago. *This will never do.*

Bilik picked his way through the maze of machinery in the dark building, heading back toward the Bird-that-Soars. Before he got to the building's entrance, his beam-light illuminated several large cables descending down a wall. He stopped, for they reminded him of power conductors. He followed them to a large dust covered cylinder that was tilted at an angle.

Yes! He thought. *This looks like a type of iron melting equipment.* He climbed a worn metal ladder up to its top, examining it in detail. Yes, it was primitive, but it was an iron-melter. He felt a surge of hope. However, it was not large enough to make a propulsion tube in one pour. He carefully examined the equipment and became more convinced it was undamaged.

Now, if it had power—a lot of power—it might work. Perhaps I can make the propulsion tube in sections. He headed back to the Bird-that-Soars with images of the iron melter stored in his biocomputer. He began to formulate a plan.

CHAPTER SIX

On his second trip to the surface, Bilik took time to observe the alien natives who were primitive mammals. He set up remote devices to eavesdrop on their conversations and fed the recordings of their language to his biocomputer.

Downwind of their crudely built dwellings, he could smell a combination of strange food, unwashed bodies, excrement, and burning vegetation. The natives wore clothes made from roughly woven fabric or animal skins.

Those in the ship above readily believed his stories of the natives' filth and poverty. After all, they were mammals. He also discovered the large joint in the middle of their lower limb was opposite to his, which explained their strange gait.

Bilik's language biocomputer steadily increased its vocabulary and relentlessly drilled him in the local language. The natives' speech seemed high-pitched, full of squeaks when compared to the cadence of his own language. It took almost a full cycle of seasons of relentless drilling by his language biocomputer before Bilik felt confident enough of his alien language skills to approach a native. He chose to contact a native who lived alone by the river in a primitive and odorous dwelling.

He screwed up his courage and walked up to the native who was sitting on a log next to a dwelling.

"What's yer name, stranger?" the hairy-faced creature asked. His digits continually moved, scratching at his body.

"My name is ..." Bilik struggled to pitch the words in the squeaky fashion of his questioner. "Bilik Pudjata."

"Billy whut?"

The creature leaned against the side of his dwelling, which was crudely constructed from vegetation. A wisp of smoke curled from the top of the structure and the smell of roasting meat permeated the air.

"Bilik Pudjata."

"Billy Pertater? Like spuds?" The native plucked at a mouth opening vaguely visible beneath a luxuriant growth of hair.

"Yes, Bilik Pudjata."

"My name's Ed Pratt. Where're you from, Billy?"

"From far away." He hesitated as he recalled his stratagem. "It is a small place, called Qu'uda."

"Cooter? Can't say I've heard of it." Ed Pratt squinted at him. "What're you doing in these parts?"

"I need a new part for ... I need an iron melting place."

"Something made of iron, eh? Well, you'd better go into Defiance, then. There's craftsmen there, there is."

"Defiance?" Bilik asked. "What is Defiance?"

"Defiance? That's the city just up the road." Ed pointed in the direction of the community. "You best go there for anything made of metal." He paused. "Watch what you say, though. Ol' Vic's boys can be downright nasty if you rub them the wrong way. They be a real violent bunch, they be. You get what I mean?"

"Yes," Bilik said. *Rub them? Am I supposed to couple with them?* The subtleties of meaning in the language had begun to overwhelm him. His head started to ache from the effort of trying to understand this hairy native. He needed to check with his biocomputer on the meaning of the conversation. "I think I understand." He also wanted to bathe after this encounter. "Thank you, Edpratt."

ᘒ

Bilik, or Billy Potato, as he was now known, soon found Edpratt liked
to talk and he told him more about their culture.

They called this planet "Earth." There had been a collapse of their
civilization. The Earth people's lack of community and disorder
disturbed him. It reminded him of the primitive times before Qu'uda
developed into a civilized society, a time of savagery and chaos when
life had little value.

After hearing Edpratt's tales of violence, he assembled a suit of
body-armor used by the defenders and took to wearing it as a regular
item of his apparel. He also took up wearing a long cloak and a hat to
cover the difference in his appearance from the natives.

In time, he learned Defiance was an old city that had survived the
war and was the headquarters of something with the title "The Mid-
West Federation" in a place formerly called the state of Ohio.
Compared to communities on Qu'uda, it was small, and without
saying, very primitive.

After his third visit with Edpratt, he accepted an offer to eat a meal
with him. The food was flavorful, but he found it difficult to digest
until his stomach made peace with the local bacteria. Eventually, he
acquired a taste for roasted meat, which was an exotic item in the
Qu'uda cuisine.

He began to eat meat regularly in place of algae derived meals.
Soon he found his energy was lagging and he began to lose weight. He
knew he had to do something and took the shuttlecraft back up to the
Egg-that-Flies and sought out the medical team.

ᘒ

"Look," the leader of the surgical team said. "The native food is low in
these amino acids." He pointed to the holographic display. The defi-
ciencies glowed blue and large.

"What can you do about that?" Bilik asked.

"We'll modify your biocomputer to make them for you," the
surgical team leader said. "The native species blood is red because it

has too much iron." The blood of all creatures on Qu'uda was purple-red in color. "So, once we modify your blood to chelate and discharge the excess iron, you can eat the natives' food."

Secretly this pleased Bilik, for everything on the ship, including the crew, now seemed, well, bland.

Bilik's skin also had become dry and scaly. The surgical team discovered the dye used to make him look similar to the natives did not protect him from ultraviolet radiation coming from this planet's sun.

Once again, the medical team modified him to make him more adaptable to this new world. He also obtained a combat helmet with a broad brim that looked somewhat like the hats worn by the natives for protection from the weather.

It was time for Bilik to return to the surface. Since their arrival, the northern hemisphere had gone from a season of warmth and lush growth to one of ice and snow. It was equivalent in time to more than one full year in the native planet's time. The rate at which plant life grew during the warm season was far faster than on Qu'uda. This was a rich and fertile planet.

CHAPTER SEVEN

"Hey, you." Al Luciano swaggered through the crowded market, his breath steaming in the cold air. "Yeah, you, Billy-the-Freak. C'mere, gimme your hat and coat."

A flurry of snow curled off the edge of a nearby red brick building.

Billy looked up from under his wide-brimmed hat. He hiked up his long, loose-fitting gray cloak off the pavement and took a step back. He'd adopted the long coat to hide the difference in the way he walked compared with the natives. In addition, it provided protection against the harsh climate.

"Why should I give you my hat and coat?" He continued to examine a cabbage he'd just picked up at a produce stall and wondered what it tasted like.

"I'm going to a New Year's Eve costume party an' I wanna look real strange." Al nudged his companion, Big Jim Dilworth, who towered over him. "Like you, spud-head. So gimme." Al was five feet six inches tall, with a face that held a perpetual frown.

Billy put the cabbage down. "You cannot have my hat and coat." He pulled the coat tighter. "I need them to keep warm."

"Hey, spud-head. Are you stupid or what? When I tell you to give me something, you give. Get it?" A touch of red blossomed in Al's face.

The shoppers became quiet, craning their heads to watch.

Al approached Billy with hard, exaggerated movements. He glanced at his companion, Big Jim, who was a large human. "I'm gonna teach you a lesson, you stupid freak." He swung a roundhouse blow.

Billy recoiled. He'd already learned he was much quicker than the natives, and stronger too.

Al missed. He glanced at Big Jim as if to make sure he was there. "Jim, grab him." His voice went up an octave. "I'm gonna teach this wise-ass a real lesson."

Big Jim lurched forward, hands reaching.

Billy hopped to one side and lashed out with his foot, striking Big Jim on the ankle. It made a sharp, thudding sound.

The big man skittered sideways and landed hard on the wet street. He wrapped his hands around his ankle and began to whimper.

"Why, you little shit ..." Al reached for Billy.

Billy caught Al's arm and twisted it. It cracked.

Al flopped to the ground like a wet burlap sack, right arm at an awkward angle, and began to howl like a baby.

Billy hurried away onto a side street.

The following Thursday, market day in Defiance, found Main Street wet, littered, and noisy with an eager bustle as though on parole from winter's icy prison. Snow piled alongside the red brick buildings had grown dingy and crystalline, aged by a warm south wind. Drizzle drifted down from a sullen, lead-colored sky. Puddles of muddy water filled the potholes in the street.

Billy's boots squished as he walked from stall to stall. He was fascinated by the variety of food, which changed with the seasons. However, he was disappointed by the quality of the clothing and tools. As he crossed the street to see more stalls, he heard a voice boom out over the market's noise.

"Yo, Billy-the-Freak. Hold it right there, don't move." Oaky Littlewood, captain of Old Vic's guards, had a voice that boomed like a mallet on sheet steel.

The three men with him pointed their flintlock rifles at Billy. Shoppers backed away with a wave of nudges and whispers. For a moment the only sound was the flapping canvas of the stalls' awnings.

"Billy-the-Freak," Oaky said in a loud voice. "You're under arrest for assaulting Mr. Al Luciano and Mr. Jim Dilworth."

Billy searched for the meaning of assault. "I did not assault them. They attack me. You must arrest them."

"Say what?" Oaky's eyebrows rose. "Are you for real?"

"They attack me. I did not assault them."

Oaky raised his hand. "This guy is really weird."

The guards' guns came up. The crowd flowed back like a wave retreating from the beach, making hissing sounds like that of surly surf.

Billy stood alone in the center of the street.

"Go on, you little freak, run." Oaky made a gesture like that of a cat touching a mouse. "Run, save me the trouble."

Billy nodded, for he was sure Oaky had just told him he was free to go. He started to cross the street.

A guard sighted his rifle and fired at point-blank range.

Billy felt a flash of surprise as a hammer blow struck him in the chest. He staggered and fell. For a moment, his world disappeared in a wave of pain. He opened his eyes—smoke was everywhere. It was difficult to breathe. He could see Oaky's men laughing and pointing at him.

"Damn, I hope I didn't ruin the cloak Al wants." The guard who had fired the gun nudged one of his fellow guards.

"Look at the poor little guy, he's bleeding to death." Individual voices in the crowd had a crystal-clear quality, though faint and distant. "They gunned him down in cold blood."

Billy's anger boiled up, ugly and hot. He sat upright.

Silence fell.

Billy pointed his hand at the closest guard and activated his personal defense system.

The biocomputer drew upon the emergency energy cells. The lasers in the holographic projectors alongside his head discharged four times, each with a loud cracking noise like that of a gunshot. One by one, the guards toppled to the ground. Each had a small round hole in the center of their foreheads. His anger left him as fast as it came.

Animals, nothing but savage animals, he thought.

Billy struggled to his feet.

No one spoke. No one moved.

Billy lifted his hand off his chest. Dark blood dripped from his fingers. He struggled to his feet but could only stand hunched over. He looked up at the crowd, but none met his eyes.

He staggered away, leaving a trail of dark drops on the wet road.

Billy wasn't sure how he reached the Bird-that-Soars. It was an hour's walk east from Defiance and hidden deep within a swampy area. Once on board, he peeled away his clothes. Pain came in waves as he pulled the armor cloth off his chest and out of the shallow wound. The cloth had retained a flattened lead slug, which he removed.

His biocomputer started pain deadeners and growth stimulants. Numbness slowly spread. Thoughts of his early years on Qu'uda floated through his mind. Life had been easier and more comfortable. These thoughts, too, faded away as a narcotic-fueled sleep descended.

Billy woke the next day, needing water and to relieve himself. His chest still throbbed with pain. He had been unconscious for almost a day. Sleep again came quickly, and the following day, he woke hungry. He knew that meant his body was on the mend. As he recovered, he had time to think and make plans. *It is time*, he realized. *I've got to take control and organize these mammals.*

CHAPTER EIGHT

Billy returned to Defiance several weeks later.

"Billy, you're alive? It's a miracle." Everywhere he went, people expressed surprise.

By now, he knew he was faster and stronger than the natives. His personal defense system could out-shoot them, too. When a man threatened him with a gun, Billy killed him without hesitation. Soon, he could walk anywhere in Defiance. It was as though all the men with guns had disappeared.

Billy walked down Clinton Street, the main street of Defiance, between the red brick buildings and glass-fronted shops. It was time to visit the man who ran the Mid-West Federation and get him started on making the propulsion tubes.

He knew the leader's name was Old Vic, and he used the largest building in Defiance as his nest or home. He planned to ask Old Vic to help him with his project to make parts for the ship. He approached the ornate, red brick building the natives called the Court House.

It was time.

"You little shit." Old Vic Caputo, leader of the Mid-West Federation, stepped out of the Court House's front door. He held a sawn-off double-barreled shotgun.

Billy turned at the sound of his voice.

People scrambled off the sidewalk.

"Kill my men, will you?" Old Vic raised his gun.

Billy felt time slow down. He jerked his head up and fired his lasers. Old Vic stumbled, one hand clutching his shoulder. The gun wavered in his other hand. Shaking, he raised the gun and fired.

The muzzle blast took Billy's hat off.

Billy steadied his aim and fired his lasers.

One of Old Vic's eyes became a small black hole and the second laser discharge made a hole in the center of his forehead. The gun fell from Old Vic's hand. He pitched face-first onto the street, twitched once, and became still.

Billy put his hat back on and carefully adjusted it. He glanced around to see if anyone else would challenge him.

The street remained silent. Pale faces peeked around corners of buildings, from doorways and every window. Now he knew he could use their fear to control them.

Billy beckoned to two men cowering in the entrance of the Court House. "You," he said. "Come here. Take that." He pointed to Old Vic's body. "Get rid of it."

The men hesitated, glancing around.

Billy raised his hand and pointed. "Did you not hear me?"

"Yes, sir. Right away, sir." They hurried over to Old Vic's body and picked it up off the road. They headed south on Clinton Street, the corpse hanging limply between them.

Billy watched until they were out of sight. *So much for getting Old Vic's help*, he thought. *However, his organization still exists.*

He picked up Old Vic's gun and walked into the gloomy old courthouse he'd learned was the Mid-West Federation's headquarters. Within, white, staring faces retreated before him. Billy cornered a man who forced a weak smile. "Take me to Old Vic's room."

"Yes, sir. Anything you say, sir."

The man led Billy to a neatly dressed man who sat behind a polished desk in the large office. "This is it," he said and scurried away.

Billy pointed his hand at the man behind the desk. "You will serve me. If you don't, I will kill you." He'd found these creatures responded better when afraid.

"Yes, sir. Absolutely. Whatever you want."

"I want a function-responsibility diagram," Billy said.

"A what?" The man's mouth opened, and his eyebrows knitted. "What is it you want?" He stared. "Sir," he said.

"I want to know who does what and who reports to whom."

"Oh, you mean an organization chart." The man scrambled to the same side of the desk where Billy stood. "Please." He pushed a chair forward. "Sit here. I'll give you a picture of old—" He hesitated. "I mean the Mid-West Federation. I'm Olny Hornyak, executive administrator. I'm only too happy to help you."

"Is there a power generator nearby?"

"A power generator? Ah, what kind of power?"

"For electron flow generation."

"Ah, electron? Generation? Er, electricity? Well, that sounds like pre-Collapse technology. Ah, you need to talk to one of the old codgers," Hornyak said. "Do you mind if I ask why you need electricity? We really have had no need of it for such a long time. It's really quite passé."

"Which old codgers?"

"Ah, let me think. Ah, well, Kevin O'Neil, yes, he should know. Would you like me to get him for you?"

"Now."

"Ah, now?" Hornyak swallowed. "Yes, of course. Excuse me a moment." He hurried to the door. "Greenwood," he yelled into the hallway. "Get your ass in gear and bring Kevin O'Neil here. Take two guards and no arguments. Immediately."

A small, mouse-like man appeared. "You mean the old dude?"

"I'm not telling you twice, Greenwood, move it."

"Yes sir, Mr. Hornyak, I'm on it."

"Mr., ah, Potato. Is that how you prefer to be addressed?"

"Call me Billy."

"Ah, yes, Billy." He paused. "I'll have Kevin O'Neil here as soon as is possible. What else can I do for you?"

"Which was Old Vic's room?"

"Ah, you mean his executive suite?"

"Yes."

"Step this way. I'm sure you'll find it is quite suitable to your needs. If you want it changed in any way, please let me know, and I'll take care of it. That's what I do, take care of things." The smile on Hornyak's face widened. "And I'll bring you the organization chart."

∿

A stocky, balding man dressed in patched clothes shuffled into the office, hat in hand, which he held close to his chest. A fringe of gray hair framed a heavily lined face. "I'm Kevin O'Neil," he said.

"Is there a power generator nearby?" Billy stared across the wide, empty desk. He'd removed all the pictures from the wall and drawn the curtains to reduce the bright sunlight. He still found the executive suite to be much larger than what he needed. At least it was warm.

"Power generator? Now, I haven't heard anyone use that term in many a year," Kevin said. "I assume you mean an electrical power generating system?"

"Yes." Bilik guessed it was their term.

"It's funny, but one of the last things I did before the war started was to mothball three gas turbine generators just outside Defiance."

"Do they still work?"

"No. Well, maybe." Kevin frowned. "Turbines need fuel. I mean, they burn natural gas and produce a stream of hot gas that spins the turbines. There isn't any natural gas, at least none that gets to Defiance."

"How much power did they generate?"

"They were rated at fifteen megawatts each and each could supply enough for several communities. They were back up for the GM casting plant, I mean the foundry."

In Billy's mind, that spoke of plentiful capacity. He had an idea how to make them work. "Where are they?"

"They're outside the city limits." Kevin raised his hand. "Now, I don't know if they're still usable. They've been dormant a long time. Hell, maybe someone has screwed with them."

"Where outside the city limits? How far?"

"Northeast of the city, about a fifteen-minute walk."

"Show me."

"When?"

"Now."

ᘛ

Under several layers of tattered blue plastic film, which was covered with a thick layer of dirt and debris, Billy found three generators.

Yes, he thought, *primitive, but usable.* It would be easier to work on them inside Defiance's defense perimeter. That would be nearer to the shops of the craftsmen and other facilities, which lay across the Maumee River. *Maybe this Kevin O'Neil knows how to move the generators.* He did not want to use the Bird-that-Soars so close to this alien community.

"The turbine generators must be moved to the industrial complex next to Defiance, near the foundry. Can you do that?" Billy asked.

"Let me see." Kevin scratched his head. "If I remember correctly, the power company brought those units in on railroad flatcars. The rail lines are old but should still be usable. They go through Defiance to the old foundry," he said. "Let me walk the rail lines and inspect them. I'll have an answer for you tomorrow. Is that soon enough?"

"Yes, do it," Billy said.

"Glad to see somebody's finally getting things fixed and back in shape," Kevin said. "It's about time."

ᘛ

Kevin stood in the entrance to Billy's office with Olny Hornyak behind him. "I went over the rail lines. They look fixable; maybe take a couple of days to replace the bad ties. Also, I'm gonna need several teams of horses and a crew to handle their move. The substation has to be moved, too." He scratched his head and began to describe the tasks ahead. "Gonna hafta clean up the rail line, too ..."

Billy cut him short. "Just do it. Hornyak, get this man horses and workers. If he needs anything else, get it for him."

"Yes, Billy. I understand." Hornyak raised his eyebrows.

Billy turned to Kevin. "If you have a problem, tell me."

ᘓ

It took several days for Kevin O'Neil to realize what Billy wanted, especially when he used strange words he didn't understand. When Billy described the power unit that mysteriously appeared overnight as a fusion drive, Kevin was convinced Billy was crazy. It was unlike anything he had ever seen. Nevertheless, he followed Billy's orders, for he knew it was death to refuse. Besides, he was curious to see what might come of them.

The task of combining the fusion drive to the turbines quickly became more complex. Men had to be trained to operate lathes, mills, and other machinery. Kevin recruited two individuals as assistants, Freddy Crosby and Joyce Vargas. They even understood the fundamentals of electricity.

Kevin had already informed Billy there were no "rail lines" between Defiance and the iron-melter to the east. It would be impossible to move them over what remained of the roads. He realized they would have to run power lines to the iron-melter on the other side of the Maumee River.

Billy realized the goal of making repair parts for the ship had just become more difficult.

ᘓ

The project to get the turbine generator running took almost a half-year of Billy's attention. When the Jones brothers challenged Billy's leadership, he killed them, and the remaining men worked harder. Once the power generators began to produce electricity, Billy found many electric motors in the old foundry still functioned. It didn't take long to move them into the workshops in Defiance which had depended upon men walking on treadmills to power the lathes and milling machines.

The electric motors revolutionized life in Defiance and increased output of goods. People flooded into the city when they heard good-paying jobs were available that did not require long days of hard labor.

Billy still had to get the electricity to the iron melting equipment. First, line crews scavenged electric wire from neighboring communities and then strung power lines from Defiance to Waterville on the Maumee River. That took power nine-tenths of the way to Perrysburg, where the iron melting equipment was located.

When Billy learned bandits had attacked crews working on the power line to Perrysburg, he mobilized guards to protect the workers. However, there were not enough weapons to arm them properly and guns took a long time to make. Billy set up a weapons-building factory equipped with electric motors powering the machinery. After inspecting the way the locals made the weapons, he made several changes and the output of guns rapidly increased.

The demand for guns grew.

CHAPTER NINE

"Mata ChaLik."

"Yes?"

"The Egg-that-Flies' orbit decays faster than first estimated," Cha KinLaat DoMar said. "The drag forces on the Egg-that-Flies at perigee are higher than first estimated. It has to do with the density of this planet's atmosphere."

Cha KinLaat had started to undergo gender change, which produced sexual urges she did not yet understand. Over half the crew had already become female and many of those had already mated. "There are about one thousand orbits left, or about five hundred of this planet's days before we must leave."

"Are you sure?" Mata ChaLik said.

"Yes, data confirm it."

"Keep checking. Notify me of any change." Mata ChaLik had already sent a signal for Bilik Pudjata to contact him.

"Yes, Mata ChaLik?" Bilik now spoke more rapidly and in a higher pitch, almost like the aliens. "What do you want?"

"When will you have the propulsion tube completed?"

"I don't know. I have not started making it yet—"

"I did not ask for excuses." Mata ChaLik spoke precisely. "I asked you, when will you have a complete propulsion tube?"

"I'm not sure—"

"Then spend some time thinking about it. The ship's orbit decays more rapidly than first estimated." Mata ChaLik exhaled noisily. "I didn't send you to the surface to develop a relationship with the aliens. Provide me a schedule of when and how you intend to make the propulsion tube before the next sleep cycle begins." He spoke in the harsh tonalities of his native continent, Ma. "That is an order."

"Yes, Mata ChaLik, leader of the Defenders of Qu'uda."

Mata ChaLik had spoken in such a way as to remind Bilik of his status.

Bilik realized he had been moved to the outside fringe of Qu'uda society. He did not like being treated as an outcast, especially when he would be the one to save them from disaster.

"I understand," he said.

ॐ

"Pull the wire now," Chip Wilson yelled.

"Hey-yar, giddy-up, hey-yar." Charlie cracked his whip.

The draft horses surged forward. Heavy wire squealed over a pulley as it was pulled to the next pole.

The sun was hot and Chip's arms ached with fatigue. Sweat ran down his back and his belly rumbled with hunger. He had worked through morning without a break on the last section of power line from the Maumee River to Perrysburg over the flat lands of north-western Ohio. From the top of the pole, he could see their destination, the old factory just outside Perrysburg, a half-mile away through fields of swaying prairie grass.

Soon, he thought, *this will be done.*

While Chip worked, he thought about his job. It had all started when Billy Potato became the leader of the Midwest Federation.

Gee, the man sure spoke funny, kinda grunted, and looked weird. It wasn't just his five-foot height—it was his odd build. He had wide hips and a neck that blended into his shoulders to make him look, well, pear-shaped. His hands had only three fingers and he had a face quite unlike anyone else. Still, no one made fun of his oversized head with its ever-present hat, or his flat nose, bulging eyes, or his pasty white complexion.

No one messed with Billy after he took out Old Vic and killed the Jones brothers who had refused to take orders and threatened him. All Billy had to do was raise his hand and someone died. That gave him a big edge in arguments.

However, Chip recalled that Cora, his wife, said the women felt safe around him. Billy left them alone, unlike Old Vic and his gang of predators. Since Billy had taken over, food production, manufacturing, and health care—all had improved. So, when Billy gave Chip a chance to lead a line crew east into the lower Maumee valley, he took it.

"Hey, Chip, look, hicks on horses." A lineman, who had yet to start to shave, pointed. "To the east."

Four horsemen in drab brown homespun clothing with Mongolian style recurve bows slung over their backs, slowly wended their way toward them.

"Quick, break out the guns," Chip called to his crew. "Those are Clan horse warriors." He clambered down the pole and grabbed a gun.

Todd Sinkton led the Clan patrol. He was older and by nature, more cautious than his companions. Being on long-range patrol made him even more so.

"Halt," Todd said. "Kyle, what d'you make of the situation?"

Kyle peered at the group clustered around a pole. Heat rose off the sunbaked land in waves. "I don't think they're gonna shoot," he said. "They ain't lined up in any kind of formation, but they do have guns." He had the keenest eyes of the group.

"All right, get out the white cloth." Todd took a deep breath and scanned the horizon. In all directions, tall prairie grasses waved in the gentle breeze. *Perfect for an ambush*, he thought. Every Clan farm settlement in this area had been burned out. *Was it bandits? Or the Fed?* "Keep your bows limbered. Hit the dirt if they raise their guns."

The patrols used recurve bows because they could be shot faster than muzzle-loading rifles. He turned in the saddle and pointed. "Kyle, stay back and watch. If trouble starts, leave and report in."

"Let's go." Todd raised a white cloth and walked his horse to within ten yards of the armed men. "Howdy. I'm Todd Sinkton of the Clan." He slipped off his horse.

"I'm Chip Wilson, line crew chief of the Midwest Federation," the stocky man said. "What're you doing here?"

"We're looking for trade opportunities in the western territories." Todd noticed they pronounced their words somewhat differently. "We've been visiting some of our folk out here." He didn't say anything about what they'd discovered. "We've been watching a while. We can't figure out what you're doing. It looks like you're stringing rope from the poles." He kept his voice polite. "What're you really doing?"

"We're running electrical line from our power station in Defiance to Perrysburg. We're opening up the lower Maumee valley." Chip used the name the Fed had called these lands prior to losing them to the Clan. "The Fed's on the move. We use electricity to run our factories." Chip spat on the ground in Todd's direction. "More people join the Fed every day. It's the place to be."

What the hell's going on? Todd thought. *What're they doing with this electricity stuff?* Previously, the Fed had always been a collection of farm communities on the Maumee and Auglaize Rivers. Years ago, the Clan had made it clear to the Fed they claimed the empty territory southeast of the Maumee River all the way to Waterville.

Todd noticed everyone in the Fed party had a black powder gun. In fact, he thought, they look as good as the best made by the Clan. *These Feds are acting like they own this land east of the Maumee River.* "Forgive us simple horse folk, but what does electricity do?" He'd heard of electricity, but only in tales from the past.

"It's a form of power used to drive machinery," Chip said. "We use electricity to run our machines. We don't walk the treadmills anymore." He nodded with assurance.

"Oh, I see." Todd knew he had to get this information back to the

Elders right away. The Midwest Federation had discovered something and was expanding into Clan territory, and maybe even destroying Clan settlements. "Ol' Vic's been busy."

"Not Ol' Vic. Billy Potato is our leader now," Chip said. "The Fed's doing much better under him."

"Billy, what's his name again?" Todd asked. "That doesn't sound like any Fed family name I've ever heard."

"Billy Potato." Chip pronounced the name slowly. "He got us electricity. He's got big plans for us. He wants to get the foundry going again. Iron and steel is in Defiance's future, lots of it." He glanced around.

"I see," said Todd.

"Well, we'd better get back to work. See you."

"Billy Potato." Todd nodded. He'd got the name. "Thanks for your explanation." He got the hint to move on. However, he hadn't had a chance to ask about the burned-out farms. "Well, we must be on our way."

"Chud, did'ja know the Fed has a settlement east of the Maumee, just outside of Perrysburg?" Todd took a swallow from a large stein of beer. They were sitting in the shade of a limestone-walled house in the harbor.

The harbor on the Maumee River was an outlet for the Clan's manufactured goods, a place to trade for grain from Fed farmers, wine, and fish from Erie islanders. The harbor was a gateway for settlers and supplies going to the empty western lands.

"Perrysburg?" Chud was the leader of the Clan fort at the mouth of the Maumee River. He enjoyed his home-brewed beer, which he considered to the best in the area. He sampled it every day to assure himself of its quality.

"Naw, I didn't know that. That's Clan territory, isn't it?" He already knew the Fed had a settlement, but figured it best to act surprised. *Hell*, he thought, *they're a lot closer than the Clan. I gotta live with them.*

"Damn, the boat for Rivermouth left this morning. It won't be back for at least a week and a half, maybe two." Chud shook his head. "You waiting for the next one? Maybe we can catch up on things, over a beer or two."

"No, it's too close to harvest." Todd shook his head.

Chud realized Todd had made the decision to ride the whole distance to the Hill. *Damn*, he thought. *That might be a problem.* He drank more beer. *I hope this too, will pass.*

CHAPTER TEN

"Footsie, you baby, you don't have a care in the world. As long as your tummy's full and you've got a warm lap, nothing else matters." Taylor stroked the gray tabby cat's head. It looked up, squinting its eyes.

The study had grown cool. Even though it was close to midday, the room was dim. The gloomy light of winter revealed a battered wood writing desk, two tall book cabinets, and a sideboard with a half-filled decanter. At the far end, an iron box stove popped and crackled, radiating warmth.

"You know, Footsie, the Clan could be twice its present size if we had decent medical care." The cat stared intently at him. "I wish we had a vet and vaccines for you. I also wish I had something more potent than willow bark extract for my aches and pains."

"Do you know there were idiots back in the pre-Collapse days who wanted us to go back to nature?" He stroked the cat. "Man, they sure got their wish. Six months of this life would have cured 'em.

"Hah, now everyone has BO, bad breath, and stringy hair. Who knows what shampoo or deodorant is? All those things we took for granted."

The purring cat flexed its claws and offered up its chin.

Taylor smiled as he remembered earlier years. *At times*, he thought, *he'd pay anything to get a good glass of wine, like a racy Burgundy or a mouth-filling California zinfandel.* Other than the few bottles secreted away, there were no more good reds. *Yes,* he thought, *the islanders produce nice white wines, but nothing like the chardonnays from California or France.*

It was six months since younger members of the Council, who enjoyed the title of "Elders," had voted him out as war leader. Taylor missed the excitement of managing the Clan and the attention it brought. He thought about the new Elders' complacency with the status quo. *They don't know what they're missing. We lived like kings and threw it away in a tantrum of selfishness and hate. This generation thinks it's on top of the world. They think they know everything about life.*

Taylor straightened his cramped legs. The cat jumped down, stretched, and moved close to the stove. *Damn, I miss central heating more and more.* With time to spare and no good lights, Clan life offered little to do in the evenings other than sing, drink, swap yarns, or go to bed early. No wonder the farm families are so large.

"Um, excuse us, may we come in and talk with you, sir?"

The voice startled Taylor.

The cat dove under the sideboard, tail bushed.

It was Klaus, his house guard, with a group of young men.

"What d'you want?"

"Beg your pardon, sir. I'm Joe Del Corso, Al Del Corso's second born. We're from the east branch of the Rocky River."

Taylor nodded. He hadn't recognized him.

"I'm a junior administrator for the Clan. All of us are leader-candidates. We, er, that is, the others and me need to learn the history of the Clan from you. The Elders said we have to record it. They said it's part of our leadership training."

Joe Del Corso was a stocky, muscular man, not yet twenty years old, showing the first signs of a beard. He wore a long, embroidered brown leather coat with no collar and heavy, roughly woven wool trousers. His boots were tooled leather high-top lace-ups. He introduced his four, fellow leader-candidates.

Taylor nodded. "So, you want to learn the Clan's history?"

"Yes, sir," they said as a group.

"D'you know why the Clan formed?" Taylor asked.

"Yes, sir. It was the Collapse, sir. It was the time of troubles and war." Del Corso nodded. "Our people joined together for protection." Everyone knew that.

"We still have troubles and wars. Every man must be ready to fight for the Clan at any time." Taylor pointed to O'Connor. "Charlie, what's different today from the time of the Collapse?"

"Er, I think that we're more advanced than at the time of the Collapse," O'Connor said in a hesitant manner.

"What's high technology?" Taylor pointed to Tim Van Minh.

"High technology is the science of the Pre-Collapse civilization." Tim's words came out in an almost rote fashion.

"What's your opinion of the science of the Pre-Collapse Civilization?" Taylor used a neutral tone of voice.

"I'm not sure," Tim said. "Some of its science is very useful. Some is, well, mysterious. What I mean is, it refers to devices and methods that seem, well, impossible. I believe the scientists of the pre-Collapse civilization couldn't distinguish reality from their wishes. Some of the things they claim to have built are just impossible, for example, their claim they sent people to the moon. It's too far away. The escape velocity is too high, and the amount of energy needed, well, it's just unattainable."

"I see." Taylor now understood why the Elders had sent the next generation of leaders to him. *They don't know beans about our past.*

"Have you read any books from the time before the Collapse?"

"Yes, sir."

"Where're they kept?" Taylor asked.

"They're in the library." Tim pronounced "library" carefully, as though it were a foreign word.

"Fine. Let's meet there tomorrow morning, an hour after first light." Taylor waved his hand to dismiss them.

That night, Taylor dreamed. This time his dreams did not wake him, for the dreams were about life before the Collapse—they were about the good life.

꩜

"Joe, did old MacPherson agree to tell you about any pre-Collapse weapon systems?" Elder Jon Beach asked.

The Elders were in the small, walnut-wood paneled room behind the council chamber. The two Elders sat in overstuffed chairs near the wood stove. They had not invited Joe Del Corso to take a seat.

"He's going to tell us about the history of the Clan. He didn't say anything about weapon systems." Joe felt nervous. *Why don't the Elders just ask Taylor?* "Sir, is this important?"

"Ah." Beach paused. "We believe it's necessary for you, as a leader-candidate to obtain some of the knowledge we already possess. You need to gain MacPherson's insight of the times before the Collapse. D'you understand?"

"I think so." *A test*, he thought. *I can handle it.* He knew this group of Elders held the power to make or break him as he climbed the ranks. *I need an edge, something to get ahead.* Maybe this was it.

"Lately, MacPherson's been spending too much time alone. We don't want to lose his knowledge," Beach said in a quiet voice.

Charlie Ramsey, the other Elder nodded. "So, when do you next meet with MacPherson?" His eyes were partly closed, his head back against the worn red brocade of the chair.

"Sir, we're meeting tomorrow, an hour after first light, in the library." Joe did not feel comforted by Beach's explanation.

"Be sure to get him to talk about the pre-Collapse weapons." Ramsey handled much of the Clan's military affairs. "Listen very carefully. Don't tell him of our interest."

"Yes, sir." Joe's sense of unease grew with their emphasis on weapons. He knew that the Elders hadn't agreed on who would be the leader to replace Taylor. Rumor was, the vote to get rid of Taylor came from a deal between Ramsey and Beach. The power struggle within the Council of Elders for leadership of the Clan continued. No one had succeeded in getting the votes to get elected war leader.

CHAPTER ELEVEN

The morning sun outlined the fresh snow and evergreens in stark shadows and brilliant whites. Thin bands of blue-gray smoke lay over the valley. Water in the ragged black openings of the ice on the river tinkled with a faint, brittle sound.

Taylor pulled his heavy brown wool coat tight and strode toward the center of the hilltop fortress, snow squeaking underfoot. He felt alive—there was a purpose to his life.

"Good morning, gentlemen," he said as he entered the library meeting room.

"Good morning, sir." The assembled leader-candidates rose to their feet and answered in unison.

Shelves full of books lined the high-ceilinged room. Pale sunlight streamed through a row of tall windows that were opaque with frost. A half dozen polished wood tables surrounded a solitary wood stove.

"Please, be seated," Taylor said. "Del Corso, send for water and glasses. Stolz, the stove is your responsibility."

"Yes, sir," Del Corso said. "I've already sent for water."

Taylor gathered his thoughts as he walked back and forth in front of the group, rubbing his hands together. Heavy boots moved restlessly on the bare wood floor. There were several muffled coughs. "We're here to learn about the Collapse."

Stephan Kuchinski exchanged a knowing smile with Hans Stolz. "Sir, my mother told me some of the history of the pre-Collapse civilization," Kuchinski said. "She never really explained why such a powerful empire fell so fast to the barbarians." The stories of the bloody battles where Taylor MacPherson had led them to victory were common knowledge.

"Well, I wish I could say civilization collapsed because the barbarians were at the gate, but that's not true. A lot of barbarians lived behind the gate." Taylor hesitated. "First, let me tell you what there was before ..."

༒

Jon Beach got up from the table in the small back room of the Travelers' Inn, its whitewashed walls decorated with faded paintings of landscapes scenes of Vietnam. The air was filled with aromas of garlic, hot oil, and cooking meat.

He closed the door to prevent eavesdropping. Customers in the main section of the restaurant paid him no attention as they ate the Vietnamese food that was the restaurant's specialty.

Joe Del Corso stood in front of them.

"We've all heard MacPherson speak about electricity," Beach said, gesturing toward the four Elders at the table. "What we don't know is how it was used in the weapons that existed before the Collapse. That's what you're supposed to do, Joe. So ask questions, encourage MacPherson to talk about electricity. Don't let on why you need to know."

"Yes, sir. I think I understand what you want." Del Corso knew Beach came from a large district of the Clan and had political aspirations. "Is there anything else?"

"No," Beach said. "Ramsey, can you think of anything?"

"Nope, just find out how electricity is used in war." Ramsey ran his eyes over the other Elders. It was his habit to poll the Elders, who usually gave orders as a group. "Okay, Del Corso, meet us here tomorrow. Same time," he said. "We expect you to have some answers by then."

Del Corso still had an uneasy feeling. *Why didn't they ask Taylor directly? What were they hiding?*

Taylor spent the next week reviewing the conditions preceding the Collapse: An overpopulated world competing for dwindling resources —particularly petroleum; the war in the Middle East that spread to involve all of the industrialized nations; and the use of sophisticated weapons that took destruction to both coasts of the USA.

Taylor also touched upon the social deterioration of the USA that had been exacerbated by the heavy tax burden caused by the intergenerational Ponzi schemes called entitlements.

"That," he said. "Just made the polarization between the haves and have-nots even greater. When the Collapse came, brought on by nuclear strikes of Islamic fanatics, the social fabric ripped asunder. It was almost like civil war."

Getting the leader-candidates to understand the degree of destruction took Taylor several days. It was only after he took them on a field trip through the ruins of downtown Cleveland, they began to grasp the true magnitude of the Collapse.

It was a day of picking their way on horseback among the ruined towers of the former downtown, buildings with shattered windows and dark, moldy interiors. Faded evidence of fierce fires left dark stains splashed against the side of some structures.

Debris and bare, whitened bones littered lobbies of former apartment buildings. Even so, the main bridges across the Cuyahoga River separating the east side from the west remained intact and littered with rusted hulks of cars and trucks. The trip back from the central city took them through areas where burned hulks of houses and gaping holes of former basements formed the "badlands" of the suburbs. It was land no one wanted, for it was filled with too much debris to be useful for farming.

"What caused this?" was a frequent question.

Taylor could only tell of his experiences fighting gangs seeking to exploit and pillage anyone who had food or fuel.

"In the first year after the Collapse, famine killed many. It was only after the Clan became organized and raised crops we became able to feed ourselves."

"Yes, but what caused the civilization to fall?" Tim Van Minh persisted with the question of why and how it had happened.

"It was a war and a surprise attack destroyed our infrastructure. You see, we were very dependent upon electronics in all aspects of our lives. When the enemy used the EMP weapons, it destroyed our technology and civilization ground to a halt." Taylor attempted to explain how pervasive electronics were in the pre-collapse civilization, but could see that it was beyond their ken.

The high technology weapons baffled most of them. It was clear to him Tim Van Minh understood enough mathematics to appreciate some of the pre-Collapse engineering.

It was odd, Taylor thought, *how young Del Corso kept asking about electricity and whether it was a weapon*. Others, however, focused on the big picture. He felt a sense of achievement in holding their interest and generating a multitude of questions.

"Sir, then the war was the Collapse?" Kuchinski asked.

"Almost, but not quite." Taylor shook his head. "The war destroyed the productive capacities of the industrialized nations and the basic infrastructure. The government lost its ability to rule when the war decapitated their leadership. Biological weapons spread diseases in the densely populated areas. People died in droves. In the end, the destruction of the transportation system worked as a quarantine against the diseases sweeping the land.

"Anarchy arrived. What the war did not destroy, the riots did. The hungry, the unemployed, the poor, the illiterate, but most of all, the opportunists became the barbarians. They pillaged the land, taking what they wanted by force and violence. There were no leaders to step into the void and restore order. There were only local strongmen who imposed their will by force. Some good, some just, but most were petty despots who hoarded the remaining resources for themselves."

Memories of the violence and hardship came flooding back. He stared out the window.

The leader-candidates stirred. "Sir, what happened to all those people?" Del Corso asked.

"That's an excellent question." Taylor frowned. "You see, back then, feeding the world was a delicate balancing act. Perhaps famine followed, I just don't know. I listened to my short-wave radio from time to time to see if anyone was broadcasting, but I've heard nothing on the commercial frequencies." Taylor did not mention burst transmissions and conversations he occasionally overheard on the Ham frequencies. *That*, he thought, *would only confuse them.*

"How much did the USA population decline?" Del Corso asked.

"If what happened in Ohio was typical, then the population of the USA is now probably less than a million," Taylor said.

"Why, sir?" Kuchinski asked.

"The nukes actually killed less than one percent of the populace directly. The rest died later from disease, starvation, exposure, and violence. Perhaps ninety percent of the people died in the first year after the Collapse." Taylor saw the shocked look on the faces of the young men who had never heard over four hundred million people inhabited the US prior to the Collapse.

As Taylor walked home after the meeting, he saw there were more wagons and people on the Hill than usual. *Strange*, he thought, *I don't see this much activity after harvest is over and the granaries are filled. The only time we bring in more grain is when a siege is expected.* He'd not heard any talk of war; there must be another reason for moving the grain.

The pathways were now clear of snow. Water ran off the roofs into the cisterns making a busy, cheerful sound. The sun felt warm.

Perhaps, Taylor thought, *there'll be enough hot water from the solar heater for a shower.*

In the valley below, a forge banged away. It had been quite busy lately making small items. The sound reminded him of arrowhead manufacture. The Clan didn't make arrowheads for trade, only in time of war. So, it must be something else other than arrowheads. He felt a little out of touch.

Taylor realized the Hill had become less of a living area and more of a business district. That would change instantly if there were danger from the outside. The Hill was the one place capable of withstanding attack by a superior force. In a time of danger, people would flood in. The Hill had resisted many attacks and each time, its defenses had been strengthened. Now it was a city surrounded by a deep moat and a fortress on top of a cliff as the place of last refuge. It was secure. It was his home.

ᘯ

That evening, the leader-candidates asked questions about weapons technology. They'd found nothing in the library about which weapons were used or how they worked.

"Sir, you've made no mention of electricity. Yet it was everywhere in the pre-Collapse civilization. Was it ever used in the war?" Del Corso asked. "For example, as a weapon?"

"Joe, I'm not sure what you mean," Taylor said. "Electricity was a very convenient form of energy. All of the weapons we discussed today had controls operated by it. In fact, I can't imagine them being possible without electricity."

ᘯ

Later that night, as Taylor lay in bed, he puzzled over Joe Del Corso's questions. *Why was a junior administrator interested in electricity?* That was the second time he'd asked about it.

Taylor regretted not setting up a university, but survival had been too important. *If I created one now, where would I find the instructors? Who had the knowledge and experience to pass on?*

Only his small laboratory in Berea kept a spark of technology alive. Some instinct, a leftover pre-Collapse notion of privacy, made him keep it secret even from the Elders.

Maybe I should discuss setting up a university with them, but they listen to me less and less. The Elders had no interest in technology they couldn't use in war or sell at a profit. *So why does Del Corso keep asking about electricity?* It was out of character. *Has Joe discovered my laboratory, or is he fishing for a political angle?*

Win Van Minh, the owner of the Travelers Inn, had noticed the comings and goings of Del Corso and the Elders. He said nothing but positioned himself in the next room against a panel that allowed him to hear through the wall. It was unusual for the Elders to meet outside of chambers, so he listened carefully.

"Look, the Fed is making a push in our direction, burning farms and bringing electricity," Jon Beach said. "They must have reason to believe we're going to back down from them."

"The last time we fought, we hurt 'em," Charlie Ramsey said. "Their Guards are no match for my Horse Soldiers." Ramsey had assumed command when Chris Kuchinski had taken time off to have a family. He had consolidated his position by the time Chris returned to ride with the Horse Soldiers. He had no intention of letting her take his place as military commander. That had been part of the reason for ousting MacPherson, who had close ties with Kuchinski. "Their bows don't have enough range and they can't shoot straight."

"Now they all carry guns," Beach said.

"Still doesn't matter," Ramsey said. "My Horse Soldiers can get at least six arrows off in the time it takes to reload a gun."

"What about electricity and other wizardry? MacPherson said the pre-Collapse weapons aren't possible without electricity." Beach's voice rose. "D'you think the Fed has found some of these ancient weapon systems? If they have, do we have any defenses against them?"

"No pre-Collapse weapons have been used." Sean Monahan had a reedy voice. "Your worries may be smoke in the wind." He waved a thin hand in the air.

"There's always the first time," Carver Washington said in his gravelly voice.

"Have Del Corso ask MacPherson about different weapon systems." Beach's voice pitched higher as he wagged a finger. "Get him to describe how they operate or how they were used. Maybe then we can devise some useful tactics against them."

"It sounds almost as though you're ready to send my Horse Soldiers out against the Fed." Everyone knew Ramsey brooked no opposition to his leadership of the Horse Soldiers.

"Well, they're taking over our territory. To me that's almost the same thing as a declaration of war." Beach's voice had almost become a whine. "I've got young families who need land. My district has too many people and not enough farmland. We need land."

"I hear you, man, and the western lands are the way to go. Are they worth starting a war?" Washington said slowly. "Against a foe that may have a superior weapon?"

"We've got to do something. I ordered grain moved into safe storage and cisterns filled on the Hill. I also started the arrow-works," Beach said. "That's still not enough."

"Making more work for your people?" Washington had a trace of a smile on his face.

"Clan protection comes first, and I resent the implication of your comment." Beach rose to his feet, finger wagging in Washington's direction.

"Easy, easy." Ramsey gave Beach a quick glance. "Maybe we should send some of my Horse Soldiers out west. We could let them know they can't burn our farms and run their electricity lines into our area without consequences." He smiled, looking at Beach out the corner of his eye. "Maybe you'd like my Horse Soldiers to stick a few arrows into some Fed people to remind them who they're dealing with. Or maybe you'd want them to go to Defiance and burn a few houses?"

"No, no," Beach said quickly. "I'm not asking for a declaration of war." He glanced around. The other Elders were smiling. "Instead of that, how about capturing a few of these Fed workers? Ask them some questions and then send them back. That way, we can send a message without starting a war." "Might work," Monahan said. "It'd get their attention."

"Yeah, but if we send the Horse Soldiers out, let's send a platoon or two. It's mighty tough to get folk with guns to surrender to a patrol," Charlie Ramsey said. "My soldiers don't like to eat crow when talking to the Fed."

"Sounds like a decision to me," said Beach.

"As soon as the weather breaks, I'll send a couple of platoons out west," Ramsey said. "In the meantime, have Del Corso keep pumping MacPherson. We'll meet here in one week." Ramsey always liked to get the last word in.

CHAPTER TWELVE

Chip Wilson twisted his hat and shuffled his feet. It was his first visit to Billy's office in City Hall, a large, opulent room with heavy mahogany furniture and a thick oriental rug.

Chip bit his lower lip before he spoke. "Sir, we've already collected a couple hundred tons of steel. We'll get the rest from the old refinery down by the mouth of the Maumee River." He lowered his eyes.

Billy had learned about the visit of the Clan horsemen late last year. He'd ordered the land around Perrysburg cleared of Clan humans and their homes burned. That, he knew, was the way to get rid of troublesome vermin.

"You can go," he said.

I must get the electric furnace working, and soon, Billy thought. To get a propulsion tube with the right properties, the iron must be free from impurities. His calculations showed it would take ten pours from the primitive metal melter to make a complete propulsion tube.

By the start of the next warm season, Billy thought, *I shall have the tube made. It should take only eight days to complete each pour.*

The undamaged iron-casting facility in Perrysburg only needed the dust, debris, and bird droppings removed. A team of workers had already started on the job. Cleaned up and connected, the furnace would be ready for operation.

Billy's two brightest trainees, Freddy Crosby and Joyce Vargas, had repaired the furnace's switch-gear and controls. He'd set up a gas-generator to make hydrogen, which when distilled, provided fuel for the fusion units. The process would give off oxygen, which he needed to purify the iron.

Billy had Kevin's men collect heavy angle iron to make frames for the huge boxes that held the molds. Workers screened sand brought from Lake Erie beaches and stockpiled it in the molding area. Other workers brought red clay from the Vermilion River valley on the edge of Clan territory to use as a binder for the sand used to make the molds.

As Perrysburg grew, Billy found it required more supplies.

A steady stream of horse-drawn wagons brought provisions from Defiance. It was a jolting trip over the pothole-plagued highway that led to the only remaining bridge across the Maumee River. Initially, bandits harassed the supply wagons, slowing the work. After a brief campaign, Fed guard units captured the bandits and forced them to repair the road. As the road improved, traffic sped up.

Billy realized the warm season was coming to an end and felt a sense of accomplishment. The workers had finished the electric line and opened a machine shop to make parts for the furnace. The unit of Fed guards sent to Perrysburg built a ditch and revetment defense around the foundry while off-duty. More workers arrived over the warm season, opening shops and starting a weekly market.

Farmers took over the empty farms nearby to supply meat and game to the newly opened market. Some had even planted a winter wheat crop, which would be ready by the start of the next warm season.

Soon, he realized, Perrysburg wouldn't need food from Defiance. *Yes, I will make the propulsion tube soon.*

"Golly-gee, my butt hurts," Todd Sinkton said. "I've been in this saddle way too long."

Ramsey had assigned him to guide the platoon of Horse Soldiers sent to the mouth of the Maumee River. He'd been on horseback for the entire week.

"Bitch, bitch, bitch. All you ever do is complain." Shig Matsuo laughed as he rode alongside Todd on an old road. "Here, you've got a chance to see the beauty and richness of our western lands." He pointed to the flat horizon, vividly green shimmering under the bright summer sun.

Yesterday, they had passed south of Sandusky Bay and now headed northwest through the flat area that had reverted to marshland. From the road's elevation, they could see ditches and waterways, lush with rushes and sedges and full of waterfowl.

"All I hear is your complaints about a blister on your bum." It was Shig's first trip away from home. "Where's your spirit of adventure? It's a beautiful day and we're on our way to redeem the honor of the Clan." Shig had just been promoted to squad leader.

"Let me share something with you, Shig." Todd winced as his horse jolted him. "It's the definition of adventure. D'you know what it is?"

"No." Shig cocked his head to listen.

"Adventure is some poor bastard having a bloody miserable time in a God-forsaken place, miles and miles away from home with no friends or help and surviving to talk about it. High adventure is being farther away, having an even more atrocious time, and in serious risk of losing his life."

"Ah, you have no sense of adventure." Shig laughed. "We're almost there. At least, if what you said was true." The column halted beside a pond streaked with floating green algae and rimmed with reeds. A flock of iridescent mallards, squawking noisily, ran across the water's surface straining to get airborne. Blue herons, motionless on stalk-like legs, stared at them, their long necks swiveling.

"See those things over there?" Todd pointed to the tiny finger-like objects jutting into the clear blue sky. "That's the old petroleum refinery at the mouth of the Maumee. It'll take us an hour to get there."

As they rode on, Todd brooded. He was getting too old to spend his life out on the frontier. He missed his wife and children. *Why did it have to be me who has to bring the troops out west?* He knew the answer was he'd brought the news to them about the Fed's electricity and knew the area. *However*, he thought, *do the Clan Elders have any idea what we go through? Do they even care?*

As the sun sank toward the horizon, the column worked its way through a maze of crumbling roads and flooded, reed-filled ditches. The flat land, no longer drained, was now swamp and nourished vast flocks of waterfowl. The old power plant, jagged and torn from a long-ago explosion, dominated the area. The main building was now a mound of brick and concrete rubble. The smokestack had somehow survived to stand tall and straight. It was now the lookout tower and lighthouse for the Clan's harbor at the mouth of the Maumee River.

When Billy equipped the factories in Defiance with electric motors to drive their metalworking machines, gun production rose. That caused a shortfall in black powder. As a result, farmers put in niter beds that matured over the winter to produce a large supply of saltpeter in the late spring. The Fed traded guns with the Lima-Findlay Alliance to get sulfur from the old refinery. By late spring, the black powder shortfall had become a surplus.

The Fed army doubled in size. The captains of the guard used the bandits as an excuse to get more recruits and guns. After the army eliminated the bandits, they turned their attention to brigands in outlying areas. The Midwest Federation incorporated some of the smaller and more distant farming communities. The Fed's influence and territory grew.

Electricity gave the gun makers and factories a voracious appetite for steel and there was never enough until Billy found that steel rails from the old railroads were made from high quality steel. Though the metal in the rails was good enough to make guns, it required a lot of machining. Captain Ed Kerr sent out Fed guards on patrol who also collected steel scrap for the furnace. He wanted the furnace to cast steel rods and bars for the factories to make more guns.

The guards ranged widely seeking sources of scrap steel. Each patrol made it a point to bring salvaged scrap back. Soon, they found the old oil refinery just south of the mouth of the Maumee River was an excellent source of scrap metal. The refinery became a regular destination for patrols.

ↄ

Chud Pepperdine stared out from the lookout toward the south. As leader of the Maumee Harbor, he wanted to be first to know when the Clan contingent would arrive.

The harbor was tucked in the lee of a twenty-foot-high wall made from large gray limestone boulders. It was an old dredging impoundment area surrounded by water on three sides, which provided shelter for the harbor from storms.

Within the impoundment, long since filled, was the Clan's settlement. It stood well above the water level of Lake Erie and was home to a small village. Neat limestone cottages with bleached thatch roofs stood apart from the rows of gray wooden barracks that could hold two hundred troops. To the east were a dozen weather-beaten warehouses. All the buildings huddled close to the shore side of the impoundment up against the wall that protected them from direct attack.

The narrow road on top of a rocky break-wall was the only connection from the impoundment area to the shore. A gaunt gray guardhouse sat astride the road as an integral part of the fortifications.

The anchorage for the harbor was far from the road, well out of bowshot range. Fishing sloops and multi-mast merchant vessels bobbed at anchor, their rigging rattling in the breeze. Several dozen families who lived at the harbor had defended it from Fed raids in the past.

Chud, as leader of the Maumee Harbor, had reported the raids to the Clan. The Clan had promised reinforcements, but never delivered them because the Elders were convinced the harbor was impregnable.

However, when they received Todd's report last fall of the Fed's incursion at Perrysburg, the harbor now received regular boats with the supplies long requested from Rivermouth, the main port on the Rocky River.

Now he waited for two platoons of Horse Soldiers to arrive—seventy-two of the Clan's best. He could see the Clan contingent riding along the road on the break-wall.

"Chud, you ol' pecker." Todd punched him on the arm in a playful fashion. "It's good to see your ugly mug. I swear you get bigger and fatter each time I see you."

"Todd, you skinny, frog-faced little shit, you haven't changed a bit." Chud smiled. "You still getting a sore ass from riding that bony nag? I tell you, you ought to come and live here. Bring your family; learn how to live right. Maybe then you'd put on some weight."

"Yeah, sure Chud," Todd said. "Give up my farm and all I own, just to swill beer in this rat-infested swamp?"

Chud was always pleased to have company, but he saw impatience flash across the faces of the tired soldiers arranged in columns behind Todd. This was a chance to hear some news and learn what his old friends back on the Hill were doing. He knew something was brewing, for this was the first time in years two platoons—six whole squads—had been sent to the harbor, not to mention the sailboat that came earlier in the week, loaded with provisions and hundreds of bundles of arrows—ten thousand in total. He was sure something had twisted the Elders' britches, but they hadn't told him.

"Chud, this is Commander Chris Kuchinski," Todd said.

"Your fame precedes you, Commander Kuchinski."

"Hello, Chud." Chris Kuchinski was tall, with a lean wiry build, and seemed almost ageless. She had a grown son, a long-dead husband, and a proud history of fighting for the Clan.

"There's hot water in the bathhouses. Supper in an hour in the meeting hall." Chud's voice boomed over the now-silent clan soldiers. Still talking, he led the weary soldiers to the stables and the barracks.

After a hot shower and a change of clothing, Todd felt better. A generous dollop of lanolin had eased the pain in his sore butt. He made his way to the large meeting hall made from rectangular blocks of limestone. From within, he could hear the clink of dishes over the voices and the occasional burst of laughter.

Once inside, Todd peered into a tureen of fish chowder. Small red skin potatoes, onions, and big chunks of fish swam in a rich creamy broth. Melted butter streaked the surface along with tiny flecks of red pepper and chopped green cilantro.

Damn, he thought. *That smells good.*

He watched the children bring in fresh-baked bread, crisp and crunchy. Chud kept glasses filled with the dry white wine that came from the Erie Islands. Meanwhile, helpers ladled chowder into the soldiers' bowls, while at the same time, Chud kept the conversation going. It was dark before the yawning soldiers finally pushed themselves away from the tables and headed back to the barracks.

CHAPTER THIRTEEN

The next day, Shig Matsuo led his squad across the causeway and formed up. He had been given the task of scouting out the area and gathering information. He also had been told to capture a few Feds as long as it didn't require a pitched battle. It would be a long ride to the Perrysburg area, where Todd and the scouts had encountered the linemen.

Barely underway, wending their way along the bank of the Maumee, as they drew close to the old refinery, Shig heard a loud clang.

"Whoa." He raised his hand.

The line of soldiers became motionless.

In the distance came the crashing sound of metal hitting against metal.

"What in hell is that?" Shig stared at a maze of strange equipment, rusted and overgrown with weeds and vines.

It had an odd look—almost magical—with tall metal structures reaching abruptly for the sky. It smelled alien, like the oil they bought from the fierce mountain people in Pennsylvania.

Shig put his index finger against his lips and gave the signal to dismount. "Benny," he said, voice pitched low. "Go take a look-see, quiet-like, and get back to me."

The young scout nodded and disappeared into the vegetation.

Shig motioned for the remainder of the squad to secure their horses.

In less than ten minutes Benny reappeared. "Sir," he said, slightly out of breath. "There're a bunch a people doing stuff with the, er, whatever." He pointed at the refinery towers. "About eight of them."

"Are they armed?"

"They've got guns, but only two look like guards."

"Have they heard us?"

Benny squinted his eyes. "Naw, I don't think so. They're too busy doing whatever it is they're doing."

"Okay, listen up." Shig huddled his squad together. "This group will do fine. We want to capture them. Don't shoot unless you absolutely have to. We want them alive. Got it? We're sending them a message, not declaring war."

Shig pointed to Benny. "Lead us to them, nice and quiet."

Benny led the squad quietly toward the sounds, through mounds covered by tall weeds. As they approached, voices and the sound of metal banging against metal got louder. The scout held up his hand for them to stop as he peered around the edge of a crumbling concrete block building.

Shig crept forward to join Benny and saw a half dozen people working on a tall metal structure. There were two guards leaning on their guns, talking. He motioned for the squad to pull back.

"Okay, you, Jones, take four to the left. Burke, you take four to the right. Wait until you see me move in, then all move at the same time. We've got to get the jump on them, before their guards have a chance to use their guns, okay?"

Silently, the soldiers surrounded the work party. "Freeze," Shig yelled. "Don't move, hands up."

At the sound of Shig's voice, the Clan soldiers, a dozen men in their characteristic drab brown, rose as one, with bows drawn and aimed.

"Drop your guns and you won't get hurt."

The workers and the guards stared. One by one, they dropped their tools and guns. Slowly, they raised their hands.

"Burke, have your men get their guns." Shig motioned for the rest of the soldiers to spread out.

Burke brought one of the guns to Shig. "Take a look at this." He held out a shiny, polished rifle.

Shig inspected it and saw that it was new, rifled and well made. In addition, the black powder looked as good as any wet-milled powder made by the Clan. They didn't look like a typical farmer's gun. Workers were carrying fine quality weapons? Didn't make any sense to him.

Shig went to the prisoners. "Okay, you're under arrest for trespassing on Clan property."

"But we were just collecting scrap...." One of the prisoners said.

"Shut up, get in line." Shig gestured to the Clan soldiers. "Alright, let's get the prisoners back to the harbor." He pointed to the north, in the direction of the lake.

The soldiers marched back to their horses and remounted. They herded the prisoners before them and directed them alongside the river until they came to the causeway.

"Halt," Shig called. "Blindfold the captives. They're not to see our defenses." After putting rags around the prisoners' heads, the soldiers linked them together with rope and led them onto the causeway and into the harbor.

"So, where did you say you live?" Chris Kuchinski raised her eyebrows as she glanced across the table. The room was warm and lit with only two candles. Two large guards stood by the closed door. Voices chattered outside, faint through the thick walls.

The blond-haired youth looked up, lower lip quivering. "I already told you twice. I come from Perrysburg." He was the youngest of the prisoners.

"How long have you lived there?"

"We moved in last year."

"How many live in Perrysburg?"

The prisoner shrugged. "I dunno. A lot. Most of us do some kind of work for the foundry."

"What were you doing on Clan land?"

"We didn't know it was yours. We thought it was just a junky ol' place by the river no one wants." The prisoner's long blond hair drooped over his forehead, almost covering his eyes. The whiskers on his chin still resembled peach fuzz.

"I know where you were. I asked you what you were doing." Chris's voice grew louder and harder.

The prisoner winced. "We was collecting scrap metal."

"Why?"

"For Billy's foundry." The prisoner sniffed, as though about to cry. "We've been getting it from that place for over half a year. We didn't know we was doing anything wrong." His head lowered, and his shoulders sagged.

"Would you like something to drink?" Chris's voice softened and became gentle, almost sympathetic.

"Yes, that would be nice."

Chris snapped her fingers and pointed at the table. "Get me a jug of water and a couple of glasses."

"Yes, ma'am." The guard saluted and went out through the door.

"Tell me where you got the rifles you were carrying. The ones with the mark that says the Midwest Federation." Chris offered a trace of a smile and leaned back in her chair.

The prisoner looked up and took a deep breath. "They came from the rifle works in Defiance. It's one of the new factories."

"New factories?" Chris raised her eyebrows.

The prisoner shrugged. "Ever since Billy got electricity running, all the factories now use it. People don't have to walk the treadmills no more."

"How many people have these new rifles?"

"All the guards have them."

"How many guards are there?"

"I dunno. A lot."

Chris motioned to the soldier bringing a jug and two glasses and pointed to the table in front of the prisoner. "Bring him something to eat, too."

She went to the door and glanced out, her eyes settling on Shig Matsuo. She closed the door behind her. "You, commandeer a fast boat and go to Rivermouth." She was sending him to the harbor at the mouth of the Rocky River. "Take the Fed guns with you. The Clan needs to know this. It can't wait."

Shig arrived at the Hill two days later.

CHAPTER FOURTEEN

"Shig, are you certain the Midwest Federation are recruiting new soldiers?" Charlie Ramsey's voice echoed hollowly off the council chamber walls. The meeting was closed to the public.

"Yes, sir," Shig said. "The Fed guards said their ranks now number several thousand." It was the same answer as before.

Ramsey weighed the reply and considered the source: poorly educated farm boys given guns and sent out to scavenge metal. Most couldn't count to a hundred if their lives depended on it. However, they did have guns as good as any made by the Clan, or possibly even higher quality. The regular Fed guard units would have the same or better.

"You're sure there's an iron foundry in Perrysburg?" He'd already heard the answer but hoped for another tidbit of information. "Powered by electricity brought from Defiance?"

"Yes, sir." Shig nodded. "They said they were gathering iron for use at the foundry. They had orders to bring only rusty steel—no shiny steel—to make something."

"Okay, Shig. Dismissed."

If all that steel were used solely to make guns, Ramsey thought, *that'd be a tremendous number of guns. If that's an indication of the size of their army, the*

Clan is in trouble, deep trouble. His guts lurched. "If the Midwest Federation has started a foundry just to make guns, then they must have war in mind," he said. "Plus, they're burning Clan farms and taking our land."

"Before we convince ourselves we're being invaded," Carver Washington said as he stroked his chin. "We need more facts. Why don't we send a diplomatic mission?"

"Well, how about a formal letter to the Fed's new leader, this Billy Potato?" Sean Monahan said.

"Yeah, and mention the Western Lands agreement." Ramsey referred to the territorial concessions the Clan had extracted from them after the last war. "Something to remind them to get out of our western lands."

They discussed the language of the Council's letter to the Fed. They finalized it with the statement: "If the Midwest Federation does not comply with these reasonable terms, your actions will be regarded as an invasion of Clan territory."

～

Shig returned to the Maumee Harbor by the same fast sailboat that had brought him to Rivermouth carrying a letter from the Clan Elders. A cold front had passed. The wind had switched around to come strongly out of the northwest. Every time he struggled into the boat's small cockpit to get fresh air to ease his nausea, water spray soaked him anew. He was sick of sailing.

It was a relief to get both feet on the dock at Maumee Harbor. After a change into dry clothing, he reported to Commander Kuchinski, who sent him immediately on to Perrysburg with the Elders' letter and the Fed prisoners. Even with a white flag and a squad as escort, he feared an ambush.

The Fed guards at Perrysburg let Shig's group in while covering them with a bristling array of guns. A Fed captain accepted the letter, which had the wax seal of the Clan Elders.

"These men." Shig pointed to his prisoners. "Were trespassing on Clan land. We're releasing them into your custody as a goodwill gesture. We expect you to punish them for their crimes against the Clan. If you wish to send a reply, carry a white flag. You won't be harmed."

"Understood." The guard captain's mouth looked as if he'd bitten into a bitter Osage orange.

꒰

"The orbit of the Egg-that-Flies decays more rapidly than originally calculated. It is calculated it will fall from orbit in one hundred and twenty planetary revolutions. You must have the parts for the propulsion tube within sixty planetary revolutions." Mata ChaLik BuMaru's voice resonated with stress.

Bilik consulted his biocomputer. "Mata ChaLik, I can make the parts in time. That is not a cause for concern," he said. "However, the tribal group to the east, the Clan, threatens war over the use of the iron-casting facility. They lay claim to it. You must watch them for me."

Bilik needed Mata ChaLik to monitor the activities of the tribal groups. Perhaps that way, those in the Egg-that-Flies would learn of the unpredictable nature of the Earth people.

꒰

Next morning, Billy called Captain Kerr into his dingy makeshift office at the foundry and dictated a letter for the Clan representative at the Maumee Harbor. He wanted to meet with the Clan emissary.

"I wouldn't meet with the Clan representative from the harbor if I were you," Kerr said. "It won't be productive."

"Explain, Captain Kerr," Billy said.

"Well, you're the leader of the Midwest Federation. You should only meet with the Clan's leader. Or, an Elder who has the authority to negotiate for them."

"I must talk with them, you said so."

"Don't meet with this underling." Kerr looked away. "That'd

suggest that we, the Midwest Federation, is desperate for peace. As leader, you'll lose status in their eyes."

"Status is not important. Castings are more important. I need the iron foundry. I do not need trouble from this Clan entity," Billy said. "Send the letter."

Chris Kuchinski met Billy Potato in the pasture outside the entrance to Perrysburg, flanked by contingents of both Clan Soldiers and Fed guards.

Chris towered over Billy. "Sure, I'll send your message to the Council of Elders, Mr. Potato. But I'm not a Clan Elder. If I made a commitment in the name of the Clan, they'd hang me." She shrugged. "Only Elders speak for the Clan. I'll make sure they get your letter."

Billy stared at her before speaking. "I will meet with your Clan Elders because I want peace. We cannot leave Perrysburg because the iron foundry is here."

"Why is that so important?" Chris asked.

"If we have peace, we can trade iron from the foundry with the Clan," Billy said. "We could show you how our factories operate. Even how the iron foundry works. Only if we have peaceful relations with your Clan."

Chris nodded to indicate she understood. "Sure, Mr. Potato, I'll pass your message on to the Clan Elders." She noted he'd made no mention of the Fed leaving the western lands.

After the meeting, Chris sent a message to the Council of Elders. Within four days, she received orders to take a letter to Billy at Perrysburg. At the same time, the Council of Elders ordered Chris to get the harbor ready to receive a fleet of boats. They also ordered her to step up patrols around the Harbor to prevent the Fed learning about what would arrive on the boats.

ᕋ

"Look, if we go to war with the Fed over an iron foundry in Perrysburg, where's the payoff?" Charlie Ramsey's words echoed off the back wall of the empty council chamber. Again, the public had been excluded from their meeting. "Can we run it? Will we have the electricity to power it? No. If that's the case, we'll still lose, even if we beat them. We'll have casualties and losses for nothing in return. I won't waste my Horse Soldiers for nothing, no, sir."

"Well, I suppose we could call out the Militia if the Horse Soldiers are afraid to take on the Fed." A trace of smile crossed Beach's face. Few Horse Soldiers came from his district. For him, an expedition carried little political risk.

"Oh, sure, I can just see the Militia marching to Defiance," Ramsey snapped. "That's not the point and you know it." He moved his chair backward with a harsh scrape.

Beach smile widened. "Really?"

Ramsey took a deep breath. "The Fed's new guns may be just the tip of the iceberg. There may be other surprises waiting for us.

"We can either forget about the western lands and develop farms closer to Rocky River, or we can prepare for war." Ramsey jabbed the palm of his hand with his index finger. "Mobilize the entire Clan and put a large army in the field. If we're going to tangle with the Midwest Federation, let's go in with overwhelming force to guarantee victory."

The council chamber was silent for a long moment. The Elders knew the consequence of war. Total mobilization would disrupt everything. Farm output would drop, factories would empty of workers, and their standard of living would fall. The production shortfalls might be made up with booty from the Midwest Federation, but then again, maybe not.

"Well, what about the electricity?" Washington raised his eyebrows as he leaned forward to look at Ramsey. "That squad leader, Shig what's-his-name, spotted power lines going into the old factory. What would happen if we cut the electric lines leading to Perrysburg? Would that work? Maybe we should try that before we mobilize. What kind of force would it take?"

"That's an idea. It just might work." Ramsey pursed his lips. "Use a small expeditionary force and cut their lines where they're difficult to repair. We might even draw the Fed forces out of Perrysburg into the open where our Horse Soldiers have the advantage."

"Well, I suppose so." Beach nodded. "That way we wouldn't have to commit too many resources. What d'you say?"

The Council members nodded agreement.

"Meanwhile, don't let any of this get out. We don't want our people talking about pre-Collapse weapons or electricity. Have Del Corso pump MacPherson again. Maybe something will pop out of the old fart's addled head." Beach had summarized their course of action as though he were in control.

Annoyance flickered over Ramsey's face. "We'll bring the Clan forces up to six full platoons at Maumee Harbor. They have facilities to handle that many. More would be a logistics problem. We can supply them with materiel from inventory at the Rivermouth arsenal. I'll take care of the arrangements and give Kuchinski detailed orders. If there's no other business, this meeting is adjourned."

Again, he got in the last word. The Council nodded and rose to leave. He smiled as Beach glowered.

ᘒ

Tim Van Minh appeared at the entrance to Taylor's office. "Sir, may I speak with you for a moment? Privately."

"Sure, Tim." Taylor closed the door and pointed to a chair in front of a fading fire. "What's on your mind?"

"Sir, my father asked me to give you his regards." Tim briefly bowed his head. "He wishes you still led the Clan."

"Tell him thanks, but no thanks."

"He asked me to tell you something he learned." Tim glanced over his shoulder as though concerned that someone could hear him. "Joe Del Corso has been meeting with Clan Elders in a back room at my father's Inn. Your name was mentioned several times. My father heard some of what they said."

"I see."

"He asked you join him for lunch at the Inn."

"Thanks, Tim." Taylor smiled. "Don't mention this to anyone. Tell your father I'll stop by tomorrow."

After Tim left, Taylor thought about what he'd said. *So, young Del Corso is cozying up to the Clan Elders? It was a fast way to power as long as he could deliver. If he screwed up, his career in Clan government was over. Were his questions about electricity from the Clan Elders? Or were they onto his laboratory? Did it have something to do with the Fed?*

From now on I'll be careful about what I say to Del Corso. He felt disappointed, for he had known the Del Corso family for a long time. *Then again, I don't have much to do with the younger generation. Hells-bells,* he thought. *That's what every member of the older generation eventually gets to: The younger generation is really screwing things up.* He laughed. *I'm no different than the rest of my generation in the way I look at the young.*

CHAPTER FIFTEEN

"The Clan Elders acknowledge Mr. Billy Potato's thoughtful proposals and promise to provide a response within thirty days." Chris Kuchinski looked up from reading the Clan Elders' letter to Billy in his grimy office at the foundry in Perrysburg. The sound of workers' voices and metal banging came through the open window.

"That's all?" Billy asked.

"Yes, that's it," Chris said. "Here, look for yourself."

Billy passed the letter to Captain Kerr. "Read it."

"He's right. It doesn't say anything else."

Well, I'll be damned, Chris thought. *Billy can't read.*

The Clan's letter worried Captain Kerr. He pressured his informant in the Maumee Harbor for news and learned boats had brought hundreds of bundles of arrows. He also found out the Horse Soldiers had set up a patrol screen around the harbor and were watching the settlement at Perrysburg. He made sure his guards stayed away from the Clan's forces to avoid a confrontation. In the open, their horse-mounted soldiers using bows had a clear advantage of the Fed's foot guard. He knew the only way to beat them was with vastly superior numbers.

"We should bring three or four command units in and give this Clan force a good thrashing," Kerr said.

"No," Billy said. "Bring one command unit from Defiance. More would be too many. Casting parts concern me more."

$$\wr$$

Three days later, a Fed guard command unit of two hundred and fifty men straggled into Perrysburg carrying only their new black powder rifles and ammunition. They arrived without a vanguard, no supplies and in groups that bore no semblance to their units.

Their ragged disorder dismayed Billy and he took command of their training. He searched his biocomputer for military guidance to turn the guards into an effective fighting unit. He made the guards march in ranks, to maneuver and fire in rolling volleys.

Toward the end of the first day, two guards in the guard unit from Napoleon stepped out of formation. "This marching is bullshit. I know how to shoot." The burly man shook his head.

"Yeah," said his wiry companion. "I'm tired of it, too. I know how to fight." He spat on the ground. "Probably better than the little shit does." He gestured toward Billy.

The guard units from Defiance, who had seen Billy's response to insubordinate behavior, remained silent, motionless.

"You." Billy pointed at the burly man. "And you." He gestured to other of the pair. "Step forward."

"Me?" The burly man raised his rifle in Billy's direction. "What the hell d'you want now, shorty?"

Billy jerked his hand upward. His lasers fired twice. Both men toppled to the ground with holes in their foreheads.

The assembled guards froze, eyes fixed on the two bodies.

"Who else does not want to take orders?" Billy pivoted his hand toward the staring guards.

No one said a word.

~

Commander Kochanski rode with an escort alongside the Maumee River. At Perrysburg, two Fed officers escorted her through the west gate to the foundry where Billy waited for their parley.

"Commander Kuchinski, welcome." Billy steered Chris out the east gate and past the foundry to a Fed command unit assembled in an open field. "In honor of your visit, I've assembled the guards. Come." He pointed. "Review them."

Two hundred and fifty Fed guards stood at attention in a tight formation, neatly dressed, weapons gleaming under the bright late afternoon sun.

Billy raised his hand and made a chopping gesture. The Fed guards marched back and forth, performing a series of complex maneuvers.

"At ease," Captain Kerr yelled. "Dismissed."

Chris saw the guards march to the settlement, still in formation. "Your guards march well." The guards had new guns, all identical. "Very, er, nice." She forced a smile. *What the hell's going on?* she thought. *This doesn't look at all like the previous Fed guard from Defiance. These guys look like real soldiers.*

"The guards need more practice." Billy guided Chris to the barracks to meet the Fed guard captains. "I do things differently than Old Vic."

"I see." Chris took in the details of the settlement's defenses. An earthen revetment, still fresh and free from vegetation, surrounded the settlement, which had a log palisade on top, too. They headed into a large clapboard building within the barracks complex where there were rows of tables laden with food.

"Join me," Billy said. "Let us eat together."

"Okay." Chris sat at the head of the table next to Billy.

"Commander Kuchinski." Billy leaned toward his guest over a plate of food. "The Fed will let you know when any of our scouts go near the Maumee Harbor."

"Oh," Chris said, her mouth full of food. "Why?"

"So we have no trouble."

"Mmm?" Chris swallowed before saying more. The duck was

cooked to perfection and much better than her normal rations while in the field. "How're you going do that?"

"We'll send a messenger one day ahead of time." Billy offered her a bowl of stuffing. "You can escort them with clan soldiers while they are in the area near the harbor."

"Hmm." Chris raised her eyebrows as she put more food onto her plate. "Why?" She pointed to the platter of meat.

"To prevent them from going where they shouldn't." Billy passed Chris the meat and a gravy boat filled with a steaming sauce. "We want no trouble."

"Sounds good to me." *Curious,* Chris thought. *The Fed has in effect, agreed to the Clan's claim on the land.* "That should work." She chewed her food slowly, savoring it. Uncertain what to say without consulting the Clan Elders, she chose to change the topic. "You know, Mr. Potato, this is a damn fine meal."

"Good." Billy's face cracked in a caricature of a smile. "Let's enjoy it." He picked at his food, eating little.

The guard captain named Pete Cutler leaned across the table toward Chris. "Our guards wiped out the bandit gangs in the south Maumee River area." He waved his fork as though to emphasize the point. "They were robbing people on the road between here and Defiance. One gang had more than a hundred men. They didn't stand a chance against our guards." He covered his mouth and belched. "We blew 'em away. More beer?"

Chris declined the offer with a smile. "Did they have guns?"

"Some." Cutler took a long draft of beer. "Most had bows."

"How many guards were in the unit that defeated them?" Chris realized this Fed guard had drunk a lot of beer.

"About an equal number, I'd guess." Cutler belched again. "Our discipline and tactics were better."

"Good." Chris forced a smile. She raised her glass in salute to the guard. *So,* she thought. *The Fed guards have fought some battles recently.* "You must be proud of your men."

Mercy, she thought. *I've gotta find a bathroom, and soon.*

CHAPTER SIXTEEN

Cha KinLaat recalculated the orbit of the Egg-that-Flies several times. Each time she got the same result—the time until impact was now only about one hundred days away. Cha KinLaat, along with most of the crew no longer believed Bilik could make the propulsion tubes in time. Rumor had it Bilik was training Earth people in the art of war. Stress had brought the change—Cha KinLaat was now completely female and fertile.

From the dawn of time, the Qu'uda had survived in the aftermath of every disaster by changing into the female form and mating. It was their way of responding to threats to their existence. The hormones released during periods of prolonged stress caused the change in their hermaphroditic form, causing most to become female. They buried their eggs in a safe place to hatch until the danger was over. More than three-quarters of the crew were now female and openly competed to couple with the remaining males.

Cha KinLaat heard the Keepers-of-the-Egg had started evacuating the ship, using the one remaining Bird-that-Soars. The egg bearers feared for their eggs and there were not enough incubators. They knew that incubation on board the ship in zero gravity would increase the deformities in developing fetuses. They had to find a place on Earth with sun-warmed mudflats to ripen their eggs.

Cha KinLaat had the assignment, as environmental analyst, to locate a hatching area. It was not as difficult as she had feared. There were so few places on this planet with the right conditions for hatching eggs. A constant, moderate temperature was only found on islands in this world's tropics. Now she was female, she longed to be with egg.

Cha KinLaat found a suitable location off the southern peninsula of the continent where Bilik was supposed to make the propulsion tube. It was a large island with few natives and had extensive swamps and waterways flooded by the ocean. It was almost like a part of Qu'uda except there were no mountains.

Cha KinLaat was very thorough in her presentation and meticulous in her delivery. The Keepers-of-the-Egg praised her work. She noticed Mata ChaLik BuMaru kept staring at her.

Perhaps he will couple with me. Her urge to mate was strong.

Mata ChaLik gave the order to prepare the ship's power supply reactor for conversion into a fusion bomb. If the Qu'uda had to make their home on Earth, they did not want the Egg-that-Flies to come crashing down on them. The bomb would detonate at apogee to propel the ship's fragments far from the Earth.

"Bilik Pudjata," Mata ChaLik called on the comm-net.

"Yes?" Bilik said.

"Be advised," Mata ChaLik said. "The Keepers-of-the-Egg have started to evacuate the ship." It was the Keepers way of expressing no confidence in Bilik; they no longer believed he could make the propulsion tube on schedule.

Bilik felt fear clutch at him. *I have slipped far in the community's opinion.* Rejection meant death.

"Mata ChaLik BuMaru, I hear, and I understand. You no longer have faith in me." He paused and drew a deep breath. "I have failed, I am shamed in front of the entire community. I am cast from the community, I no longer belong...."

Bilik started the ancient refrain that led to ritual suicide. It was the fate of all Qu'uda who fell from the community's grace or those too old and a burden on the community. He continued with the ritual, familiar and feared, the eventuality of every Qu'uda. "... I shall cut out my biocomputer and crush it beneath my claws, tear off my clothing, destroy all that I value, and remove every trace of my offending presence for I no longer belong within the community—"

"You should have done better." Mata ChaLik interrupted Bilik's recital of the ancient refrain. "It was not my decision. It was the entire community. I am tainted by your incompetence." His groan was one of shame.

Bilik heard Mata ChaLik's groan. *His responsibility for my failure may cast him out*, Bilik thought. *He is vulnerable. If I die, he may have the same fate. This means I may have a chance.*

Something made him speak up.

"There are one hundred sleep cycles before the orbit of the Egg-that-Flies becomes unstable," Bilik said. "The latest schedule to produce the propulsion tube shows at least sixty-four days of slack time after completion. That is plenty of time to assemble the propulsion system. You, Mata ChaLik BuMaru, have said you can complete this work in less than thirty-two days."

"Yes, that is true." Mata ChaLik's voice rumbled with uncertainty.

"Then why should I be cast from the community?"

"You know the reason." Mata ChaLik said.

Usually it was obvious to any expelled Qu'uda why they were beyond the fringe of the community. Bilik had been away from the Qu'uda on the Egg-that-Flies; he had not participated in the community's consensus. He knew his modifications and lack of a female aspect had made him anathema to the crew. This was not his fault—they'd asked him to become like this. Now they did not want him.

"The schedule slippage is your fault," Mata ChaLik said. "If you had interacted with the community every day, perhaps they would have been more understanding."

"Yes," Bilik said. "I can still get the parts made in time. Consider the alternative. Without a new propulsion system, everyone is condemned to an uncertain life on this planet. You must consider all the risks."

Living on a strange planet under a blazing yellow-white sun with its dangerous ultraviolet radiation, without the Egg-that-Flies' facilities, a place with few locations suitable for hatching their eggs and hostile natives. It would be a life of permanent exile, with no chance to leave and little chance of rescue. That might push some of the Qu'uda to suicide. The ship's gene pool was perilously small—all were needed for their species if they were to survive on this planet.

"Perhaps." Mata ChaLik took a deep breath. "You are right. Perhaps there is still enough time to make the propulsion tube. As Defender-of-the-Egg, I must save the Egg-that-Flies if at all possible."

"Yes?" Bilik held his breath.

"You must continue your work." His voice was high-pitched, as though he were being tortured. He was going against the consensus.

"Ah." Bilik released his breath.

"However, since there is but one Bird-that-Soars, we must continue the evacuation. We have reached the point of no return." Mata ChaLik clenched his claws, as though grasping the load of responsibility more firmly. "My decision to support you will fly against the consensus of the community. By doing this, I, too, am moved further from the center of the community. Report to me each day of your efforts to make the tube. Your only contact with the community will be through me. You may no longer use the Bird-that-Soars other than to send us completed parts."

"You must provide surveillance data from the Bird-that-Soars," Bilik said. "The eastern savages may attack the iron foundry. The Midwest Federation's army can defeat them, but only if they are not surprised."

"You cannot have the Bird-that-Soars for surveillance," Mata ChaLik said. "Its schedule is to carry people and supplies to the new settlement. Did you not understand?"

"I must know if the eastern savages are about to attack. Please,

Mata ChaLik, have the Bird-that-Soars fly over this area as it descends to provide me with surveillance data. The Midwest Federation guards are not like our defenders—if surprised, they might break and surrender. That would be a fatal setback."

"That may be possible," Mata ChaLik said. "I'll see if it can be done."

~

Captain Kerr resumed command and set the guards to work, strengthening the settlement's defenses. He wanted to be sure if the Clan's cavalry attacked, they would pay dearly.

Billy awakened to a chirp from his biocomputer indicating a high priority item. He focused on the visual display of surveillance data. It showed a force of Clan Horse Soldiers leaving the Maumee Harbor in the faint light of pre-dawn. As he watched, they formed into columns and turned south along the bank of the Maumee River. Behind, a column of carts and wagons as large as the cavalry unit followed.

Billy summoned Kerr. "Clan forces are moving toward Perrysburg."

Kerr frowned. "Er, did my scouts report in to you, sir?"

"No, my friends told me," Billy said.

By the end of the day, Kerr's scouts confirmed the Clan Horse Soldiers were, indeed, moving south. They reported that six platoons, or more than two hundred Horse Soldiers were heading toward Perrysburg.

~

"Burke, are you ready?" Chris Kuchinski called to the sapper who was crouched over a bundle of fuses that trailed from the parapet on the bridge over the Maumee River. All of her forces were on the east side of the river.

"Yes, Commander, the charges are in place and set." Burke looked up as sweat dripped from his brow. "We're ready." For the past several hours, he'd packed bags of black powder around supporting columns and into every crevice adjacent to the columns. "This," he said. "Ought to do the job."

Burke's buddy had tried to cut the wires carrying the electricity with a knife and had died in a sheet of blue flame. He had burns all over his body and reeked like roasted pork.

"Platoon Leaders," Chris called. "Withdraw to the east bank, dismount, and hold your horses." She nodded to Burke who held the bundle of fuses in his left hand. "Ready?"

"Ready." Burke held up a small oil lamp.

"Light the fuses and get out of there." She joined her men over two hundred yards away.

The black powder exploded, brightening the evening sky, shaking the bridge with a violent, rippling boom. Smoke and dust briefly obscured the center of the bridge and rose to coalesce into a black, mushroom-shaped cloud several hundred feet high. Support columns sagged, splintered. The bridge groaned, and one part of the central span slowly collapsed into the muddy waters of the river below. Wires sparked brightly, like the blue-white flames of hellfire.

Chris crossed herself. The electrical flashes made her think they were tampering with an evil force.

ⵎ

Machines stopped abruptly, lights went out. All work stopped in Perrysburg. From faraway came a sound like that of an extended peal of thunder. A dark cloud briefly appeared on the horizon, fading quickly.

All electrical power had stopped.

Billy contacted the Bird-that-Soars to get surveillance data. If the power station in Defiance had failed, he would have to leave immediately, even if the Clan held the bridge.

Surveillance images started to flash in front of his eyes. They showed the City of Defiance with brightly lit streets—its power generating facilities were undamaged. The surveillance images flashed eastward to the bridge over the Maumee River. A span of the bridge was down. From beneath the bridge, something sparked and flashed. As the image magnified, he saw Clan Horse Soldiers around fires and rows of tents—they had settled in for the night.

While the Clan soldiers controlled the bridge over the Maumee River, no repairs could be made to the power lines, and without power, no metal would be cast. That had been the only point of weakness in his plan, and the Clan had found it.

CHAPTER SEVENTEEN

"Look at the surveillance images," Bilik said. "The eastern savages cut the power lines."

"When will you get the power back?" Mata ChaLik BuMaru asked. "Are they going to attack?" *Great Egg*, he thought. *Everything is so difficult on this barbaric world.*

"I don't think they will attack today," Bilik said. "This will delay the schedule for casting the tube. I don't know how long the repairs will take. The road to Defiance is blocked."

"What do you propose?" Mata ChaLik had a sense of foreboding. *My reputation is on line for this bumbling incompetent.* "Well?"

"It will be difficult if not impossible to protect the power line." Bilik hesitated. "I'm not sure ..."

"You must do something."

Bilik took a deep breath. "It is becoming impossible to conceal our technology from the natives. We have to take action, and soon."

"Like what?"

"Move the iron melting equipment to Defiance. That would get it out of the territory claimed by the eastern savages."

"How?" Mata ChaLik asked.

Bilik Pudjata paused. "Use the Bird-that-Soars."

"I must talk with my fellow Keepers, for that would expose us to these savages. That is a dangerous step." Mata ChaLik said. "I'll let you know after we confer."

Mata ChaLik later learned Bilik had worked his craftsmen around the clock to prepare the furnace for the move.

ↄ

"Where the hell are those Feds?" Chris Kuchinski paced back and forth in front of tents flapping in the rising wind. Overhead, clouds gathered. She stared at the sea of waving grass. "I was sure after we'd blown up their bridge, they'd come. They can't get past us to go to Defiance, and they can't get reinforcements. We should have them just where we want them."

Chris worried about being encircled and pinned against the river. Before the troops settled in for the night, she sent for her aide. "Stanek, as soon as the scouts get in, send them to me," she said.

Rain began as night fell.

ↄ

The morning dawned gray and wet, the long grass bent and dripping.

"Hey, Shig," Todd Sinkton called. "This's an adventure with a mud flavor. Great, right?"

Shig didn't answer; he just shivered.

Todd watched the patrols return and report to Commander Kuchinski they'd seen no sign of the Fed forces. They told of seeing Fed guards cleaning ditches around the settlement.

"Damn," Shig said. "All we ever do is sit around. When are going to see some action?"

ↄ

Commander Chris Kuchinski waited most of the day for the Fed to make its move, but no one appeared. Chris called a conference of the platoon leaders under darkening skies. Once assembled, their faces carried many frowns, and they glanced at each other uneasily. Her face clearly showed her growing annoyance.

"We've got food on hand for another three days. We can get more from the harbor. We have only enough for another week," Chris said. "The Feds haven't come out. It's almost as though they know we're here." As she spoke, the rain intensified.

"The longer we're here, the greater the risk is the Fed will bring up a larger force. In the meantime, we're moving into the old town, Perrysburg, to get out of this weather." She referred to the abandoned part of the community separate from the foundry. "We'll attack in the morning." She glanced around. "Comments?" The discussion quickly focused on the logistics of the move to Perrysburg and the tactics for the morning's attack. After the meeting, they struck camp.

つ

Overnight, a cold front arrived and cleared the air. Under a brilliant blue sky, a northern breeze rippled the long, green prairie grass. Even the larks seemed to welcome the change in weather, singing a cheerful symphony as they soared ever higher.

After breakfast, as the Clan forces assembled on the west side of the Fed settlement, out of range of bow and gun, Chris examined the main entrance. As she sat on the horse, she overheard several soldiers talking.

"Man, what a nice day. It's just perfect for a battle—cool, dry, and lots of good light," Sam Heimlich said to a grizzled warrior named Mitch Doaks as they approached the west side of the Fed settlement.

"There ain't no such thing as a good day for battle." Doaks spat on the ground and squinted at Heimlich. "When you die, the weather don't mean shit. If the ground's mud or dust, it's all the same. When your number's up, you won't care if the sun is shining or not." The corners of his mouth turned down and a frown knitted his brow.

"Doaks, knock off the chatter," Chris said. There was more truth in Doaks's remarks than she cared to hear. "And you, Heimlich, you should know better than to say things like that." Chris discouraged talk of glory. She'd been in battles since the Clan had formed. Too many. Dying on a battlefield was never glorious.

She turned on her horse and beckoned the youngest and least experienced platoon leader. "Peterson. Take your platoon to the east entrance of the Fed settlement. Set up a screen to catch anyone leaving. Have your fastest rider ready to let me know if they try to leave. If they do, slow them down, and we'll take care of them when they get into the open. All right, move it."

After lining up the horse-mounted soldiers, Chris ordered platoon "A" to charge at the front entrance of the Perrysburg settlement.

The gate withstood their charge and the Fed guards' guns ripped through the Clan Horse Soldiers, leaving a half dozen dead.

"I knew this wasn't going to be easy," Chris said to no one in particular. "I hate fortifications." She watched the horsemen reform and wait for her next order. "All dismount except the patrols. Platoons "B" and "C" forward on foot. We need to find their strong points. We need to pound the crap out of them for a while."

Damn, she thought. *It's going to turn into a siege.* She knew her Horse Soldiers' fighting skills held no advantage against fixed defenses.

Clan soldiers probed the settlement's walls. Before long, they identified all of the strong points. Out of range and from behind makeshift barricades, Chris ordered the Clan catapults to lob black powder bombs at the towers and strong points on both sides of the west entrance of the Fed fort. She watched as the bombs split the main gate, loosening its hinges.

It's time to try again. Chris sent the Horse Soldiers forward on foot. They advanced in leapfrog fashion until they were within bow shot range. Popping up, one at a time, the clan soldiers picked off defenders as the catapults continued to throw bombs. Gunfire from the Feds' defenses slowly became less and less. The main gate sagged on its hinges.

"Sir, the gate's almost down." A guard interrupted Billy while he worked on the furnace. "What should we do, sir?"

Billy did not look up from his work. The furnace, the transformer, and the switch-gear were almost completely disconnected and ready to go. He transmitted a message. "Mata ChaLik, bring the Bird-that-Soars here, immediately."

"I cannot come," Mata ChaLik said. "I'm delivering supplies to the evacuation base. I will not arrive before the middle of the night."

"I hope that is soon enough," Billy said.

CHAPTER EIGHTEEN

Billy shivered even though he wore thick, synthetic armor fabric. It was late afternoon and the cool, dry air blowing in from northern Canada had grown colder. The gate at the west entrance was almost destroyed, along with many of the guards' defensive positions. He knew the deep ditch and embankment would stop a direct cavalry assault.

So, he thought, *the attack must come through the gate.* "Captain Kerr, fill carts with scrap iron and put them behind the gate to block the entrance."

"If they attack through the west entrance, it'll be Horse Soldiers supported by archers on foot," Kerr said. "Maybe we should run some of that unused power cable across. It would break up their charge."

Billy nodded. "Do it." After Kerr left, Billy took out the hand projectile gun he'd brought down from the ship. It would be the first time he'd used it since training. It fired small, high velocity pellets propelled by hydrogen-oxygen explosions. The weapon had a small, high-capacity battery that rapidly dissociated water into hydrogen and oxygen, which cycled the gases into the propulsion chamber under high pressure. When fully loaded, the handgun had sixty-four spherical metal pellets with an effective range up to thirty feet.

It is time. I must join this fight, Billy thought.

He visited the Fed guards huddled behind the metal-filled carts and piled up debris behind the main entrance. He went from one defense position to another and gave the guards advice. Even though he moved quickly, an arrow hit him and bounced off.

The Fed guards who saw Billy take the arrow gave a weak cheer.

"Always keep at least half your guns loaded. Only shoot when another gun is reloaded." Billy repeated the same advice at each defense post. "Have loaded guns ready at all times. If they charge, you will need all of them."

The guards took his words as an order. Their rate of fire slowed as they increased their stock of loaded guns.

ᘉ

"The Feds aren't firing as often," Chris said. "I think they're losing heart. It's time to show them what we can do. Shig. Get Squads "A" and "B" mounted," she said.

"Yes, Ma'am."

"Shig, lead the charge."

"Mount up." Shig raised his voice to his squad.

The platoons of "B" squad joined his and they dressed their ranks. Shig reviewed their formations. It was by the book, in tight lines, the rows orderly. "Ready? Forward." They trotted out in tight formation.

As his horse moved under him, Shig felt a tremendous surge of excitement. *This is how victories are won. What tales I'll have to tell.* He felt invincible; he knew he was destined for greatness. *My children—even my grandchildren will ask about this great victory.*

"Charge," Shig yelled and cracked his crop on the horse's flank. The sound of the horses' hooves pounding on the ground grew into thunderous pounding. He felt like part of an avalanche, unstoppable, about to roll over everything in its path.

"Clan, Clan," the Horse Soldiers screamed and lashed their horses to even greater speed. It was now a race, a contest to be the first into the Feds' settlement. Volley after volley of arrows flew over their heads. *Our archers are keeping them from firing*, Shig thought. They drew close to the gate. *Nothing can stop us now.*

Shig saw a cable stretched across the shattered gate opening between the ruined towers rise and become taut. Beyond was a barrier of carts. He slowed his horse and prepared to jump the cable. As the first rank jumped over the cable, they slowed. Several horses failed to clear the cable. The rest accelerated toward the line of carts. *Oh, shit*, Shig thought. *It's going to be a mess.*

Shig heard a voice yell, "Fire."

A horizontal sheet of flame and smoke erupted from the barrier.

That's a lot of gunfire.... It was Shig's last thought as a large caliber lead ball smashed through his chest, lifting him out of his saddle. He slumped forward and as the horse halted, he slid down the horse's withers and died.

ᘏ

Men and horses collapsed into screaming heaps. The front rank of the charging Horse Soldiers stumbled to the ground.

The second rank of the Horse Soldiers halted before the shattered gate, behind the mass of bodies and screaming horses, unable to advance. The Warriors stood in their stirrups and fired their bows at the rate of one arrow every ten seconds. Desperation drove their efforts. At close range, the long arrows from their recurve bows proved deadly. The sleeting storm of arrows overwhelmed the muzzle-loading rifles of the Fed guards. The guards began to retreat from the hail of arrows.

ᘏ

Billy took out his handgun and stood up, took a deep breath, and pointed it. As fast as he could pull the trigger, pellets struck Clan Horse Soldiers with deadly accuracy. One after another, they fell. He continued to fire.

Kerr arrived at a trot with a group of reserve guards, moved into position behind the carts, and lined up. On his signal, they fired a rolling volley from less than fifty feet at the Horse Soldiers confined in the narrow entrance and between the gate's towers.

As the thunderous echo faded, a new chorus of men and horses began screaming anew. Courage was no longer enough.

Riderless horses reared, panicked, and thrashed about with steel-shod hooves, pulping the flesh of man and beast. Blood frothed pinkly. The mass of panicked man and beast dissolved into chaos.

The remaining Horse Soldiers retreated.

Billy noticed the attacking force had committed only a small group to the charge; at least two-thirds of the Clan Force remained. He estimated there were over forty clan soldiers down. Thirty-two Fed guards had been killed in the attack and many more wounded. *We have less than one hundred effective Fed guards left*, he thought. *We're outnumbered.*

"Bilik Pudjata," Mata ChaLik called over the comm-net. "It is taking longer than planned to unload the Bird-that-Soars. Everything has to be moved by hand—things are different here than on Qu'uda. We cannot arrive for at least another one-third of a planetary rotation."

Bilik silently noted he had tried to convey that point earlier to those on the Egg-that-Flies. *Sometimes*, he thought. *You have to experience Earth to understand it.*

Bombs from the Clan catapults once again began to fall onto the settlement, starting fires, which spread rapidly, sparing none of the dwellings. The sheet-metal-covered iron foundry was the only building not hit, into which people started to crowd. Even though the pace of the bombardment eased, bombs fell through the afternoon.

As night descended, the rain of explosive projectiles stopped. The breeze out of the northwest freshened, becoming colder. Flames flickered in wrecked and burned-out buildings. Drifting smoke made the area around the foundry a dark and hazy hell of shouting voices and screams of pain.

Billy mobilized teams of civilians to put out fires, rebuild defenses, and to dig a ditch in front of the gates. He treated the wounded, but without medical supplies, he knew only the lightly injured would survive.

His tactics biocomputer warned him of the danger of a night

attack. It advised him to use rocket flares to discourage them. He knew the Feds had no flares. He sought a substitute in his archives. One alternative was a balloon that carried a flare.

Billy found the needed components in the foundry's laboratory.

"You, yes, you, come here," he said to a startled guard. "Take this metal strip and straighten it out. No, stretch it, that's right, more, more. I need it straight."

"Like this?" The guard asked as he pulled the magnesium ribbon over the barrel of his gun to remove its curl.

"Yes." Billy took fifty feet of straightened metal ribbon outside. He vented hydrogen from his handgun into a large plastic bag. When full, he sealed the balloon and added a small plastic bag with just enough ballast so that the balloon had a slight positive buoyancy. He tied the magnesium ribbon to the bottom of the balloon and slowly played it out. The balloon rose slowly, drifting sideways in the gentle breeze.

Billy lit the end of the magnesium ribbon. The balloon rose into the night sky with a brightness that equaled a full moon and drifted toward Perrysburg, clearly illuminating the land below. He watched to see if there were any attackers in the vicinity of their defenses—there were none.

As the flare slowly moved over Perrysburg, it gained altitude, casting its pale light over the land.

"Look, there's a light shining at us," Pete Watson said.

"Huh?" The Clan Warrior standing guard duty beside him looked up. "What the hell's that?"

"It's coming closer." Watson's voice rose higher, entering into the register that signaled panic. "Quick, warn the others. It's gotta be an attack." As he spoke, the light rose higher into the night sky, coming ever closer.

"It's, it's in the air." Watson wanted to crawl under the nearest bush and cover his head. The light flickered intensely blue-white. *Something is above it*, Watson thought. *Is it a daemon that steals men's souls?*

Clan soldiers stared at the strange light in the sky lighting up their entire encampment. All they knew was it had come from the direction of the Fed settlement. Some spoke of weapons their parents had told them about the Collapse. Others were sure it was an evil spirit.

The light reached a point directly overhead, flickered, and exploded. Something drifted, flapping toward the ground, like a bird of death in a darkness that now seemed even more oppressive.

Search as they might, they found no creature or carcass of anything resembling the bird that had flown through the night.

Chris put the Horse Soldiers on alert, fearing a counterattack.

The darkness yielded only distant, desperate cries of the wounded in the Fed's settlement.

CHAPTER NINETEEN

"All right, y'lazy sods, get up," Elroy Stanek's piercing voice split the pre-dawn darkness and awakened Chris Kuchinski.

She yawned and rose. A pink rim on the eastern horizon promised a day of fine weather.

"Rise and shine. Let's go get 'em." In spite of Stanek's call to war, breakfast came first. The Horse Soldiers never attacked into the sun at first light, nor did they ride on empty bellies.

Later, she met the platoon leaders to review the scouts' report. She was uneasy about the coming day and wanted to check on their preparations. Going into battle always made her feel jittery, and the episode with the strange light the previous night didn't help. No one knew what had caused it. The Fed had too many things that reminded her of the pre-Collapse technology Taylor talked about.

Chris learned from scouts the west gate had been reinforced and even now, work continued. While riding close to the Fed lines, they'd drawn fire. There was fresh dirt by the entrance and a new ditch blocking it. She'd learned from the quartermaster there were only sixty black powder bombs remaining—just enough for one more attack.

This assault has to work, Chris thought. *Otherwise we'll have to wait until we get more black powder bombs, which meant getting another shipment from Rivermouth.* She knew if she came back with casualties and no victory, Ramsey would use this as an excuse to post her on the frontier far from any action and a sure end to her career.

"How about using some of the farmers' hay wagons as protection for our archers when they advance on foot?" Platoon leader Doaks asked. "Them Feds don't have catapults to throw bombs at us. They only got rifles."

"Good idea. Add planks to the wagons, and maybe a layer of sod," Sinkton said. "That'd give the archers more protection."

"Do it," Chris said. "Doaks, Sinkton, it's your job." She paused. "This time, we'll use the wagons for cover, we'll attack the gate and the secondary barrier. The Horse Soldiers will leapfrog the archers once they make an opening in the Fed lines." She knew she had to be positive even though she did not feel like it. "This'll work."

ॐ

"Something coming," A Fed guard called, pointing west. He was on the top of the foundry building, acting as a lookout.

Captain Kerr climbed up. Six four-wheeled hay wagons piled high with boards slowly moved closer through the tall grass. Barely visible behind each was a cluster of brown-shirted men.

"Damn." Kerr hurried down from the vantage point and sought out Billy. "They're using wagons to cover their advance. They'll be harder to stop this time. There're more of them this time. They've committed all of their forces to this attack."

Billy stepped away from Kerr and spoke through his communications system to Mata ChaLik. "The Bird-that-Soars must come, and soon. Our defenses cannot hold out much longer. If the savages break through, I cannot stop them." He'd worked all night. He knew many of the guards were on the ragged edge of exhaustion. "Do you understand? Come at once."

"I hear you, Bilik Pudjata. It may be possible to get the Bird-that-Soars there soon. Is it wise to let them see it? Perhaps I should bring it after dark," Mata ChaLik said. "What will the Keepers think?"

"If you don't come immediately," Billy's frustration boiled over. "Your concerns about what the others think will be meaningless. Do you not understand? The savages are about to overrun us. If they do, there won't be any new propulsion tube," he spoke loudly in his native tongue.

Kerr inched closer to Billy, staring at him. "Omigod," he said to his aide. "He's having a fit."

Billy ignored him.

"Yes," Mata ChaLik said. "I'm just beyond your horizon. I'm setting a course for you now."

"Approach the foundry directly," Billy said. "Just do it."

"But, but ..." It was obvious that Mata ChaLik had not expected Billy to speak in this fashion.

"Yes?" Billy was breathing heavily.

"Nothing. I'll arrive soon."

The Clan's archers had a rhythm. They fired volleys of arrows while the wagons were pushed forward, then moved up and did it again. Explosive bombs sailed over their heads and landed on the settlement's defenses. Gunfire from the Feds' outer perimeter began to decline.

"What's that noise?" Pete Watson asked Dutch Malley. They were part of the crew firing bombs from a catapult.

"Sounds like a swarm of bees."

"WHAAAHOOOOM." A giant bat-like creature screamed across the sky. As it passed overhead, its shadow covered an entire platoon. It had a mottled appearance, a beak-like nose and two oval holes looked like black, sunken eyes. It continued to scream like a banshee from Hell.

All fighting stopped.

Clan and Fed fighters stared at the thing in the sky. "What the hell is that?" Pete Watson's jaw sagged open.

The Bird-that-Soars raised its main airbrakes, which made it look as though it had flapped its wings. It swept over them again, its two staring eyes ever larger. Its landing struts unfolded, just like the talons of a bird of prey ready to stoop.

The Bird-that-Soars passed low over the foundry and rolled into a banking turn. As it came back, its engines grew louder as its thrust vector nozzles rotated forward to reduce its velocity. It came to a hover, howling its ungodly song. Slowly, ever so slowly, it descended on the foundry. Dust swirled and rose in a billowing cloud.

2

Billy ran from the foundry, waving his arms to get attention. "Get inside. Get in the building, do it now. Get under cover." He knew that the downdraft from the Bird-that-Soars would be fierce. "Captain Kerr, get everyone inside now." he said. "Use force if necessary but get everyone in the building before the flying machine arrives."

No one had to be told twice. The rush for the door started. Most had fled at the sight of the sky monster. Once inside the foundry, they huddled together amid sooty machinery festooned with cobwebs. Some had been caught by the wind from the Bird-that-Soars in the scramble to get inside and been knocked to the ground. The injured moaned; others swore steadily like they were chanting a mantra. Those who were convinced it was a monster from Hell crossed themselves and prayed loudly, invoking the names of their favorite Saints.

The Bird-that-Soars hung a hundred feet above the foundry on its eastern side. As it hovered, its biocomputer acquired images of the iron melting equipment's lifting points. Its lifting grapples rattled down.

"The flying machine belongs to my friends. It will save us," Billy called. "Guard captains, get your men under control."

Inside the cavernous foundry building, amongst the gloom and black machinery, the guard captains looked at each other, faces long and uncertain. They said nothing.

"The flying machine has come to take the iron melting equipment to Defiance." Billy raised his voice, so all could hear him.

A crowd gathered around him, silent and sullen.

"It will not hurt you."

They had been attacked by Clan soldiers; bombarded by explosives; and now, a flying monster hung over their heads. Fear filled the air with its rank smell. It was common knowledge Billy would kill them if they disobeyed his orders; they'd seen him do it many times.

At the far end of the foundry, the flying machine's screaming engines grew louder. Something clattered and clanged. Machinery screeched. The furnace jerked upwards to disappear through the opening in the foundry's roof. Black clouds of dust roiled out between the grimy steel columns, spreading rapidly, and filling the air, making it difficult to see.

The noise from the flying machine increased briefly to a shriek then faded. At the eastside of the building, the noise sighed down in volume and pitch.

The crowd grew still, quiet, listening.

Silence fell.

"Guards," Billy called. "Assemble everyone by the east door of the foundry. Now." His voice cracked. "You will ride in the flying machine back to Defiance."

For a moment silence reigned.

All at once it seemed that everyone tried to speak. Voices babbled loudly. The civilians, exhausted, dirty, some wounded and most frightened, were on the edge of panic. Many screamed their fears.

"Silence," Kerr yelled. "Silence."

BOOM. Kerr fired his gun over their heads.

The crowd froze, silent.

"Quiet, damn it," Kerr yelled. "Be quiet. Listen to Billy Potato." He climbed on top of a workbench. "Has he ever misled you? Has he ever deserted you? Hasn't he fought alongside you and risked his life for you?" Downward chops of Kerr's fist marked time with his words. "Why would he deceive you now? He hasn't and won't. Listen to him and do what he says." He glared at a sea of pale faces. "If you don't, then by God, you'll answer to me," Kerr's voice echoed off the metal walls. His face was red and grim. He reached for another gun and cocked it.

It was as though he'd dared the crowd to challenge him. None did. There was a fragile measure of order, but just below the surface, panic still simmered.

Billy clambered awkwardly in his strangely disjointed fashion up onto the workbench next to Kerr. Billy was almost hidden beneath his ever-present cloak and wide-brimmed hat. He seemed tiny next to Kerr's height and muscular build.

"Thank you, Captain Kerr." Billy gave his caricature of a smile and glanced from side to side. "The flying machine is here to help us. It belongs to my friends. It will take the iron melting equipment to Defiance. I will ride in the flying machine." He paused. "You will come with me. It has much room." Billy gave his version of a smile. "It is quite safe."

There was a hiss as the crowd drew a collective breath. "Between here and Defiance are Clan soldiers, so it will be much safer to come with me in the flying machine." Billy turned and looked at Kerr. "Right, Captain Kerr?"

"Yes," Kerr said without hesitation. "All my guards are going, too." He glared at the crowd.

There was a murmur of nervous voices.

"Remember, if you stay," Kerr said. "The Clan soldiers will come and get you and you will die at their hands."

The crowd stirred.

Billy held up his hands and got an uneasy silence. "Good," he said. "The flying machine is outside the east door."

Many in the restive crowd averted his gaze.

"It is ready for you," Billy said. "It has room for all. Bring only what you can carry in your hands—nothing more. I shall go first." He jumped down from the workbench. "Follow me." He marched toward the door.

The crowd parted fluidly before him without a word.

Outside, the Bird-that-Soars sat perched on its ungainly struts, looking away from the building. At its rear, a ramp extended like a giant metallic tongue between the two openings of its engines. Suspended beneath its wings was the iron-casting equipment, almost like a mother hen protecting her chicks. The circular openings on each side of the ramp softly crackled and pinged.

At the base of the textured metal ramp, Billy turned and beckoned for them to follow. He marched up the ramp, past the two engine openings at the rear of the craft, toward its doors.

He could hear people start to talk. He kept moving. He stopped when he reached the top.

Billy looked back. Captain Kerr's men herded the civilians out the foundry's door. They had stopped at the bottom of the ramp and stared at him. Billy beckoned that they should come. He turned and walked inside where he stopped to listen.

Yes, I can hear their footsteps—they are coming.

Inside, the open compartment stretched for about two hundred feet and was thirty-five feet wide. The ceiling, twelve feet high, was strongly reinforced with curved beams and fitted with glowing orange light panels. The textured metal floor glittered and had flush-fitting metal loops set at regular intervals. Bright green webbing hung from its walls. At the far end, the wall was bare of webbing and had two metal doors. In between the two doors was a large square panel of a dull, gray material that looked like textured glass.

It took a quarter-hour until the last person entered the Bird-that-Soars. Some were afraid to enter the belly of the sky monster and fled —more willing to take their chances with the Clan soldiers. Others, more curious, tried to go further into the Bird-that-Soars, but no door would open for them. Some came out of a sense of duty or fear of Captain Kerr; others had to be prodded on board. Some sat huddled, almost catatonic. Some—not all of them children—sucked their thumbs.

The compartment resonated with babies crying, moans of the wounded, and the near hysterical chatter of those who had more fear than curiosity. The air was thick with the smell of smoke, unwashed bodies, vomit, and voided bowels.

"These will now close." Billy pointed to the clamshell doors at the rear of the flying machine. "Soon, we'll leave. The trip to Defiance will take ten minutes." As he spoke, the doors folded in and closed with a metallic clunk. Fans began to blow, bringing fresh air. The stench lessened.

A high-pitched whine started. It rapidly increased in pitch and volume—more felt than heard. There was a rumble and a loud clunk. The noise increased further. The flying machine made a lurch, tilted slightly, and began to vibrate gently.

CHAPTER TWENTY

When Chris saw the strange flying monster arrive, she wanted to bang her head on the wall and wake up to find it was only a bad dream. The sight of a strange apparition hovering like a hawk over the old foundry with its unending scream was like nothing she'd ever heard before. Finally, it disappeared behind a blackened hulk of a building, its sound fading as though it were gone.

"You, Watson," Chris said. "Go and find out what's happening in there. Don't pick a fight just find out what they're doing. Got it?"

"Me?" Watson wrinkled his nose as though he smelled something bad. "My platoon's on the catapults—"

"Move it, Watson," Chris yelled. "Don't give me any crap."

"Yes, ma'am." Watson's voice was sullen. The squad leader mounted slowly and gestured without enthusiasm for his men to get on their horses. They trotted toward the settlement in the wide line they used when scouting hostile territory.

※

The squad rode around the perimeter but saw no one. As they rounded the eastside of the foundry, Watson saw it. Before them was the flying monster, huge and close. "Whoa." Watson reined his horse to an abrupt halt. "I don't like this one bit."

The strange flying machine was still and silent. At its front were two oval openings that stared like black, bottomless eyes. The mass of the machine hunched over spindly legs, like a raptor about to devour its prey.

"We've seen enough." Watson looked around as though he was being watched. "It's time to go back." He gave a signal and the squad executed a turn around the corner. Once out of the monster's sight, they spurred their horses into a gallop and raced back.

೨

Watson reined his lathered mount to a halt.

Chris stepped up. "Did you see any Fed guards?"

"No, ma'am." Watson's eyes were wide. "We had to leave. The flying monster saw us. We're lucky to get back alive." He was flushed and breathing hard.

"Did you go completely around the settlement?" Chris asked. She already knew the answer because the squad had returned in the same direction they had left. "Well?"

"No, ma'am. When we got to the eastside of the foundry, the monster was there. Its eyes, it was watching us—"

"Yeah, yeah," Chris said. They were afraid. *Crap*, she thought. *I better send a larger force.* "Doaks, take two platoons in there," she said. "Don't attack the flying monster. Just find out where the Fed troops are hiding."

"Yes, ma'am."

೨

Doaks guided the platoons through the broken gate and picked their way into the deserted settlement. Guns lay scattered on the ground as though thrown carelessly away. Everywhere, buildings had roofs burned out and doors off their hinges.

"Sheesh," Doaks said. "It's kinda spooky." The streets were

deserted, silent. "Let's go that way." He pointed toward the hulking black building that dominated the Fed settlement. It was in the opposite direction to that which Watson had taken.

As they approached the east end of the black building, several people ran off. When they reached its corner, the scream of the flying machine started, only this time it was louder.

"Let's get the hell out of here," Doaks yelled over the rising sound. The Horse Soldiers pivoted and galloped back to the west entrance. As Doaks slowed to pick his way through the entrance, he glanced over his shoulder. The flying machine was slowly rising from behind the building.

"Omigod, it's coming after us," Doaks yelled.

He flogged his horse with his crop. "Move it, dammit, move it." It took but a moment for the mounted men to break free of the shattered entrance, their horses' hooves pounding the turf.

To Doaks the flying machine looked as though it were a giant primeval bat whose eyes saw everything, and it soon caught up with him.

Some of Doaks's squads even reached the main contingent of Clan soldiers. Order evaporated as the flying monster approached. When it passed overhead, a powerful wind struck, knocking both man and beast to the ground. The group of men and horses directly under the flying monster were tossed around like autumn leaves, scattering them in all directions.

On the forward wall of the ship, the gray panel glowed into luminescence. It coalesced into a detailed image of the land below. "Look," someone said. "It's the foundry."

The panel showed a picture from a viewpoint high above. A group of Clan soldiers appeared on the screen. They were riding hard. Without warning or reason, they began to fall to the ground and tumble around. As the Clan soldiers got up, they scattered in all directions.

The guards near the screen raised a weak cheer.

The view screen soon captivated the passengers. Land seemed to pass across the screen at an incredible rate as it followed the highway. When it showed the Maumee River, they saw that the bridge was missing a section. The view screen became a source of entertainment to those sitting near it—except to those who were still afraid. A few recognized some of the dwellings on the screen.

"Er, excuse me, Mr. Potato." Captain Kerr quietly tugged Billy's sleeve. "Just who're these friends of yours? I've seen a lot of the civilized world. But this here flying machine is something else. I've even been to St. Louis and seen the miraculous Great Arch. Even there, I never saw a flying machine. My folks told me about flying machines from the times before the Collapse. I always thought they were just tales of magic." Kerr paused. "Just who are these friends, sir?"

"My friends come from the same place as me." Billy hesitated. He realized that the trip would be over before he could give an explanation. "It's a long way from here. It's not even in this country. It is a place not affected by the Collapse. We saw signs the Collapse had taken place. We did not know what it was and came here to find out." Billy said. "I never realized my coming here would cause trouble with your neighbors."

The engine pitch started to drop.

"We're almost there." Billy glanced at the people huddled on the floor of the cargo compartment. They were dirty and many bore wounds. Less than half the guards stationed at Perrysburg were on the Bird-that-Soars. These people had suffered in the siege.

"I did not know the iron melting equipment would cause trouble, but it is needed. I don't have time to explain more. We must get ready for our arrival."

"Arrival?" Kerr cocked his head. "Where?"

"Defiance," Billy said. "We'll be there in a moment."

"Right," Kerr said.

Everyone knew that it took a day to go from Perrysburg to Defiance by wagon. Whatever this flying machine was, it just didn't bump and bang enough for something moving fast.

"When we get to Defiance, put guards around the iron melting equipment. Send a courier into the city and inform the people the flying machine is not dangerous to them." Billy glanced at the screen. It showed an empty meadow. "Captain Kerr, your questions will have to wait."

A clunk and a bump vibrated the cargo hold. The high-pitched whine faded into silence. The passengers became quiet. The doors sighed, clunked, and swung open. In the west were buildings and to the north was a broken-down factory.

Kerr stared at the distant city. "Why," he said. "That looks a lot like Defiance. It can't be ..."

"Captain Kerr." Billy's voice was harsh.

"It is Defiance." Kerr had difficulty breathing. "Yes, sir?"

"Give your orders." Billy's face was impassive. "Get everyone out quickly. My friends cannot wait."

"Yes, right away." Kerr shook his head. He pointed to a Fed guard. "You, you're in charge of getting these people out of here."

"Me?" The Fed guard's eyebrows went up.

"Move it." Kerr's voice had a hard edge.

The disheveled survivors of Perrysburg straggled into Defiance. The townspeople watched silently from the doorways of the old red brick buildings. It was as though the survivors were something strange, touched. The news of a Clan raid on Perrysburg was ominous, particularly to the older citizens. The appearance of the flying apparition was even stranger.

The Bird-that-Soars unloaded the iron melting equipment at the derelict General Motors' foundry. Once free of its burden, it rose fifty feet off the ground and moved to the northeast, away from the city, looking like an ungainly bird. Once across the wide Maumee River, it roared fiercely and climbed in an almost vertical direction. In a matter of seconds, it disappeared from sight.

In the quiet hours just before dawn, Billy watched the Bird-that-Soars return with a huge bundle of iron and steel structural members salvaged from Perrysburg. It was material needed to build the framework that would hold the molds. Once the ship deposited its load on the ground, it rose high into the sky and vanished. It was time to get back to work.

CHAPTER TWENTY-ONE

"Commander Kuchinski? Are you all right? Say something, please." Stanek's round face came into focus.

Pain throbbed in Chris's left arm.

"Are you all right?" Stanek's eyebrows knitted together.

"I don't know." Chris sat up. "My left arm hurts." She motioned to Stanek to help her rise. The effort made her grit her teeth. "Thanks, Stanek." Her left arm was bent in an odd way and it hurt like hell.

Bodies littered the field. Only now did she realize how powerful the wind from the flying machine had been—it had thrown man and beast in all directions. Bloody streaks on the green grass led to broken bodies, with at least fifty soldiers down, some moaning and a few crying for help. Others lay motionless and silent. Injured horses made screaming noises like those of tortured humans.

Chris shook her head. "Things have really turned to crap. God dammit, Stanek," Chris said. "Put those horses out of their misery." She noticed a couple of the soldiers had soiled themselves and made mewling sounds like that of babies—they had head injuries.

Jesus Christ, Chris thought. *Just from the passage of that damn flying machine.*

"Stanek," Chris called. "Where's that flying thing?"

"I'm not sure." Stanek scratched his head. "The last I saw, it was heading west over the river."

"Establish a watch. I don't want it sneaking up on us."

"Yes, ma'am." He turned to go.

"Get Sinkton," Chris said. "I've got a job for him."

As she waited, one by one, the screaming horses went quiet. She felt chilled. She struggled to pull a blanket over her shoulders. The injured arm made it difficult.

"You sent for me, ma'am?" Todd Sinkton asked in a quiet voice as he adjusted the blanket around her.

"Thanks," Chris said. "Yes. Scout out the settlement. See if the Fed guards are still there. Do it without attracting attention. Take men who know how to be quiet." Every beat of her heart caused her arm to throb.

～

Todd returned within an hour. "There's no one there. Not a soul in the settlement."

"Is everything still there?" Chris remembered seeing something hanging under the flying monster.

"Well, it looks like a bunch of big stuff, like the melt equipment, is missing from the foundry."

"Foundry? Why d'you think it was a foundry?" Chris asked.

"Look." Todd handed her a piece of iron.

"What's this?" Chris turned it over. One side was flat and the other was rounded.

"It's a metal splash. They're usually found in pour areas of foundries. There's a lot of this on the ground where the equipment was taken out. Also, there's a pile of scrap iron stacked up just outside the building."

"Are you sure?" Chris asked.

"Yes, ma'am," Todd said. "I worked at the foundry at the Hill during the summer. That was before I got a land grant to start a farm. This kind of thing is typical. 'Cept this place is huge. They must have poured tons and tons of iron here."

"Thanks, that'll be all." Chris saw no reason to stay in Perrysburg any longer. "Stanek." She called the officer over. "Let's get moving. We're going back to Maumee Harbor." The sky had darkened, and the wind picked up.

Crap, now it's gonna rain.

It was the first time she had experienced anything like this. For the past ten years the Clan had not lost a battle. It had taken but a moment for that machine to wreak havoc. Even though the enemy had fled the scene, it didn't feel like a victory.

As she rode back to the harbor, Chris worried about sending the news of the expedition's failure to the Clan Elders. *I'd better take some witnesses to testify as to what happened, she thought.*

The Elders were famous for asking probing questions, variations of the same questions again and again, ready to pounce on any discrepancy. Her stomach soured at the thought. Every step of the horse jolted pain up her arm.

~

At the harbor, Chris demobilized the units from the western frontier and sent them home. They'd carry the news of husbands and sons who would not return. The soldiers who had come from Rocky River would stay in the barracks at the harbor.

"Stanek," Chris said. "You're in charge. I'm going to the Hill." She tightened her lips.

"Yes, ma'am."

"There's something I want you to do while I'm gone." Chris guessed the odds of her returning to command were slim to nil once the Elders heard her story. "Look, I think there's a spy in our ranks. If not there, then in the harbor somewhere."

"You think so?" Stanek plucked at his lower lip.

"Yes." Chris frowned. "The way the Fed never came to the bridge after we cut their power lines makes me believe they knew we were there. Not even their scouts."

Stanek nodded. "You're right. They never did come to see what had happened." He looked into the distance, thinking.

"While I'm gone, keep your eyes and ears open for information. Look for someone who leaves the harbor frequently, someone who regularly visits Fed territory. Ask around, you know, quietly."

"Got it." Furrows appeared between Stanek's eyebrows.

Chris took a sloop, which made a fast voyage to Rivermouth on a steady wind out of the south.

The boat sailed a course close inshore where the water was flat. The sloop sailed on beam reach, slicing through gentle swells of clear, almost turquoise waters, with its white sails fully filled, rigging thrumming. The lean black hull left a dancing trail of sparkling bubbles in its swirling wake.

In the shallow areas off Cedar Point, Chris could see the boat's shadow racing across the rippled sandy bottom. At Avon Point, over deeper water, seagulls began following the sloop, dipping into its wake to seek the small fish brought to the surface by its turbulence.

Chris saw little of the trip back—her mind was elsewhere. She played the encounter with the flying machine over and over in her mind's eye. She reviewed and analyzed her actions. *I think I did all that was possible under the circumstances,* she thought. *Until it appeared, I was sure of victory.* The more she thought about it, the surer she was it was a flying machine—a technological terror out of the past. Even so, that would be no excuse and she feared her career was over.

"Commander Kuchinski," Jon Beach said slowly like he was talking to a child. "Do you realize what you're saying? A flying machine?" He leaned back. His chair squeaked in the quiet emptiness of the council chamber. "Please, even you can do better than that." He waved his hand as though to dismiss her.

It wasn't until after the Elders interviewed the witnesses separately and in private their attitude changed.

"So, what are we going to do about this?" Beach asked.

"Better talk to MacPherson," Carver Washington said.

"Do we really have to involve the old fart?"

"I agree with Carver," Ramsey said. "He's from the time before the Collapse. He knows about such things."

"I don't know." Beach frowned. "I think he's long past his prime and well into his dotage."

"Put it to a vote." Ramsey polled the Council with his eyes. All voted for it except Beach. "Let's get him in here."

"Flying machines? Electricity?" Taylor's voice rose. "Do you know what this means? Those are products of a technologically advanced society." He stroked his chin and looked down. "The Fed is far from that. They're a bunch of farmers. Sure, they might be able to make electricity. A flying machine? Never." He stared at the Council of Elders.

"We learned about the Fed's electricity last fall," Beach said. "Our scouts found men putting wire on poles near Perrysburg." He leaned forward with a knowing look. "Since they were in Clan territory, that caught our attention—"

"What? You mean to tell me you knew the Fed had electricity six months ago?" The lines between Taylor's eyebrows narrowed. "You've been keeping it a secret? Haven't you paid attention to anything I've said? Electricity is essential to rebuild our civilization. And you kept that to yourselves?"

"Er, yes, it's a Clan secret." Beach often sought cover for his actions by invoking Council authority.

"What?" Taylor said. "Why? Trying to figure how to make a profit from it? Or is it a political angle?" He lowered his voice. "I would've gone to the Fed in person to get electricity for the Clan. Even if I had to crawl on my hands and knees." He wagged his finger at them. "Electricity is a key technology." His voice rose. "And you kept it your dirty little secret. It could, no, will lift us from this miserable, grubby existence into a real life and you hid the knowledge."

The Council was silent. They looked at one another. They refused to meet Taylor's stare.

"Let me see." Taylor stared briefly at the ceiling. "I suppose it was one of you who sent Joe Del Corso to weasel information out of me on how to use electricity as a weapon."

Beach and Ramsey averted Taylor's sweeping stare.

"Gentlemen." Taylor's voice was controlled—even polite. "I'm sorry that you think me untrustworthy." He bowed his head and turned to go.

"Taylor, please," Washington said quickly. "We need your help, your expertise. Help us understand what's happening. We don't know how to deal with this." He spread his hands. "I never favored keeping this electricity thing a secret." He hesitated. "It was a mistake. I'm sorry. Can you help us overcome our mistake?"

"Carver, since you asked, I'll help." Taylor's shoulders sagged as he looked at Washington.

Washington stared back without flinching.

"Not tonight, I'm tired. In the morning. Send me the eyewitnesses who brought this story to your attention. I need to question them to find out—"

"We've already questioned the officers involved," Beach said with a wave of his hand. "They'll return to their posts tomorrow. The Council will provide you with the details—"

"Beach, you don't know squat." Taylor's voice echoed off the chamber's bare walls. "You never listened to me, never asked any questions about the pre-Collapse times. You wouldn't have a clue as to what questions to ask." He wagged his finger. "Your details would be as useful as tits on a boar hog." Taylor paused at the door. "I'll talk to the witnesses tomorrow."

ᘓ

Outside the council chamber door, Taylor saw Chris Kuchinski.

"Chris, did you see the flying machine?" Taylor found he had a sudden thirst for answers.

"Yes," Chris said.

"Describe the flying machine; how did it fly?"

"It was big. It made a terrible noise," Chris said. "It was misshapen —it didn't look like any aircraft I remember."

Taylor frowned.

"Maybe I could make a drawing of it, then you'd have a better idea of what I saw."

"Good idea. We'll do that tomorrow." Taylor nodded. "What happened at the bridge when you cut the electricity line?"

"Well, a soldier tried to cut the wires." Chris hesitated. "There was blue fire all around him. When he fell off the pole, he was all burned." She hesitated. "And he smelled like roasted pork. We used five hundred pounds of black powder to blow up the bridge. When the wires touched the ground, they flashed. Later, we found beads of copper all over the place."

"Come to my home tomorrow morning, an hour after first light." Taylor nodded. "We need to talk more."

CHAPTER TWENTY-TWO

"I'm sorry I'm late." Chris Kuchinski stood at the steps leading to the door of Taylor's home. Wind blew her gray-streaked hair around her long face. A yellowed sling held her left arm. "I had to clear coming here with Elder Ramsey. I've got to follow the chain of command, or I'll be in even more trouble."

"Hah, more chicken shit," Taylor said. "Chris, we're going for a hike up-river. I've got something to show you."

They walked along the old footpath bordering the east branch of the Rocky River through the dense woods of the former park. They talked about the incidents at Perrysburg and renewed their friendship. Chris's account revealed she had a good memory and an eye for detail.

In Berea, Taylor led Chris through the maze of damaged and abandoned buildings in the former Baldwin-Wallace University to an ivy-covered building. He unlocked a door, which opened silently on well-oiled hinges and took her to the top floor. It was a laboratory where two technicians started an old gasoline motor and powered up a generator. In an adjacent room, Taylor turned on a computer. Its screen glowed, as text scrolled across it.

"Is this really a computer?" Chris asked.

"Yes. It's my little secret," Taylor said as he input commands to the computer. "The Elders won't support my ideas, so I pay for it and keep it to myself." The screen flickered. The colorful graphical interface appeared.

"Jeez, what's that?" Chris only vaguely remembered pre-Collapse technology. It gave her a similar feeling like when she had first seen the flying machine. Except this time, she had no fear. It was like being a little girl all over again.

Taylor loaded a memory device. He swore several times as he struggled to get the command sequence right. An image of a machine appeared on the screen. "Take a look." He pointed. "These are pictures of aircraft from pre-Collapse times. This one's the C17 troop transport. It's in the size range you gave for the flying machine. What do you think?"

"No, no. It's not even close." Chris pointed. "Those wings are too long and too skinny."

Taylor manipulated a control. A series of images scrolled rapidly. "What do you think?"

"Gee, I didn't remember this many aircraft in the pre-Collapse times." Chris reached out and touched the screen.

Taylor scratched his head. "You say that it rose straight up? Do you mean vertically?"

"Yes, with a great sound and a violent wind." Chris remembered the passage of the flying machine. "It also flew horizontally after it rose above the factory."

"I see." Taylor gestured with his hands. "Did the flying machine tilt or turn upright?"

Chris smiled at the miming effort. "No," she said. "It didn't sway from side to side."

"How about this one?" Taylor said. It was a Harrier jump jet. "Are you sure it was larger? How about this?"

"No, that's not it," Chris said. "I wish I could be more helpful." She bit her lower lip, worried that she might be accused of dreaming up the incident. "It did have openings in the front somewhat like this one. Except they were on the very front of the machine."

Taylor scrolled rapidly through the remaining images.

"That's it, that one," Chris said quickly. "Oh, no, for a second I thought it was the machine."

"That's the Space Shuttle." Taylor looked at her. "What made you think it was that one?"

"It has the same sort of boxy appearance. Its wings look similar except they seemed like they had been cut off. They also looked like there was a set of shelves perched on top. It also had two air intakes at the front. It has the same type of legs as this one." She pointed at the landing gear.

"Are you sure?" Taylor watched her carefully.

Chris stared intently at the image. "Yes, this part." She pointed at the tail fin. "Was shaped differently. It came more toward the front." She traced an outline on the screen.

"Damn," Taylor said. "I wish I had a graphics program to create an image." He paused. "Well, what did it sound like?"

"It made a scream and a roar like a tornado," Chris said. "It was so loud it made the ground shake and my ears ache. Its wind knocked my horse to the ground. That's how I broke my arm."

"You had to be very close when that happened," Taylor said. He hesitated. "What did its wind smell like?"

"Smell?" Chris frowned. "It didn't smell."

"Many pre-Collapse aircraft used oil as a fuel," Taylor explained. "It has a distinctive odor, y'know like a lantern."

"Oh, I've smelled oil burning, I know what you mean." Chris nodded. "This didn't smell like that. If there were any smell at all, it was like when a stove gets really hot. I don't mean the wood smoke smell—the hot metal smell. Do y'know what I mean?"

"Yeah, I think so. We're getting nowhere fast," Taylor said softly. "Do you think you could make a sketch of it?"

"I'll try, but I'm not an artist." Chris made several sketches of what she had seen.

Her drawing showed it had sharply swept-back wings that turned up at the ends. It had two air intakes near the front and two engine outlets at the back. Yet it took off vertically and could hover.

Taylor gave up trying to identify the flying machine. "This isn't like anything I've ever seen before. It has to be something that was new or top secret in pre-Collapse times. I don't know what it is. Now, Chris, you must swear to never reveal the existence of this equipment. Promise?"

"Taylor," Chris said. "Don't you trust me?"

"Sorry, I forget sometimes." Taylor laughed. "Join me for lunch?" Warmth crept into his voice. "My housekeeper probably has a pot of soup going. There'll be plenty for both of us."

"Thanks." Chris relaxed. "I'd like that."

That afternoon, Taylor went to the Council of Elders. "I cannot identify the flying machine. However, Commander Kuchinski and I have prepared sketches." He passed the drawings around. "Without knowing what type of flying machine it is, I can't tell what kind of threat it presents nor what it can do. I just don't have enough information."

Ramsey smiled. "We have the responsibility to lead the Clan and protect it from outside dangers. We must know what we're facing. What about electricity? How does the Fed use it as a weapon?"

"Electricity." Taylor hesitated, thinking about the question. "First, it's not used directly as a weapon. If you touch a wire carrying enough electricity, it'll kill you. Armies never used electricity as a weapon or a means to kill in combat. I don't believe the Fed uses electricity as a direct weapon." He took a deep breath.

"I think the Fed is using electricity to make weapons. The guns Commander Kuchinski brought back are new and well made. They have high quality machining and consistent dimensions. That concerns me. I believe machines powered by electricity made those guns. Listen carefully, this is important. With electricity, fewer people can make weapons faster and better. Whoever has electricity will be better armed."

"Yes, but our archers can out-shoot an equal number of men with guns anytime." Beach frowned, indicating he didn't think it was a meaningful threat.

"The real value of electricity in war is the economic benefit. It frees up the labor supply and provides greater flexibility in manufacturing. Simply put, with electricity you have greater material output and can put bigger armies in the field."

"Does the Fed now have a bigger army?" Beach asked.

"It sure sounds like it." Ramsey's eyes seemed fixed on a spot on the distant wall. "Remember Kuchinski's report from her visit to Perrysburg? The Fed showed off their new forces—even bragged about them. That sounds like it."

"Electricity and technology are almost synonymous," Taylor said. "Electricity can drive motors more powerful than the largest mill race. If we had electricity, we could move our manufacturing away from the rivers to the food surplus areas. Electricity would replace manual labor in our factories."

"So?" Beach's expression showed he'd heard Taylor's sermon before. It was obvious it bored him as much today as it did the first time.

"We need electricity." Taylor raised his voice. "We've got to find out how the Fed does it, so we can get on with rebuilding our civilization. Let's make peace with the Fed and find out how they make the electricity. Let's negotiate with them—we can give up the western lands we don't need."

"Mr. MacPherson. Thank you for your opinions," Ramsey said coldly. "I think you've overlooked the fact the Fed trespassed on our lands, killed our settlers, and has taken a large iron furnace from us. I don't like the Clan being treated that way." Everyone knew he was still angry about the expedition's defeat.

"Yeah, that's right," Beach said in a loud voice. The proposal to give away western lands would sit poorly with him when his people needed living space. Everyone knew the value of iron. "MacPherson." He dropped all pretenses of politeness. "You stated that electricity is not a weapon. Correct?"

"Yes, but you're missing the point—"

"Excuse me, MacPherson." Beach raised his voice. "This is our meeting. You've given us the results of your interrogation of Commander Kuchinski. For the record, I note you haven't been able to identify the flying machine, nor given us the answers we need." He paused. "Now you want us to surrender Clan land to the Fed? That,

MacPherson, borders on treason. If you've forgotten, the Council makes the policy for the Clan, not you." His voice had risen to a shout.

The council chamber was totally silent.

Ramsey cleared his throat. "Thank you, Mr. Beach. I think the word treason is a little strong. I understand your feelings. The Fed has trespassed, killed settlers, and stolen an iron melting furnace. Why should we negotiate with them?"

"Damn straight." Beach looked surprised.

"All in favor of sending an ultimatum to the Fed to make reparations and return our iron furnace?" Ramsey glanced from side to side at the Elders present. "The language will be worked out in camera. Those in favor?"

"Aye," Beach said.

"Nay." A frown filled Washington's face.

The rest of the Council approved the motion.

Washington said nothing. It was well known he did not like war. Ever since his eldest son had fallen in battle, he opposed sending young men out to face hot lead and cold steel.

CHAPTER TWENTY-THREE

Todd Sinkton carried a message from the Elders to the Midwest Federation using the sloop from Rivermouth. There was little wind on Lake Erie—a typical midsummer's day. The boat spent most of the day with its sails slating aimlessly under a cloudless sky and a brassy sun. When the sun set, the moon rose, big and golden. Soon after, a gentle offshore breeze started. By midnight the sloop ghosted into Maumee Harbor.

A nearby cock crowing brought morning too soon, waking Todd. After a quick breakfast, Todd learned his old friend Chud had been arrested on suspicion of passing information to the enemy.

After the disaster at Perrysburg, a hunt for an informant started and Chud's compulsion to talk got him into trouble. Todd knew if Chud had passed information to the enemy, he would hang.

Todd set off for Defiance with two soldiers as escort. He knew once he crossed the Maumee River, there was a real chance of catching a stray arrow or lead ball even while carrying a white flag.

Their horses plodded along a crumbling asphalt road through flat, rich farmland filled with bountiful crops of grains, tomatoes, and cabbages, and fat cattle lowing in pastures. Farmers glanced at them but said nothing. At the city of Napoleon, a local Fed guard commander disarmed the Clan soldiers even though they carried a white flag. He accepted Todd's explanation but escorted them to Defiance under guard.

In Defiance, the civilians made catcalls as they walked amid the red brick buildings lining the main street of the city. At the Victorian-style courthouse on the town square, they were directed to go inside.

"Mr. Potato," Todd said, "I've got a message for you from the Elders of the Clan of Rocky River."

"Yes." Billy didn't even look at the envelope. "I am curious why you attacked us. We have much to discuss."

"Mr. Potato, I can't negotiate on behalf of the Clan. I'm just a messenger." Todd noticed Billy had accepted the letter containing the ultimatum sent by the Clan Elders but had not opened it. He'd heard rumors their leader was illiterate. Seeing him in person, he wondered how this freak had become leader of the Fed in the first place.

"I must get this message read and discuss it with my staff," Billy said. "In the meantime." He swiveled with a peculiar movement. "Hornyak," he said. "Provide the Clan delegation with comfortable accommodations in the guards' barracks. They must not be harmed."

"Yes, sir, Mr. Billy, right away." Hornyak smiled and nodded. "Just a moment please." He went to the door. "Greenwood," he yelled. "Get your ass in here."

A mousy little man appeared in the doorway. "Yes, sir?"

"Escort these gentlemen to the barracks. Give them the best of everything and protection around the clock. Got it?"

"Yes, sir, Mr. Hornyak," he said, "I'll take them myself."

"Thank you." *So far, so good,* Todd thought. He recognized the logic of their lodgings.

"Kerr," Billy said. "Assemble the Fed representatives and guard captains right away."

"Yes." Kerr frowned. "Anything I should know about?"

"I want the letter from the Clan Elders read to them."

Kerr moved fast and brought representatives and captains into the Court House. When he read the letter, its contents set the Court House abuzz.

"Why," Billy asked. "Is the iron furnace an issue to the Clan? Tell me, what do you think should be done?"

Pastor Jones jumped up. "Sir, I knew no good would come from messing around with that thar pre-Collapse technology." It was his oft-repeated sermon on the dangers of technology and the need for faith. "It's like there's been an evil genie let out of a bottle. Now we're cursed and only the power of prayer—"

"Yes, we know that," Ned Biehl, a representative from Napoleon, said. "The Clan must still think of us as farmers. Why don't we show these Clan people around? Let them see how much we've advanced over the last few years. Tell them we want peace, but we won't be a pushover. Offer them trade."

"The Clan forced us to cede the land east of the Maumee River," Kerr said. "When they attacked Perrysburg, we held off two hundred clan Horse Soldiers. Now they want our iron furnace." His voice rose. "Well, it sat unused for umpteen years and they never cared about it until we repaired it. It seems to me they still think they dominate us."

Heads nodded approval.

"Those days are over." Kerr stabbed his index finger into the palm of his hand. "If the Clan crosses the Maumee, they'll face two thousand or more of our guns. Let them keep the land east of the Maumee. We keep our iron furnace."

A roar of approval followed. Many tried speaking at once.

Billy raised a hand. The room quieted. "I will tell the emissaries the Midwest Federation will remain west of the Maumee River." He spoke slowly. "I will refuse their request for the iron furnace." His eyes settled on the grizzled captain of the guards. "Captain Kerr, you give me good counsel. Arrange for the Clan guests to review our guards as soon as possible."

The room erupted into a round of applause.

Billy held up a hand and the crowd quieted. "The meeting is over," he said.

After the crowd left, Billy pulled Kerr to one side. "Do not mobilize all the men into the guard. I need more men to work on the iron furnace."

"What's the rush?" Kerr asked.

"I must have the castings, and soon."

"Look, we've got to get our priorities straight," Kerr said. "The risk of war is real. We must be prepared to defend ourselves now that we've rejected their demands."

"The castings will be made," Billy said. "Without delay."

"Look," Kerr said. "The Clan is sure to attack us now. That's been their way. We've never held off their Horse Soldiers before. It's the damage to their pride, not the loss of the iron furnace, that's pissing them off." He realized Billy did not understand the ways of the city-states in the Midwest.

"Build a fence made from wire around the generators and iron furnace. Above all else, protect the furnace and generators. Prepare to make castings."

"Where do you want the fence?"

Billy sat motionless for a moment. "Tomorrow I will give you details. Have men ready to start work at first light of the morning."

"Mr. Sinkton, this is a small contingent of Fed guards." Kerr said. All of the guards in Defiance had been assembled for a carefully orchestrated review. Three command units marched ten abreast down West Second Street, saluting as they passed the front steps of the Court House. They executed a precise right turn onto Jefferson Street and returned to their barracks in the old Riverside Park.

"That's quite a military force." Todd raised his eyebrows. "This is a small contingent? You've got more forces elsewhere?"

"We only keep a small number of our guards on active duty in our cities." Kerr looked off into the distance.

"I see your guards all have guns," Todd said. "Doesn't anyone use the bow anymore?"

"The Fed guard doesn't."

"That must require a lot of black powder," Todd said.

"Right." Kerr nodded. "We've got plenty of black powder, even a surplus. We've considered offering it as a trade item now we've got our stocks built up."

Todd Sinkton raised his eyebrows. "Really?"

"That's right." Kerr smiled.

～

The next morning Billy gave Kerr sketches for a defense system at the industrial complex and around eastern Defiance.

"Er, excuse me," said Kerr. "This shows the wire fence connects to the electricity generators. Is that right?"

"Contact with electricity is painful, even deadly," Billy said. "When the fence is connected to the generators, this area will be very difficult to enter." He turned as to leave. "Crosby and Vargas will make the electrical connections. I want the power to the fence turned on every night and any time there's danger of attack. Put these lights by the fence." He pointed to a stack of streetlights. "It will give us an advantage if there's a night attack."

～

"So, they rejected our offer?" Ramsey frowned. The council chamber was empty, his voice echoed off the bare wood walls. The tall windows were closed, the air was stuffy.

Todd Sinkton had brought Billy Potato's message back. "He did say they'd stay west of the Maumee."

"But no iron melting furnace?"

"No." Todd hesitated. "I did get to see their troops. They've got a lot of guards stationed in Defiance."

"Really?" Beach looked up. "How many?"

"I'm not exactly sure—"

"Aren't you supposed to be a scout?" Beach's face sprouted a vicious frown.

"Yes, sir." Todd stiffened and looked straight ahead.

"Now, Sinkton," Ramsey said quietly. "Why don't you think about what you saw. Get your thoughts organized, especially on military details. When you're ready, maybe after lunch, stop back and let me know."

"Yes, sir." Todd relaxed. "I'm ready now."

"Yes?"

"There were three command units on parade, which would be seven hundred and fifty men if they're at full strength." Todd took a deep breath. "I watched them carefully to see if they were marching the same units around the block. I don't believe they were. Every single guard had a gun."

Beach looked like a snake watching a mouse. "Now you know?"

"Yes sir." Todd's eyes swiveled toward Beach. "I don't know the exact number. They moved too fast to count. I estimated that force at about seven to eight hundred men. Sir."

"Other forces?" Ramsey asked quietly.

"Sir. I saw more guards in Napoleon, but they weren't as disciplined as those in Defiance. They had new guns, too." Todd hesitated. "It's my estimate that both towns could put five guard units in the field, plus rural levies, which suggests a total force of several thousand men."

"Thank you, Sinkton, you may go." Ramsey turned to Beach. "Debriefing soldiers is a skill." He smiled, raising his eyebrows. "You should learn it."

"He was insolent," Beach said. "But that doesn't matter to you. What do we do about the Fed?"

"It's time to teach them a lesson," Ramsey said. "I know just the person to lead an expedition to Defiance and do it."

"Oh, who's that?" Carver Washington leaned forward.

"Bray Grant."

Washington's smile looked as though he were sucking on a bitter melon. "I see. Your son-in-law."

Ramsey nodded and looked down at the paper on the table.

"General mobilization?" Beach asked.

"No." Ramsey frowned. "We'll do this quietly. We'll use regular Horse Soldier units. We'll call it ..." He hesitated. "A field exercise. That's it. That way no one will be any wiser."

CHAPTER TWENTY-FOUR

Kevin O'Neil, a former engineer, had spent the last twenty-five years grubbing out a living as a farmer. When he heard the iron foundry construction had bogged down, he pushed himself forward and offered to help. Kevin reminded Billy he'd organized the move of the turbine generator. After some discussion, Billy gave him supervisory responsibility for the foundry's construction.

Kevin loved it. It gave him a chance to show his stuff. It was like the good old days from before the Collapse—a tough project and a tight deadline. He accepted the givens and designed around them. He cleared the old building and reinforced it to withstand the anticipated loads. At the same time, he relocated an old railroad siding. He used rail flatcars to move the molds from the generators to the foundry building—it was the best way to move such heavy objects. He supervised the installation of piping to connect the oxygen discharge system on the electrolysis unit of the fusion power plant to the furnace.

Once Kevin found he could mobilize as many men as he wanted for the job, he finished the work ahead of schedule. On his own initiative, he'd made four molds instead of the three Billy had requested. "Why don't we test the iron furnace by casting billets?" he asked. "That way we can check it without risking the mold."

"Yes," Billy said. "We need no problems."

Kevin felt as though he'd won a small victory.

ॐ

Two days later, Kevin started the electric arc furnace and lowered the carbon electrodes into the mass of scrap steel. It melted the metal with much vibration, popping, and clouds of brown smoke.

After the iron melted, Kevin's men withdrew the electrodes, lowered the oxygen lance to the surface of the molten iron, and started the flow of oxygen through it. Sparks, flames, and smoke billowed from the fiercely glowing mouth of the giant cylinder as its heat forced workers away. As the oxygen burned off the excess carbon in the iron, the ebullition subsided to a slow boil.

Kevin shut off the oxygen. The metal was far hotter than needed for casting and as it cooled, the workers skimmed the dross from the surface of the melt. They tilted the furnace and the brightly glowing metal ran into the mold, raising clouds of gray-brown smoke.

Kevin was impressed; they had poured eight tons of iron rods, more than had been cast during the entire previous year. The factories now had metal supplies that would last for three months.

Even though the electric furnace had only been half-full, it had performed successfully. The heat produced by the oxygen jet was greater than expected, so Kevin placed metal sheets around the top of the furnace to deflect the heat and provide protection for his workers.

ॐ

Billy felt a sense of relief now the furnace was operational. There was enough steel scrap to make the propulsion tube and the molds were almost ready. He'd previously approved Kevin's suggestion to move the molds near the generators to use the waste heat to dry the clay-bonded sand quickly. The first pour would be in two days.

The energy and drive of the Earth people worried Billy. Yet their capability to grasp complex ideas quickly and work under difficult circumstances proved very useful. It disturbed him there were two humans who understood the basics of electricity. Primitives weren't supposed to understand it.

Billy awakened to a sequence of chirps from his biocomputer—it was surveillance data. Time-lapse images showed a large number of boats arriving at Maumee River Harbor. The data also showed humans on horses converging at the harbor. The image zoomed closer. *Clan horse soldiers*, he thought. *So the eastern savages gather again. Biocomputer, estimate their numbers.*

In less than one second, the biocomputer responded. There were six hundred.

Billy knew he had to warn the people of Defiance.

"Captain Kerr," Billy said. "My friends tell me a large force of Clan soldiers arrived at Maumee Harbor. Warn the communities, mobilize the guards, and send out scouts."

"Er, how large is this group of Clan soldiers?"

Billy paused as he calculated the number into base ten. "There are six hundred soldiers mounted on horses," he said. "They have thirty carts and two projectile throwers."

The Clan's use of explosive projectiles worried him. He consulted his tactics biocomputer on primitive weapons and found one that appeared a good candidate to counter the Clan's weapon. He showed a sketch of it to Kevin O'Neil. "Can you make this?" he asked.

"A cannon gun? Do you mean like an old Civil War cannon?"

Billy ignored Kevin's question. He explained the concept of using hydrogen and oxygen from the fusion generator to propel a projectile from the tube. "Can you make it?"

Kevin stared at the sketch. It showed a long barrel with two large chambers that stuck out at right angles at its base. "Maybe not exactly like that." He scratched his head. "Let me work on it."

"Work fast," Billy said.

Kevin used a piece of scrap-iron tubing with a six-inch internal diameter and a wall thickness of over an inch, which came from the refinery. The machine shop fitted side chambers and inlet valves. They moved it to the fusion generator where they hooked up oxygen and hydrogen lines.

During trials, the cannon shot pouches of greased leather filled with ten pounds of rocks well over a thousand yards. Each time the cannon fired, the crowd cheered. It was louder than any firecrackers set off on Independence Day.

༄

"Bilik Pudjata, the eastern savages are moving toward the iron-casting facility." Mata ChaLik BuMaru's voice quavered, as though on the edge of panic. "What are your plans? The Keepers-of-the-Egg believe another delay will doom the Egg-that-Flies." With each orbit, the Egg-that-Flies drew ever closer to the outer fringes of the planet's atmosphere.

"Mata ChaLik BuMaru," Bilik said. "The people of Defiance are ready for this attack. The eastern savages will blunt their claws against the city's defenses. The iron melting furnace is safe." Bilik was confident. "Work will not stop; the Egg-that-Flies will have its parts on schedule."

༄

Mata ChaLik relayed Bilik's words to the Keepers-of-the-Egg. "This Bilik Pudjata creature sounds alien. He no longer humbles himself like one trying to return to the center of his community. Has he become a Prime Communicator?" DuKlaat YataBu asked. "How can that be? We have not accepted him as such. Yet he shows such a confidence. What has happened? Can we trust this creature?"

"Yes, DuKlaat YataBu," said DalChik. "Is there any reason to abandon his efforts at this time?" Since she had started to swell with egg, she was more assertive in protecting the ship.

DuKlaat declined to offer any objections.

"Shall we abandon Bilik Pudjata?" DalChik asked the Keepers-of-the-Egg. "Or shall we go forward with his plan?"

"Forward." The Keepers signaled their agreement. They were not happy. They had no alternative.

"Mata ChaLik BuMaru," DalChik said. "The Keepers have agreed Bilik Pudjata shall continue to get surveillance data." She flashed a summary of the proceedings of the Keepers' meeting to the entire community on the Egg-that-Flies. She told them the propulsion tube would be completed on schedule.

Bilik's name was at the center of the entire community of the Egg-that-Flies. And he never knew it.

CHAPTER TWENTY-FIVE

Todd Sinkton listened carefully to the briefing.

"My strategy is simple." Bray Grant ran his hand through his stylishly cut, long, blond hair, his eyes flashing as he paced back and forth in front of his officers. His walnut brown shirt had embroidery around its collarless neck and cuff. His tooled and embossed leather riding boots gleamed with brightly shined silver spurs. He slapped his hand with a braided-leather-riding crop. "Audacity.

"We'll surprise the Feds and blow through their defenses. We'll head for the inner gate before they have chance to close it." Grant smiled. "Audacity, always audacity."

The Clan forces were bivouacked in a shallow depression next to an old cemetery, a mile and a half south of the Maumee River and five miles east of the town of Defiance. It had a small creek that still flowed even though the weather had become hot. A dense stand of mixed hardwoods along a tributary to the creek hid them from the highway.

"We don't have any good intelligence," Ellis Harbaugh said.

Todd tightened his lips but said nothing. He had given Grant a detailed report on the Fed defenses.

"Look." Grant pointed at the map with his riding crop. "Two-thirds of old Defiance is surrounded by the river. The rest has a strong ditch and wall system. That's just too tough to crack with a direct head-on attack."

"Well, where do we hit 'em?" Harbaugh asked.

Grant smiled as if he'd expected the question. "We'll start by breaking their outer defenses at the east end of the city—the gate on the main road that comes in from the east."

"Doesn't that have a ditch and fence, too?" Harbaugh asked.

"Right, I know. Nothing we can't handle." Grant wrinkled his nose. "Sinkton, take three platoons to the south gate by the old factory before dawn. At sunrise, launch an attack." He pointed to the map and looked at Todd. "Here, understand?"

"Yes, sir." Todd kept his face expressionless.

"That'll draw out their defenses. We'll launch the main assault against the east road entrance with the sun at our backs." Grant smiled. "Harbaugh, you will use the catapults to take out the gate."

"I'll have to be in position before first light." Harbaugh frowned as though he'd had a great revelation.

"Right, I know." Grant nodded. "When the gate is down, move the foot archers up to cover the Horse Soldiers' advance." He smiled. "We'll blow right through them."

"Sir, what if they stop us at the bridge?"

"No problem." Grant's smile got bigger. "We'll get both the electricity, and the iron furnace. We can strip them and move 'em out, and at the same time, we'll give the city a good pounding with the catapults. Right, Harbaugh?"

"Yes, sir." Harbaugh pursed his lips as he contemplated the plan.

"They won't forget this visit in a hurry." Grant cracked his riding crop against his boot. "Any questions?"

The officers shook their heads.

The Clan Elders held Bray Grant in high regard. He was one of the new generation of Clan soldiers—highly skilled in the martial arts and dedicated to a full-time career in the military. A victory here would give him the field experience to justify another promotion. It was common gossip he believed he was from the right family and destined to eventually lead the Clan.

Todd remembered how Perrysburg had seemed easy at first, but everything had gone so wrong. He was sick of western Ohio, and his butt was sore from too much time in the saddle. And no one seemed worried about that damn flying machine.

This expedition makes me nervous, with us so deep in enemy territory, Todd thought. *Especially with know-it-all Grant in charge.* He'd tried to warn him the Fed had a lot of guns, but Grant had insinuated he was a coward.

ౌ

"Let's go, quietly," Todd said.

Three platoons of Horse Soldiers surged forward through the dew-laden grass in the pre-dawn light, out of the dense stand of white oak trees into the open field. They lined up in single file onto the berm on each side of old county highway 38 and picked up the pace. They followed the highway west, paralleling the Fed's perimeter fence. At the road due south of the old factory, they headed north toward the barely visible gate in the long, wooden palisade. The eastern horizon brightened, eclipsing the light of the waning moon.

A Fed guard called out a greeting. He hadn't recognized the Clan horsemen in the faint light.

Todd gave the signal.

Bows twanged. Steel tipped arrows whistled through the air. The two Fed guards on the towers at each side of the gate screamed as the arrows found their mark. Guns flashed and boomed. From a field behind the Clan soldiers, a cloud of quail and pheasant scattered noisily.

The Horse Soldiers moved out of gun range, where two platoons dismounted. They formed up and advanced on foot through tall prairie grass, using it for cover as they moved closer to the gate. The third platoon, still mounted on horses, continued to ride back and forth in front of the gate, shooting at the Fed guards. Still undetected, the foot archers moved close to the gate, where, on a signal, they rose and fired a volley.

Screams erupted.

Todd was puzzled. There weren't many guards. This was the closest gate to the city. He'd expected the guards at the gate to summon reinforcements from the city, but they hadn't. *We just might break-through this gate by ourselves*, he thought. *Something is wrong.*

Todd heard two loud thuds in the distance. He knew they were bombs signaling the start of the main attack. That meant it was time to retreat. He gave a signal. The foot archers fell back and returned to their horses.

Everything had gone well. Too well.

CHAPTER TWENTY-SIX

Bray Grant rose tall in his stirrups, pointed his riding crop, and yelled, "Forward."

The Clan's main attack started against Defiance's outer perimeter, which consisted of a ditch and palisade system. Two wooden towers guarded Defiance's east gate. Catapults threw bombs containing ten pounds of black powder, which trailed thin lines of smoke. The bombs hit the gate and exploded. Smoke drifted away, revealing a jagged hole.

Two more bombs sailed through the air. One bounced off the tower and landed in the grass where it exploded. The second bomb detonated inside the north tower and two guards flew out, flopping like rag dolls.

A steady rain of arrows sleeted down on the Feds' defenses as the catapults threw more bombs. The tower on the north side of the gate began to lean outward. The tower on the south side had a gaping hole at its base. Bombs smashed the gate's upper hinge, which now sagged partially open.

Grant rose once again in the stirrups and pointed to the broken gate. "It's time. Forward."

A dozen men with axes ran forward, followed by a tight formation of mounted Horse Soldiers shooting a steady stream of arrows at the towers and the palisade. Axes chopped furiously at the wood around the gate's lower hinge. Four men tied ropes to the gate. Once they had attached the ropes, the men with the axes switched to the ropes and pulled. Each time they pulled in unison, the gate creaked, sagging further. On the third pull, the gate fell with a splintering crack.

Horse Soldiers advanced through the smoke, picking their way through the debris. As they got through the gate, they cleared the defenders from the inside of the palisade walls with a deadly hail of arrows. The remainder of the battle group followed, formed up into ranks, and advanced.

One hundred yards in front of the now broken east gate was a low dirt embankment with a fence on top with five strands of wire. When the riders reached the fence, they bunched up and milled around, seeking a way past. Even though the riders beat their horses with crops, the horses balked. The fence was too high for the horses to jump.

The platoon leaders shouted orders. Half a dozen men dismounted and approached the fence. As each grabbed at the fence, they screamed and convulsed. Some staggered away, dazed; others fell to the ground and remained motionless. More Horse Soldiers came through the broken gate and stopped at the fence. Order disintegrated.

Fifty yards beyond the fence, a row of black-clad Fed guards—at least one hundred—emerged out of the ground. With smooth, mechanical precision, they leveled their guns at the Clan forces. They fired.

The leading edge of the Horse Soldiers dissolved into a disorganized mass of screaming men and horses. The Fed guards dropped back into the ground, disappearing as though they had never existed.

Three Horse Soldiers forced their horses into the fence, and upon contact with the fence, the horses screamed, rearing and bucking wildly. The horses trampled blindly on the fallen soldiers and horses, turning the ground into a bloody mass of broken flesh and mud.

As the smoke cleared, another row of Fed guards rose, with their guns pointed at the Clan like gleaming steel fingers. The second volley seemed even louder than the first. The hail of lead smashed gaping holes in the massed Horse Soldiers.

Pungent gray smoke drifted into the mélange of milling men and horses. Whinnied screams of panicked horses drowned out the platoon leaders' bellowed commands. The metallic smell of blood mixed with the odor of torn guts.

Thirty seconds later, the Fed guards rose again and fired.

The rear ranks of the Horse Soldiers broke and fled for the shattered gate, seeking escape. A full third of the Horse Soldier battle group remained at the fence, dead, dying, or injured.

಄

"What d'you mean?" Grant yelled. "Five strands of wire and a single row of Fed guards stopped you? An entire Clan battle group?" His nostrils flared. "Do that many cowards ride together?" He stared down at the platoon leaders from the devastated battle group. "Wire fences never stopped you before."

A sullen-faced man looked up. "Sir, it was like evil demon fire. I barely touched it and my arm is still numb."

"An archer is more than a match for a man with a gun," Grant said as though it were a law. "I smell something that might be smoke. Or is it your fear I smell?"

"The Fed surprised us. They came out of the ground—"

"Yes, I'm sure they did," Grant said. "If you had more courage and used your bows, you would be in Defiance by now."

"Goddamn you, Grant. Will you listen?" The voice came from a white-faced platoon leader with a torn jacket and blood seeping from his shoulder. "That damn fence burned all who touched it. It kills both man and horse."

A silent chorus of nodding heads stilled the quick comment on Grant's lips. He stared hard at the man who yelled at him as though memorizing a face. "How many guns were there?"

"At least two hundred." The man added slowly. "Sir."

"Two hundred? Are you sure?" Grant's eyebrows narrowed skeptically. "That sounds like a lot for the Fed to have on regular guard duty."

"Yes sir. There were two rows of Fed guards behind that wire fence. They were in pits in the ground."

"I know how to fix that," Grant said. "Harbaugh, move the catapults forward. Pound that fence to pieces."

"Yes sir," Harbaugh said. "I'll move them up."

"Do it." Grant turned to the platoon leaders of the second battle group. They were the reserves. "Get your men ready. When that wire fence is down, smash through the Fed lines. Show me that Clan soldiers really know how to fight."

～

Harbaugh's platoon maneuvered the catapults inside the palisade and lofted bombs at the fence, but they were too close for effective aim. They had to aim the bombs into high arching trajectories to drop them on the fence. Harbaugh's men settled into a routine, finding the correct range to lob the explosive bombs steadily closer to the fence.

Without warning, something screeched past the catapults and tore a hole in the palisade behind.

A distant boom echoed across the open fields.

Men clustered around equipment by a group of old industrial buildings a quarter mile to the west.

"What the hell was that?" Harbaugh said.

The hole in the palisade was six inches in diameter.

Two bombs exploded near the fence and a section of fence disappeared in a cloud of smoke. From behind the broken gate, several Horse Soldiers cheered.

A cart tender next to a catapult did a bloody cartwheel. Again, came the distant booming noise. The crew gaped at the pulped remains of the cart tender, stepping away from their catapults.

"God dammit," Harbaugh yelled. "Get those catapults going. This isn't a Sunday outing." The men moved slowly back to the catapults. "That damn fence should be down by now. Get to it, now."

As he finished, a catapult disintegrated into a shower of splinters. Its bomb exploded, triggering half dozen explosions from other bombs on the ground nearby, scattering the wreckage of the catapult far and wide.

"Shit." Harbaugh's face had become white. "What happened?"

"Harbaugh," Grant yelled. "Why isn't the fence down?"

"We're working on it." Harbaugh swore. "Load the catapult," he yelled. "Destroy the fence." His words came out like a chant. The catapult crew went back to work. They adjusted the catapult's throwing arm and released a bomb. It arced through the sky and blew up another section of the fence.

The watching Horse Soldiers cheered. "Yeah."

A catapult operator careened over, landing thirty feet beyond, broken and bloodied. Another hollow boom echoed over the fields.

"Move it," Harbaugh yelled.

The crew hastily loaded a bomb and slewed the catapult slightly to one side. Its bomb ripped out more fence.

Without warning, the catapult shattered into a shower of splinters, killing three of its crew instantly. Three more lay on the ground, screaming.

Harbaugh lay moaning on the ground, his head bloodied.

"Battle group," Grant yelled. "Mount up, prepare to advance."

It wasn't supposed to go like this. The Fed were a bunch of farmers; they couldn't build wire fences with weird powers or destroy catapults from great distances.

"Clan. Clan," the soldiers chanted as they picked their way through the broken gate and formed a column.

"Bows at the ready." The Horse Soldiers held the nocked arrows with one hand and reins in the other.

"For the honor of the Clan," Grant shouted.

"Clan. Clan."

"Forward, hah," Grant yelled.

The column trotted onward and the leading ranks broke into a gallop directly toward the section of the wire fence that was down. Foot archers swarmed through the gate and lofted arrows at where the Fed guard had last been seen. The soldiers slowed to avoid the shallow bomb holes and bodies of the dead and dying horses and men near the fence.

The first few horsemen passed cleanly through the wire fence, but a horse stumbled and fell, slowing them. More arrived, bunching up at the passage through the wire fence.

Without warning, something violent and bloody cut a swath through the Horse Soldiers milling at the fence. A narrow column of horses and men collapsed into a mass of shattered bodies.

"Come on, you bastards, let's go," Grant yelled.

He lashed out with his riding crop, pushing the Horse Soldiers forward. Grant's face was bright red. "Move it." Flecks of white spittle dotted his mouth. He spurred his horse and took the lead through the fence. The column of Clan Horse Soldiers moved forward again.

A row of Fed guards emerged out of the ground, guns leveled.

The leading edge of the Horse Soldiers got off a single volley of arrows. The bristling line of Fed guns erupted into a rolling volley. The Horse Soldiers in the front row collapsed under a sleeting storm of lead.

The Fed guards sank back into the ground as more emerged. Their guns fired, starting at one end of the line. A wave of fire and smoke rippled along the line of steel like a gigantic drum roll.

A large caliber lead ball struck Grant in the middle of his chest, lifting him out of his saddle. He toppled headfirst into the sodden ground, limp and lifeless. Men and horses tangled together. A mass of flesh and mud clogged the fence opening. The formation collapsed as horses and men fell, trampled underfoot. Grant was there, a part of the flotsam of broken and bleeding flesh, now anonymous in the debris of war.

Without leadership, the remaining Horse Soldiers turned and retreated through the broken gate, carrying wounded or horseless comrades. Over half their force remained on the ground behind them.

Todd Sinkton heard the battle from his position of rear-guard. So few Horse Soldiers came back through the broken east gate that he went forward to see where the rest were. One glance told him the story.

The uninjured Horse Soldiers made litters and stretchers for their wounded; it was time to leave. A group of mounted soldiers established a screen around the walking wounded and those on stretchers.

"I thought riding a long distance was a pain in the ass," Todd grumbled without any real rancor. "Carrying this friggin' stretcher is an even bigger pain in the ass." It was his turn on the stretchers. They kept moving.

ꝛ

The news of the defeat reached Maumee Harbor by mounted courier well before the remnants of the expedition arrived. Less than two hundred soldiers returned out of the six hundred.

Elroy Stanek sent word to the Council of Elders. News of the defeat spread like wildfire throughout the Hill.

Did the Midwest Federation have pre-Collapse weapons?

CHAPTER TWENTY-SEVEN

"Your guards fought well," Billy said.

"Thank you." Captain Kerr turned to watch the townspeople arrive and move onto the battlefield. They began cutting the throats of the wounded Clan Warriors and stripping them of their possessions. It was the normal practice of war.

Billy grabbed Captain Kerr's sleeve. "Stop that," he said. "Take them to the hospital."

"Who?" Kerr stared at him.

"The wounded. All of them."

"Even those from the Clan?" Kerr frowned.

"Yes, the Clan soldiers, too."

Kerr said. "But—"

"You refuse to do as I say?" Billy raised his hand and pointed it at Kerr.

Kerr flinched. "No." He beckoned a group of Fed guards and gave them orders. The guards moved quickly and began to provide help to the injured.

"Those men will provide information about the Clan. Question them." Billy stared with unblinking eyes. "They can teach your guards how to ride. With horse-mounted guards, you will have a better army.

Always be willing to learn from your enemy. Remember, they will not always be your enemies."

"Er, sir." Kerr's eyebrows rose. "You want a horse-mounted guard unit? Guards on horses?" His voice rose slightly. "What d'you mean about them not always being enemies? The Clan has been our enemy for as long as I can remember."

"If you had guards on horses today, your victory would have been total." Billy cocked his head. Across the river, in Defiance, came the sound of cheering. "What is that noise?"

"Er, sir." Kerr was unsure of how to explain the situation. "It's a celebration. Our victory came on an old pre-Collapse holiday called Independence Day. We haven't had much to cheer about for a long time, but today, we do. If I had to make a guess, there'll be a party in town tonight. You should join them. It ought to be a lot of fun and we owe this victory to you."

"Maintain a contingent of guards on the perimeter until the fence is repaired." Billy said. "We must not let our defenses down. We are still vulnerable to an attack."

"Er, sir." Kerr knew this would be difficult. "I don't think the Clan will be back any time soon. Our scouts report they're on their way to their fort on the mouth of the Maumee. They're in no condition to attack Defiance after what we did to them. We've already repaired the wire fence. What if it's connected to the generators before nightfall—?"

"Yes. Do that. Guards must be on duty at all times." Billy's voice sounded harsh. "This victory means nothing. More important to make castings."

There he goes again about those damn castings, Kerr thought. *I'll put guards on duty tonight, but not a full contingent. I've got to live with these men. Denying them leave after today's victory would really piss them off.* Now, he thought, *who're going to be the lucky volunteers?*

"Here's a toast to Billy, our fearless leader." Chip Wilson burped and raised a glass of beer. He sat with his fellow workers at a picnic table under a leafy silver maple tree overlooking the confluence of the Auglaize and Maumee Rivers.

Nearby, vendors sold food and drink from carts to the people who'd come to the park for the concert and Independence Day bonfire. Word of the victory had spread far and wide, bringing people in from outlying communities. Many drank and gossiped, celebrating the holiday and victory.

"I wonder what Billy is doing tonight?" Chip wiped foam from his lips. "I bet he's still working."

Joyce Vargas sat across from him at the scarred table. "He's always so serious." Joyce nodded. "He really does need to lighten up." She played with her glass of beer.

Joyce was a small woman with dark flashing eyes and strong features. She had high cheekbones, a prominent nose, and full lips. Her face was long with a trace of gauntness in her cheeks. Her dark red hair, almost mahogany-colored, was set off by her clear complexion. She got her coloring from her English mother and her features from her Mexican father. Her quick intelligence and sharp tongue put off many men.

"Sure, Joyce." Freddy Crosby giggled. "You're just the one to help him out of his shell. Right?"

Joyce ignored his comment. "Really, does Billy have a woman? I mean is there anyone he sees?"

Her father had taught electrical engineering at the Ohio State University. During the Collapse, he'd fled north with his wife and daughter. Joyce had learned about electricity from him and had joined the electrical repair shop as soon as Billy had opened it. There she learned all she could about switch-gear and generating electricity. No one could add much to what she already knew except Billy, who patiently answered her questions.

Chip shrugged.

"He could have any woman," Joyce said. "He's our leader."

"Naw, Joyce, Billy's saving himself for just the right woman." Freddy hiccupped. "Someone who'll love him for 'is personality." His words were slurred.

Joyce glanced at him and said nothing. Freddy was closer to the truth than he realized.

Men in positions of power fascinated her. She'd found out leaders were smart, had strong drives, and were capable of anything. Billy was a fascinating enigma, the strange little man who had deposed Old Vic. *He has done so much for us, he deserves some attention*, she thought. *And I'm going to be the one.*

"Oh, be quiet," Cora, Chip's wife said. "That's uncalled for. Billy's a good leader." She put her hand on his thigh and squeezed. It was a signal.

"My, 'tis getting late." Chip glanced up at a dark sky filled with stars. "I believe Billy has a full day planned for us tomorrow."

A few flames still flickered from the bonfire, but most of the partiers had drifted away.

"Well," Freddy said. "It's time for me, too." He drained the last of the beer from his glass and gave it to his wife, who put it into her bag. "See you."

Joyce remained seated as the two couples left. There was a group of guards nearby who kept glancing in her direction. Once she had gone with one such group and after a night of drinking, they'd taken advantage of her drunken state. She was sore for a week. *Never again*, she thought. *Bastards. Sure, there were tough farm girls who bragged about how many men they'd had in an evening, but that's not for me.*

Well, she thought. *It's time.* She made her way to Billy's quarters. As she did, she loosened the top buttons of her blouse. *Tonight's the night*, she thought. Her heart started to beat faster.

At the door to Billy's room, Joyce paused. "Billy," she called. "Are you there?"

"Come in," Billy said. "The door is open." Though the room was warm, he still had his ever-present cloak wrapped about him as he lay on his bed. His hand pointed directly toward her.

Joyce felt a flush bloom. She took a deep breath. "Billy, it's me, Joyce," she said. "I've wanted to come and see you for a long time. I think it's time that we got to know each other—better." She stopped at Billy's side.

Billy lowered his hand, but remained still, saying nothing.

Joyce smiled, pursed her lips, and blew him a kiss. *Why is it*, she thought, *the powerful ones are ugly? Here goes.*

Billy did not respond.

She ran her hands up her midriff, forcing her breasts up and out. "Did I surprise you, Billy-honey? Tonight, I'm going to be the best surprise you've ever had. Do you like what you see? Would you like to see more?" Joyce moved her hands to her blouse and slowly undid the remaining buttons, releasing her breasts. While she did, she watched him and smiled.

Billy did not move. His expression remained frozen.

"I'm not here to tease you, I'm here to have a good time with you." Joyce unbuckled her belt and then unsnapped the front of her skirt. She leaned forward, hooked her thumbs into the top of the skirt on both sides of her hips. With one motion, she slid her skirt and panties down to the floor and stepped out of it.

"Billy, you and me are going to have a great time tonight," Joyce's voice was low. "Come on, Billy, move over and let me into bed."

Billy lay on the bed, unmoving, staring at her.

"Are you waiting for me to come to you?" As she spoke, she clambered onto the bed and straddled Billy with her knees. She leaned forward. "Sure, Billy-honey, all for you. Come on, baby." Watching him, she lowered her breasts until they almost touched his lips.

Billy sat up quickly.

Joyce put her arms around his neck, smiled, closed her eyes, and tried to kiss him.

Billy ducked under her arms and with an almost impossibly quick motion, wriggled out from between her legs. He almost fell to the floor and stood up with a hop.

"What's the matter?" Joyce asked. "What's wrong?"

"Joyce," Billy said. "I cannot couple with you." He seemed to have difficulty speaking. "You are different."

His words didn't make any sense. "What's wrong, Billy? Did I say something wrong?" Joyce pouted as she knelt on the bed and held her hands out toward him. She opened her mouth wide and slowly ran the tip of her tongue over her lips, then pursed her lips. "Come on, Billy, please, I want you now." She beckoned with her hands for him to come to her.

Billy just stood and stared at her.

In that instant, Joyce realized it wasn't the hungry look of an ineffectual voyeur. It was the look of someone examining a piece of equipment.

Joyce felt a chill.

Something was wrong—he wasn't responding the way he should.

It wasn't going to happen.

Billy picked up her skirt and handed it to her. "Put on your garment." His voice was loud and harsh. "Explain your behavior."

Oh, my God, she thought. *I've done something wrong.* Sexual arousal and desire drained away. Fear ran down her spine. Billy was, she knew, their absolute, total leader. He could kill her without penalty.

Joyce pulled on her skirt and buttoned her blouse. She had come with the best of intentions, trying to be nice to him. Now, he was like a stern priest, making her feel guilty as though she'd committed a sin.

"Why did you come here?" Billy's voice was harsh. "What for?"

Joyce froze. Questions like that were trouble. The memory of Old Vic killing her friend, Patty, for giggling at the wrong time, came back. "Billy, there's something special about you. You answer my questions. You pay attention to me. You treat me with respect. I can't help it, I like you," she said, almost babbling. "You're our leader, you're powerful. You've done so much for us. You've made us rich and you've just given us a great victory."

Joyce wiped her eyes with the back of her hand and sniffled. "All of us, the whole community, are celebrating, but you aren't. You're here by yourself, all alone. I wanted you to know how much you mean to me, to all of us." Words came out, even though she wasn't sure of what she was saying.

Billy stared at her. He stood a little straighter, lowered his head slightly, but said nothing.

"It didn't seem right to me. We were having fun and you weren't. I mean you deserve to have fun, too. You work so hard and ask so little of us. I guess I went a little crazy. I came here to be with you. I've wanted to be with you for a long time, but I was afraid to tell you. You've done so much for me, for all of us, the whole community." Joyce swallowed and looked up at him.

"It was the only way I knew to show you how special you are to me." Her words came out in a rush. Tears welled up. "I'm sorry, please forgive me, I mean no harm, please don't kill me." She sank to the floor, lowered her eyes, and clasped her hands. "Please."

"Joyce." Billy hesitated. "You say nice things about me." His head swiveled to stare down at her. "It would not be right for me to couple with you. We are different, not the same. So it is not possible."

"But, but," Joyce said, "I don't care if we're different—"

"We are different," Billy said. His words came out loud and harsh. "Not possible."

Joyce flinched. "Please don't hurt me."

"I will not hurt you," Billy said. "You are the only one who comes to tell me how your people feel."

The silence grew.

He grasped her hand, raising her from the floor. "I have an obligation to respond to you, message-bearer of the community's recognition." He touched the tips of his hands together and bobbed his head. "It is an honor to move closer to the center of your community. I will do my all to justify the recognition given by your community. I am pleased to be in this community. Thank you, message-bearer." He bobbed his head again.

Joyce felt whipsawed and emotionally drained. She had gone from arousal to fear. Now he was thanking her. His behavior was almost like a gentleman in some old-time story.

He isn't going to punish me. She had the urge to throw her arms around him, to hug and squeeze him. That might be a bad move. She still wanted to see him again, sometime.

"Billy, if, I mean, can we really talk sometime?" Joyce lowered her eyes. "It'd be so nice if we could. You see, I really do want to be near you, to be with you."

Billy stared at her for a moment. "If you do your work, no harm will come to you." He paused. "As message-bearer of your community," he said. "You have the right to talk with me."

After Joyce left, Billy reviewed what had happened. A member of the community had come to him, wanting to couple, as part of their ritual to honor him.

How strange, he thought. *Is it even possible for my species to couple with them? Her body has obvious anatomical differences to mine. She told me of the community's high regard for my efforts and their acceptance.*

Billy felt a glow of pleasure. *Odd, the Earth people have the same recognition system as we do. They know to give praise. Strange, they recognize my efforts when my own species does not.*

CHAPTER TWENTY-EIGHT

"Goddamn it. No one has ever defeated our army," Charlie Ramsey said. "The Fed used evil means. This means total war."

"If the Horse Soldiers had been more careful about spies, it wouldn't have happened." Beach shook his head.

The four Elders glared at each other in the empty council chamber.

"Or your scouts had been competent," Beach said.

"Goddamn it, Beach, we're on the same side."

Outside, on the steps to the Council Chambers, Taylor MacPherson spoke to the soldiers' families.

"Our Council is looking for a scapegoat. They ignore the fact our expedition encountered an electric fence and artillery. That's pre-Collapse technology." He saw that his words were hitting home. "Our soldiers can't fight weapons like that."

He jabbed his finger toward the closed doors of the council chamber behind him. "In there, the Elders are figuring out who to blame rather than facing up to the challenge."

The crowd roared. Everyone here had friends or relatives in the

expedition to western Ohio. As of yet, no one knew exactly who had
died in the Defiance disaster.

෬

Billy rose early and walked to his new foundry. The sky was clear and
the sun was already warm. Unexpectedly, the previous night's
encounter with Joyce intruded upon his thoughts. It disturbed him. He
forced his attention back to the problem of making the propulsion
tube parts.

෬

There were only a few workers on the job at the foundry. "Where is
Kevin?" Billy demanded. "Where are the workers?"

"What?" Craig Schmitz was the foreman in charge of making the
number three mold. He'd just replaced a bad section in the mold wall
with a special, damp sand-clay mix with good bonding properties. He
was smoothing the inside of the mold with a clay slurry. He looked out.
"What did you say?"

"Where is Kevin?" Billy's voice was loud and harsh.

Since Craig didn't drink, he didn't have a hangover, but he was
tired from being up late. He knew Kevin had tried to drink the town
dry the night before and was still not at work. "Er, sir, it's a tradition
not to work the day after the July fourth celebration." Word had
gotten around that Billy knew little or nothing about the Fed's
traditions.

"This work is more important than tradition," Billy said. "Get
Kevin, now. Tradition is not an excuse to not work."

"Yes, sir." Craig took off at a run toward the sleeping quarters. He
forgot to move the mold into the hot air stream coming from the
generators to dry the damp molding sand.

෬

"Kevin, wake up. Billy wants you right now." Craig shook Kevin, who groaned and tried to bury his head under a pillow. "I think he's upset, very upset." Craig continued to shake him.

Kevin opened his blood-shot eyes. "All right, shit-head." He winced as he spoke. "This'd better be good, otherwise you'll regret it. Anyone who feels like I do ought to be left alone."

"I didn't want to wake you. I understand how you feel, but Billy's at the yard. He wants you and the crew on the job right now. I can't get the men to come. I tried to cover for you by telling him that it's traditional to take the day off after a holiday, but he's not interested in excuses."

"Damn, my head aches." Kevin groaned. "Now Billy wants to give me more headaches." He rolled over and looked up. "Aw, shit. Go get me some willow bark extract and make it snappy."

Craig grinned. It was worth taking all the crap about being a teetotaler just to see these assholes the morning after a big party. He trotted over to the herbalist, thinking, he who laughs last, laughs longest.

$$\mathcal{C}$$

It took Kevin forty minutes to report to work. "Sir, the workers are too hungover to work. If I force them to work, their mistakes will take forever to fix."

"We must get started, today," Billy said.

"If you insist. I'll try to round them up. I think we're wasting time." Kevin's head pounded, and his stomach threatened revolt. The three potions of willow bark extract hadn't yet begun to ease his headache. He thought Billy's order to mobilize the work force was foolish.

"Castings must be made. If you take a day off, how will you make up the lost time?"

"I don't know. I'm a little hungover. I'm not thinking too clearly. I feel like dog shit." He swayed on his feet.

Billy stared at Kevin and pointed a stubby finger at him. "Tomorrow, we cast iron. Every one of your men will be here. If not, they leave the Midwest Federation. Forever."

Kevin flinched. The threat of exile underlined the project's importance. Now he had to make the rounds and warn the men that Billy was unhappy. If Billy was unhappy, then Kevin O'Neil was unhappy. His hangover only increased his unhappiness. He would share his unhappiness with his workers.

Craig stood silent, at one side, as Billy directed his anger at Kevin. He took the rest of the day off.

He did not complete drying the number three mold.

CHAPTER TWENTY-NINE

"All right, you wimpy-assed bastards, get moving," Kevin yelled. "Get going, we're gonna do four pours today." Workers threw scrap metal into the furnace-loading skip even faster.

A long, steel I-beam mounted on a heavy timber frame pivoted over the electric furnace. Four horses strained against a long cable to lift the skip full of scrap steel into the mouth of the arc furnace. Ten loads later, the arc furnace was filled and ready to start.

Today, for the first time, Kevin would make the mysterious pieces Billy wanted for his friends. Every worker arrived early, even those genuinely ill, motivated by the threat of exile.

A team of snorting horses pulled the number one mold on a squeaking flatcar along rusty rails. The flatcar stopped in the pour area next to the arc furnace.

Kevin increased the current flow to the furnace and the turbine generators slowed under the load. The fusion drive reactor increased its output and the gas turbine units spooled up to their normal operating speed, howling as the hurricane of hot gases shrieked through them.

Kevin checked the turbine generators' operation. Each of the three units produced fourteen point five megawatts—their maximum design output. The reduction gear oil temperature was well within normal limits and the turbines ran true with no excessive vibration. Conditions were normal.

"They're operating well." Kevin turned and beckoned Crosby and Vargas. "Watch the generators. Inform me only if these limits are exceeded." He pointed to the gauges and headed back to the arc furnace.

"Has it melted?" Billy asked.

"Lemme check." Kevin scrambled up a ladder lashed to one of the legs of the crane and peered through a piece of dark stained glass into the furnace's brightly glowing opening. The molten metal was well below the full level—it needed more scrap steel. He signaled the crane operator to put in more scrap.

As the scrap steel melted, a steady stream of greasy-black smoke rose from the crucible. The workers loaded more scrap steel into the furnace, filling it to capacity.

"It is fully melted," Kevin said to Billy.

Billy said. "Is the mold ready?"

"Yes." Kevin nodded.

"Turn on the oxygen and lower the nozzle close to the surface of the metal," Billy said.

"Gotcha." Kevin opened valves, releasing oxygen into the hollow lance pointing at the surface of the molten metal in the crucible. When he was sure the gas was flowing steadily, he signaled the crane operator to lower the oxygen lance.

The operator used a wire cable on a block and tackle to lower the lance until its oxygen jet cut into the molten surface. A white-hot flame streamed from the surface of the glowing, molten metal in a star-like pattern.

The crane operator stopped lowering the lance.

Kevin signaled to continue, watching the surface of the iron through a piece of darkened glass. As the oxygen jet bit into the molten iron, sparks and flames grew into a coruscating column of fire. Showers of sparks and clouds of reddish-brown smoke billowed out along with waves of heat.

Kevin peered into the crucible—the metal appeared to be boiling. He signaled the crane operator. "Raise it," he yelled.

The oxygen oxidized the carbon in the iron and the increased heat boiled off the volatiles. They added lime, which combined with the acidic impurities and floated to the surface as dross. The process turned steel into pure iron.

A driver cracked the whip on a team of horses and raised the oxygen lance from the crucible. The cloud of smoke above the furnace drifted off on the westerly breeze.

Billy used a hand-held spectrophotometer to confirm the iron's purity. He waved to get Kevin's attention. "Pour the iron."

The motors controlling the crucible whirred. A fiercely glowing stream of molten iron arced into the mold. A cloud of smoke streamed out of the mold as it filled.

Kevin directed the excess iron into the bar mold, stopping when slag appeared. The operator reversed the crucible's position to dump the dross into a pit on the opposite side from the mold to become slag.

Meanwhile, a team of horses moved the mold away on its flatcar. Waves of heat shimmered above the still-smoking mold on its way to the turbines. The carter released the team of horses from the flatcar and moved them to the next flatcar, which carried an empty mold. The horses dragged the new mold into position beneath the furnace. The cycle started again as the workers refilled the furnace with more scrap iron.

Billy left Kevin in charge of the foundry. The workers ate or rested while the iron melted. They had been told the pours would continue until all four molds were filled. It would be a long day.

The second melt went faster than the first. In their haste, the workers over-filled the mold, causing molten iron to splash out, burning one worker. Work stopped until the workers carried the injured man to safety. It was already early afternoon, and two pours remained on the schedule.

"Mr. Billy, when do we break for the day?" Joe Wisnieski asked. Joe oversaw loading the crucible with the scrap iron. His wife had a new baby and he wanted to go home.

Billy stared at him for a moment. "When all four castings are poured."

Joe silently sighed and hurried back to the crane. "Okay, guys, let's move it. We've got two more pours, so let's get on with it." He acted as cheerleader for the scrap crew, urging them to fill the crucible to the proper level.

Joe peered through stained glass to check the level of the metal as it melted with the usual smoke and flame. "Yep," he said. "That's about as close as we can get it."

Kevin powered down the furnace. In the failing light, the oxygen lance cycle's show of sparks and flames was like a fireworks display, shooting sparks and flames high above the corrugated metal roof of the foundry. The after-dinner onlookers cheered. The foundry workers waved back to them, before returning their attention to mold number three.

"All right, pour the iron. Keep the flow fast and steady," Kevin yelled to the crew in charge of the tipping motors. "All in one pour, that's what Billy wants and that's what he'll get."

"You got it," The crew called back.

A stream of white-hot molten iron arched through the air.

Orange-white light flared.

KA-WHUMPH!

A deep, bone-shaking explosion ripped through the foundry. Huge clouds of reddish-gray smoke shot sideways out of the mold, billowing into the casting area. Brightly glowing molten iron arced through the red fog with a terrible yellow brilliance.

Voices screamed in agony.

As the dense cloud of smoke drifted away, glowing iron lay in puddles throughout the scrap sorting area. Two blackened bodies steamed and smoked on the ground near the shattered mold. Half a dozen workers in smoldering clothes writhed and screamed. Flames licked up the side of the crane's wooden supports.

"Get those men out of there," Kevin screamed in a voice that penetrated the cacophony of voices. "Put the fire out."

Billy appeared out of nowhere. "What happened?" he asked.

"Something went wrong with the number three mold in the middle of the pour," said Kevin. "It's too hot to go in there."

"Sir, sir, excuse me, Mr. Billy, Mr. Billy. I'm Joe Wisnieski; I was on the crane. I saw the whole thing." Joe's voice started to crack. "The side of the mold blew out all over my crew." His face worked as he spoke. "Those poor bastards never had a chance."

"The side of the mold blew out?" Billy's eyes seemed to focus on the distance. "The presence of water in the mold can cause the explosive formation of steam, extreme pressure generation, mold collapse, or explosion. Damp mold forming material," he said. He pointed to Joe. "Get the number three mold crew. Bring them to me. Kevin, come with me. I go to see the injured men."

꒰

"Hi, I'm Craig Schmitz, foreman of the number three mold crew. What happened? Did someone damage," Craig paused at the word damage. "My mold?"

"Who did the final inspection of mold number three?" Billy's grunting voice was softer than usual.

"I did." Craig's brow furrowed.

"Was the mold completely dry?" Billy asked quietly.

"Sure. We dried the mold over a week ago. We had it in the hot air for two days," Craig said. "It was dry."

"Was anything else done to the mold?" asked Billy.

"Well, yes. When I inspected the mold, I found a rough section of the wall. So I dug out the bad section and replaced it," Craig said. "I put on a real smooth coat. I don't want any junk parts coming out of my mold." He smiled proudly.

"Did you dry the mold again?" Billy's voice had gotten louder and harder. "After the repair."

"Well, no, I didn't get a chance to dry it again." Craig's face reddened. "After I worked on it, you sent me to get Kevin. Then you gave us the day off. So, it didn't get to dry."

Billy tuned away from Craig. "Kevin, this man caused the mold explosion. The moisture in the mold core material changed to steam and blew out the side of the mold. He is responsible for the delay in making castings and the deaths of two men. He must be punished. Call the workers."

"But, Mr. Billy, you took me off the job—"

"Silence." Billy was frustrated with the workers' conduct. He remembered how he had gained power over them in the first place—it was time for a reminder.

Stony-faced workers silently gathered in a grimy, sullen group in front of the foundry.

"This man did not dry the mold, for which he was responsible," Billy said. "As a result, casting is delayed, and two men died. So, he must die." He pointed to the number three mold crew chief.

"But you took me off my work," Craig yelled. "It isn't my fault that—"

Billy raised his hand. His laser cracked once.

Craig staggered a half step backward. He fell to the ground with a hole in his forehead. He twitched once and died.

"I will not tolerate any more delays. You will be more careful. All of you." Billy's voice echoed off the metal walls of the dingy building. "You must do your work properly, or I shall punish you."

The workers stared silently, eyes flashing between Billy and the still body of Craig Schmitz.

"We pour the number four mold tomorrow morning." He turned to Kevin. "If there's a problem with that one, I will deal with you." His voice echoed loud and harsh off the quiet buildings. "I must have these castings. No delays."

The workers moved away silently.

ࠑ

Billy joined the healers and advised them throughout the night, trying to save the burned workers. Two more died by morning. Four workers survived, with their burns covered by dressings Billy had sterilized.

At first light, Billy assembled the workers and explained how the accident could have been prevented. He promised a payment to the dead and injured workers' families.

The workers glanced at each other; many raised their eyebrows. Previous Fed leaders would not have cared about the accident victims.

$$\approx$$

"Get on that mold and inspect it. I don't give a shit if you've inspected it ten times before," Kevin yelled at the new number four mold foreman. "That mold has gotta be bone dry, got it?" His voice quavered. "To make sure you've done the job properly, you're going to stand next to the mold when the iron is poured. Got it?"

Kevin's fears proved unfounded for the pour into the number four mold was uneventful. The crew moved the mold to join the other molds that sat in the exhaust stream from the generators to cool.

$$\approx$$

Two days later, Kevin supervised his men as they disassembled the mold. They moved three fourteen-foot-diameter-thick-walled sections of iron tube into a large, open area not far from the turbine generators. No one knew what these casting were for.

Kevin only knew that Billy wanted ten castings. Three had been made so far and one mold was damaged beyond repair.

CHAPTER THIRTY

"What d'you mean? A wire fence stopped them?" Ramsey's eyes narrowed. "And some mysterious, unseen weapon destroyed the catapults?" His voice was loud and angry. The Chamber was crowded with soldiers' families. It was hot and humid, and filled with steamy body odors.

The platoon leaders shuffled their feet. Harv Perkins, their spokesman, swallowed. "Well, sir, whatever hit them catapults was mighty powerful. It just smashed them into smithereens." He lowered his eyes. "I never saw nothing like that nowhere never before."

It was the first time Perkins had been away from his farm in a long time. "I saw enough blood shed in the past week to last me the rest of my days. Those damn Fed guards had more guns than I ever seen, and they knew how to use 'em, too. There must've been five, six hundred of 'em. It was awful." He'd left friends behind, dead and broken, on that field at Defiance.

"Sirs, the Fed never responded to our diversionary attack on the south side," Todd Sinkton said.

"What're you trying to say?" Ramsey's eyebrows furrowed.

"Well, er, the Fed guards fired back at us, but they never got any reinforcements during the entire time we attacked them. That struck me as mighty unusual."

"Did you inform Officer Grant of this before he started his attack?" Ramsey fanned himself.

"No, sir. It didn't seem strange then," Sinkton said. "It was only later I realized they knew our attack was a feint. When I saw what happened to our main attack, it convinced me. There were at least twenty times as many Fed guards at the east gate. And they were all dug in."

The council chamber went silent. Heads in the public section craned forward, straining to hear.

"Whose responsibility was it to scout out the Fed defenses?" Ramsey tapped his finger impatiently on the table.

"Sir, some of the information came from my visit to Defiance," Sinkton said. "When I took your message to them."

"Yes, yes, I know all about that information," Ramsey said. "I want to know who verified that information in the field?"

The platoon leaders looked down, silent. It was common knowledge Commander Bray Grant based his tactics on those used by the Clan expedition against Defiance seven years ago—one of surprise and fast movement, which Grant called "audacity."

Perkins broke the silence. "Sir. I think Commander Grant observed the Fed defenses himself."

"You didn't scout the Fed defenses prior to the attack? You let Commander Bray Grant down by not scouting out the enemy?" Ramsey leaned forward, frowning.

Perkins's face got red. "It wasn't like that sir—"

"Did you expect him to do all the scouting by himself? As well as plan the attack? Everything?" Ramsey's voice had become even louder.

"No, sir."

"Then who did?" Ramsey glared at the platoon leaders.

"Well, sir, it was like this—"

"Is this another lame excuse?" Ramsey's voice reverberated through the Council Chambers. "I just want to know who was responsible for failing to scout out the battlefield properly. Well, whose job was it?"

Todd Sinkton stepped forward. "I'm in charge of the scouts.

Commander Grant wanted the attack to be a surprise. 'No scouts,' he said."

"Oh, so that's your excuse, is it?" Ramsey wagged his finger. "Because you weren't given a direct order, you failed to do your job and scout out the territory. Do you realize how many fine young people died as the result of your laziness and dereliction to duty? Do you know? Answer me, how many?"

"Sir, with all due respect," Sinkton said. "It wasn't like that. Commander Grant didn't want any scouting."

"Oh, really?" Ramsey raised his eyebrows. "So, he gave you a direct order not to scout out the Fed positions?"

"Well, no, sir, he didn't, but—"

"Then you didn't do your duty." Ramsey's voice echoed through the silent hall. "Isn't that a fact? And you didn't go to the Commander's aid after he'd been ambushed." His voice dropped. "You just let him die. You ought to be ashamed of yourself."

For a moment, the room was dead silent.

A chair scraped loudly in the public section of the Council Chambers. Heads turned. A wave of muttering swept through the crowd. A weather-beaten man in a worn red shirt stood up. "Damn you, Ramsey, this is bullshit. You sent our sons out to die under your greenhorn son-in-law. Now you want to blame others."

"Why weren't you on the battlefield with them?" Another voice called from the back of the Chamber. "Too busy making deals and money from the blood of our kin?"

Voices in the public section rose, raw and angry.

"Silence. Silence." The sergeant-at-arms bellowed. He pounded his staff on the floor. "If the public doesn't remain quiet, I'll clear the Chamber." He pounded his staff repeatedly. The noise slowly diminished.

A thin, tired-looking woman with a tear-stained face rose slowly to her feet. She wagged her finger at the Elders. "Ever since you were elected, you've always been up to something, but you've done nothing for us." Her voice quavered. "You can't even agree among yourselves and elect a Clan Leader. Oh, 'MacPherson was no good,' you said, 'too old. We need new leadership,' you said. A year has gone by and what've you done?"

The woman paused to wipe her eye. "You sent my only son out to die in the muck of western Ohio, that's what you've done." She choked on her words. "My poor little Joey, not even a decent burial." Her head sank into bony hands as her frail body sagged and began to shake.

The public section roared like an angry beast.

"Silence. Silence." The sergeant-at-arms beat on the floor with his staff as the volume increased.

The Elders looked at each other and nodded.

Beach pounded the gavel. "Meeting adjourned." The Elders filed along behind the dais and slipped out the rear door.

As they left, the chorus of catcalls and boos increased in volume.

CHAPTER THIRTY-ONE

"So, Randy, there were loud noises far inside the Fed defenses? And each time, were the catapults damaged or Horse Soldiers hurt?" Taylor busily scratched notes at the battered desk in the small, stuffy room outside the Council Chambers. The wood paneled room's solitary window was open wide, seeking but failing to catch a breeze in the warm, humid air.

"Yes, sir, I remember it distinctly." Randy Bowling was a teenage Horse Soldier who'd had a near miss. "At first, I thought it was a clap of thunder, but the sky was clear. Something whizzed past my nose and slammed into the horses and soldiers. I'll never forget it 'till the day I die. It was horrible."

"Okay. Thanks, Randy, you're a brave man."

So far, Randy had given the best description of the Fed's devastating weapon. *It was strange*, Taylor thought. *It sounds just like modern artillery. No black powder. Maybe someone had found out how to make smokeless powder. If so, their chemistry is miles ahead of ours. God help us.*

He sent for the next man who reportedly had a different tale to tell. "Your name?" Taylor turned over a sheet of paper to use its reverse side.

"M'name is Butch Henderson." The man was middle-aged, balding, and had a trace of a belly. He twisted his cap in his hands.

"So, tell me what you saw." Taylor leaned back and chewed the end of the pencil. He'd heard some fanciful tales in his quest for facts on the Defiance expedition.

"Why, sir, it was at night-time. I like to look up at the stars. Both my missus and me like the stars. Y'see, when we're apart, we both gaze at them because it brings us closer together, if you know what I mean. Most people laugh at me when I talk about the night sky." Butch hesitated.

"But, I know it better than the back of my hand. It's got its patterns, and they don't change. This world has changed a lot, most of it for the worse. Why, I remember how it was before the Collapse. It's like a dream. Sometimes, I wonder if it were really real." His eyes appeared to go out of focus.

"I'm sure we could discuss pre-Collapse times at length," said Taylor. "The night sky is the topic, remember?"

Butch's eyes rose and took on a keen edge. "I'm sorry, sir, I won't do that again. Let me see. It was about three years ago when Madeline and I first noticed there was a new star in the night sky. Well, it isn't a star. It's a satellite, something orbiting the Earth."

"A satellite?" Taylor looked up quickly. "Are you sure?"

"Yes, y'see, it moves way too fast to be a star." Butch's eyebrows knitted together. "So it has to be close, isn't that right? Now, Madeline, she's a whiz at math, she reckons it's in a highly eccentric polar orbit. I forget the details. It moves across the sky differently than anything else there."

"Why hasn't anyone else noticed it?" At that moment, Taylor remembered the strange sight he'd seen in the night sky three years ago. Were they related?

"I dunno. It sticks out like a sore thumb to us. It sort of goes from south to north." Butch hesitated. "At times it shines brightly, at other times, it'll blot out a star or two. It's pretty big, sir. I really don't know what it is. I've read a fair few books on the stars, but they don't say nothing about something like that."

"Have you worked out the orbital mechanics for this ..." Taylor paused to choose his word, "satellite?"

"Madeline has, sir. We've got it all written down."

"Can I get a copy of it?"

"I'll copy it for you as soon as I find a piece of paper."

"We'll get you paper. Don't worry about that."

"We've calculated when it appears. It's predictable."

"Good, that's important." Taylor stared at Butch. *If I ever establish a university, I'll recruit him and his Madeline. They sound like they still have a good command of mathematics and astronomy, too.* He cleared his throat. "Have you noticed anything else unusual in the night sky? More recently, for example."

"Well, sir, I got recruited for the expedition to Defiance because I've got good eyes. Mr. Sinkton has me do some of the forward observing and describing the enemy positions."

"Yes, yes. The night sky, remember?"

"Oh, yes, the night sky. I had a chance to watch the night sky a couple of times," Butch said. "Twice, I saw a big shadow sweep across the sky. When the moon illuminated it, it looked like a triangle."

Taylor made a triangular shape with his hands and cocked his head. *Butch was a scout, which meant he had keen eyesight. He hadn't been on the Perrysburg expedition; so he hadn't seen the flying machine. Maybe this was something else.*

"Well, after the shape crossed the sky, there was this distant sound, almost like the sigh of the wind coming through the shutters on a winter's night. Almost like a faint howl. I really don't have any idea what it was. It moved so fast that I couldn't figure an orbit for it." Butch's eyes got bright for a moment. "I even thought it might be a pre-Collapse aircraft, but there ain't any of those left. It always came from the southeast. Each time it was different enough to rule out an orbiting body." He lowered his head and shuffled his feet. "I'm sorry sir, to take up your time this way."

"Come back tonight and show me your satellite."

"Really?" Butch said. "You really want me to?"

"Yes, this is important." Taylor smiled. "When this war's over, I want you and Madeline to come here and tell me more of what you have learned. We can share a meal and talk more about astronomy." He had never paid much attention to the night sky. If what Butch had said was right, then out there, somewhere, was a reservoir of high technology.

Maybe, Taylor thought. *This ties in with the Fed's use of electricity—more evidence of advanced technology.* The connection between aircraft and the Fed had just become stronger.

Then a realization hit him: *The Fed had the Clan forces under aerial surveillance. That's how they ambushed us. The Fed possesses advanced technology. Maybe, just maybe, technology from the pre-Collapse civilization had survived, hidden somewhere, and now was being reintroduced. Maybe the dark ages are over.*

His emotions soared, elated by the possibility of restoring a technically advanced society. Then it came to him: *The Clan might have to face the horror of modern warfare: weapons of mass destruction.* His heart lurched. Waves of hope and despair swept through him.

$$\rightthreetimes$$

"Okay, Beach," Taylor said. "I'll tell you what I learned, later." He turned, as though to go.

"MacPherson, why don't you do it now?" Beach leaned back in his chair behind the dais, staring toward the rear of the empty Council Chambers. He avoided Taylor's eyes.

"I'll do it to an open Council. The Clan needs to know ..."

"You don't need to do that, not really," Beach said. "We're the people's representatives. We don't want to take the chance our tactics will be revealed. A spy could hear what you have to say ..."

"You're full of shit, Beach," Taylor said. "You don't have the Clan behind you. If there were an election today, I could beat you in your home district." He smiled. "Remember, I'm still an Elder. If you want to hear what I've learned, it'll be at an open meeting of the Council. Make up your minds, you can do this with me, or without me."

"I believe the Council has a right to know, and you should oblige us ..." Ramsey began.

"As an Elder, you cannot compel testimony from me, remember?" Taylor frowned. "It's open meeting or nothing."

"Er, Taylor. We'll let you know our decision." Ramsey's mouth puckered as though sucking on an unripe damson plum. It was obvious he planned to poll his constituents to gauge the degree of support before he gave the former Clan leader any authority.

"It's your game." Taylor smiled.

He'd already learned from Win Van Minh how the people were leaning. He figured the Elders wouldn't be happy with the results of the unofficial but highly effective poll conducted in the tavern.

CHAPTER THIRTY-TWO

The Bird-that-Soars glided in from the east, its high-lift foils erect on its giant delta-shaped wings. Out of nowhere, it appeared like a dark shadow, engines rumbling like the sound of distant thunder. The few residents awake in Defiance knew it wasn't a storm, yet none left the comfort of their homes to investigate. The Fed guards on duty had been warned to stay away because of the danger of the wind from the flying machine.

"The castings are in the clamps. We are ready to depart," Mata ChaLik said. "Is the area clear?"

Bilik glanced around the Bird-that-Soars. Nothing was nearby. "Depart when ready."

The Bird-that-Soars' drive rumbled back into life. As the craft lifted vertically off the ground, its engines rose to a high-pitched shriek. The ship pivoted east, raised its nose, and gained altitude as it moved away from the city. Once clear of the inhabited area, it accelerated and disappeared into the velvet black night sky.

"We're on course for the Egg-that-Flies," Mata ChaLik said over the comm-net. "The milling and welding shall be completed in eight sleep cycles. Have the next set of castings ready at that time. If this schedule is maintained, the Egg-that-Flies shall have a working drive long before it falls from orbit."

"There are no problems with the foundry at this time. I will keep you advised." Bilik prayed to the Great Egg his problems were over.

ꙮ

"Well, Mr. Potato, what do your friends think of our iron castings so far?" Kevin asked. The latest pour had gone without a hitch.

"We still need another set of castings." Billy looked up. "You pour tomorrow?" His office at the foundry contained a single desk and two chairs. There was no paper on his desk, nor any books or writing instruments.

"Yes, sir. The molds are dry and protected from the rain. The last three pours should be cool by midnight. Will we be making any more of these castings?" Kevin looked worried. "The mold frames and boxes are going to need repair soon."

"No. If these castings are good, we need make no more."

"Good. The mold makers have beaten the mold frames back into shape. Number two is the weakest. We've shored it up, but its framing needs replacing," Kevin said. "Maybe we should pour that mold last, just in case there's a problem."

"Yes," Billy said. "Do that."

ꙮ

Billy's biocomputer woke him. It had surveillance data showing Clan soldiers crossing over the Maumee. *They're entering the Midwest Federation territory again*, he thought. The biocomputer summed their numbers—three hundred—about half as many as those who had previously attacked Defiance. Enough to be a nuisance but not a major problem.

His biocomputer showed him other images. Several groups of people on foot were moving west, into Midwest Federation territory. The enlarged images showed unarmed people bringing carts piled high with hay. Other data showed more than the usual number of boats at the Maumee Harbor.

Kerr had told him the harbormaster was buying larger amounts of grain than normal. *Something seems odd*, he thought. He made a mental note to discuss this with Kerr. *Today, the last castings will be poured by the foundry. The Egg-that-Flies shall get the parts for its propulsion tube.*

Soon I shall rejoin my people and leave these Humans.

He sent Mata ChaLik BuMaru images of three completed castings. "The last three parts for the propulsion tube will be cast today. They will be ready to pick up in one sleep cycle. I, too, am ready to return."

"You must remain on Earth, Bilik, to collect all items with any connection to the Qu'uda." Mata ChaLik hesitated. "Leave no trace of our technology."

Strip the Midwest Federation of electricity and related technology? Bilik thought. *They will be weak again and easy prey for the barbarian Clan.* He shook himself. *Why do I concern myself with them? They are only mammalian vermin.*

"Mata ChaLik, I hear you. My mission is almost finished, and it will succeed." *I'm ready to return*, he thought. *I will now take my proper place in the community, close to the center.* "When will you send the Egg-that-Flies for me?"

Mata ChaLik did not reply.

"Captain Kerr," Billy said. "Three hundred Clan soldiers entered into Midwest Federation territory yesterday. There are more sailboats in Maumee Harbor. Do you know that?"

Kerr stroked his grizzled beard before answering. "My scouts have run into several groups of Clan soldiers lately. They may be up to something. Have your friends seen anything?"

Billy said nothing, only stared at the captain.

Kerr realized that Billy was waiting for him to answer the rest of the question. "Er, the sailboats. Yes, they're buying more than the usual amount of grain, with silver, too. I guess they need sailboats to take it back east."

"Why are they buying grain?"

"I don't know," Kerr said. "I don't get as much information since we lost our man in their outpost. I've sent out more scouts, but they haven't learned anything. They get stopped before they get close to the harbor. I still worry about an attack in the night or sabotage to the iron furnace, so I've tightened our defenses. That brings me to something I've been wanting to ask." He took a deep breath and put his hands in his pockets. "Can we use the iron furnace to make big guns? If Defiance had cannons, no one would dare attack us."

"After you make my castings, the iron furnace could be used to make cannons." Billy turned away.

ॲ

"Damn, I'm good," Kevin said.

After a late start, all three pours had gone well. He postponed for a final inspection of the mold to make sure they had not been harmed by rain. His precautions had worked, for the molds were bone dry.

"Yes." Billy waved his stubby arms. "Move the molds into the drying area. They'll cool faster in the airflow from the turbines."

ॲ

"Joyce. May I come in?" Billy stood in the doorway to her room. It was small with a cooking area adjacent to the sleeping area. Clothes lay spread over the bed.

Joyce looked up, surprised. "Oh, sure." She felt unsure of herself and a little embarrassed. "Excuse the mess. I was working on my clothes." She rose and went to him, standing before him.

"Joyce, this is not easy to say. I do not understand many things about your people. You honored me. You like me and I like you." Billy hesitated. He looked up and his dark eyes locked onto hers. "This will end. Because, soon, I must go."

"What do you mean? End?"

"It cannot go on. You and me. It is not possible."

"It doesn't have to end. We can still like each other. Stay for a while, we can talk. You never told me where you came from." *Some relationship*, she thought. *Not even first base, never mind the fireworks.* She reached out and grasped his hand.

Billy didn't resist.

"I have to leave the Midwest Federation. I must go back to my kind. It is far away. I have not told anyone but you. You must not tell anyone else. I tell you only because you want to be close with me, and ..." He paused. "I like you."

Joyce pulled his hand up and put her other arm around him lightly, moving closer. "I don't want you to go."

My, she thought, *I'm almost a head taller than him.* "Just when we're getting to know each other, please don't go." Something rose into her throat and she pulled him against her body. Unable to speak, she squeezed him tightly and closed her eyes.

Billy's arms slowly enfolded her. "Joyce," he said. "I came to tell you I will leave. I don't know when, but it will be soon."

Joyce stroked his back with a growing excitement. She ran her fingers over his back. His spine had a prominent ridge and his muscles felt hard, almost like iron. As she held him, she could feel his body radiate heat. *My, he'd be great to have in bed on a cold winter's night.* Yet, some of his bones seemed to protrude in the wrong places, and his shoulder blades were absent. As he moved, his muscles rippled like taut rope.

She longed to run her hands over his naked body. "Billy, stay with me, tonight, please."

Billy lowered his head and took a deep breath. "Joyce, please understand," he said. "I am different than you. It wouldn't be right, not possible." He disengaged himself from her arms. His dark eyes never left her face.

Joyce's eyes watered. A tear ran down her cheek. "Billy." She took a breath. "My heart is open to you. Please, please, don't break it." She bent and kissed his massive forehead.

Billy gently caressed her face with his three-fingered hand. "I like you, in spite of our difference, though I should not." He gently disengaged her arms, turned, and left.

CHAPTER THIRTY-THREE

"Okay, I think I know what happened. Our forces were bivouacked just east of Defiance the night before the battle. As usual, they built fires to cook their meals." Taylor paused.

Through the open windows of the library came the soaring, clicking song of cicadas. Below the Hill, water in the Rocky River barely moved. A brassy sun baked the valley, filling the air with warm honeyed aromas of summer.

The soldier leaders and leader-candidates listened intently, heads supported by hands propped up by elbows perched on polished wood tables.

"I don't think it was a spy," Taylor said. "Butch Henderson saw something fly over on the night before the attack." He paused to let his words sink in. "I think we gave ourselves away to surveillance from the sky."

The leader-candidates and the young soldiers glanced around uneasily. The briefing had been full of surprises.

"Let's assume the Fed will again be able to see us from the sky. So, we have to remain hidden until we're ready." Taylor pointed to the map on a stand. "The mobilization point will be on the east side of Defiance, here in the former Girl Scout campground." He indicated a looping road next to the Maumee River. "No fires, no cart convoys, no columns of soldiers, and no pillaging. If we intend to surprise the Fed and get through their outer defenses, we must be invisible and get to Defiance without being detected."

"Chris Kuchinski will be the field commander," Taylor said. "Now, let's discuss tactics."

"Sir, maybe we could mount the catapults on carts. Then we can keep them moving. That'll make it harder for the artillery to hit them." Kerm McClure had been with the catapults that were destroyed at Defiance. A close friend had been smashed to a bloody pulp.

"Yes, that's the kind of idea I want to hear." Taylor nodded. *If the Clan wants to go to war*, he thought. *I'll do my best to make sure we win.* He looked around the room. "Del Corso, get the catapults to Defiance. Do something creative to make them look innocent."

Del Corso nodded silently as he scribbled a note.

"How about mounting the catapults cross-ways on the carts?" Tim Van Minh said. "Then we can run them parallel to the enemy's lines and still have them facing the right way to fire."

"Sounds good. Work with Del Corso on that, okay?" Taylor wanted Del Corso involved, for his administrative skills were evident and needed. "Del Corso, get as much black powder as possible sent to Maumee Harbor. Trade for it if you have to. Del Corso, round up all the black powder rifles you can find and send them to Maumee. We may have to fight the Fed according to their rules."

"Tim." Taylor lowered his voice. "Stick around for a while." After the leader-candidates and young soldiers had left, he motioned for the young engineer to sit across the table from him. "I've got something for you." Since time was short and because he had to oversee the rest of the mobilization, he needed someone to work on his ideas. He gave Tim an outline of what he wanted before introducing him to his laboratory and its staff.

ౌ

After the soldiers and war materiel got underway, Taylor set out, insisting the Clan Elders accompany him. They traveled without their usual baggage train and special escort. They grumbled, but they came because they were aware public opinion held them in low esteem.

The battle group of Clan soldiers who had fought at Defiance remained behind to guard the Hill. Over half the militia in the Rocky River Valley, some eight hundred men and women, accompanied the Clan soldiers. The Clan expedition totaled over two thousand armed fighters.

"I hate this damn rain." Charlie Ramsey had forgotten what it was like to be on an overnight march. After reaching the Maumee River, south of Perrysburg, he'd slept under an oak tree with only a sodden blanket strung above him to fend off the rain. Water had dripped on him half the night. This morning, there was no fire to drive the chill away. "This ground is no substitute for my bed at home." His smile was a weak attempt at humor.

"If you go home now," Beach said. "Your political career is over." He gritted his teeth and swore. "That damn MacPherson out-maneuvered us. Never again."

"Rise and shine, time to hit the road," a cheery voice called out. "Today, we reach the rendezvous. Soon the fun will begin." The young leader-candidates escorting the Clan Elders seemed unaffected by the camping conditions.

By mid-morning, the clouds broke to reveal a brilliant blue sky. The sun's warmth soon dried out their wet clothing as they marched on. Taylor's group stayed well south of the Maumee River to bypass the town of Napoleon and away from the other towns and villages. Four Clan Horse Soldiers rode in front to provide a screen.

Taylor worried they would tip their hand. The Clan's forces were scheduled to arrive at the rendezvous point east of Defiance by the end of the day.

"MacPherson, are you sure you did the right thing?" A frown creased Ramsey's face. "Hanging that Horse Soldier?"

Taylor sighed. "Look, I don't want some fool soldier compromising our mission by running around like a wild man, robbing and raping. My orders are clear: No looting, raping or abusing the civilians. If anyone else does that, they'll get the same treatment. And their family will pay restitution to whomever he harms. Got it?"

Ramsey nodded as anger flitted over his face.

"Let's move it." Taylor estimated they'd be at the rendezvous point near Defiance by noon.

჻

Butch and Madeline Henderson reported to Taylor. "Before it started to rain," Butch said. "We heard a real faint sound, far away. We ain't sure it's the sky thing. When we're on the move, the cart and the horses make too much noise. Sometimes, I think I hear it, but I can't be sure." Butch looked at his wife.

Madeline looked down before looking Taylor directly in the eyes. "On the last clear night," she said in a high-pitched voice. "We watched the object in the polar orbit. I think it's becoming unstable. The light from the object has started to occult. That means the body has started to tumble. It may be entering the upper atmosphere on the perigee pass and the parasitic drag is causing rotation. Without good observational data, I can't estimate when the body will be captured by atmospheric drag. I suspect it'll be soon."

The thin, almost mousy woman sounded to Taylor like a lecturer from a pre-Collapse university. "How big is this body? Any idea where it'll impact?"

"I don't know, at least not accurately. The orbital mechanics are easy to calculate. We've estimated its closest approach is in the Northern Hemisphere, near the North Pole. When it goes over here, its altitude is between two hundred to five hundred miles. It's quite bright in the night sky; it's big, maybe a klick long, perhaps two."

"Holy mackerel." Taylor took a deep breath.

"I wouldn't want to be within a hundred miles of its splashdown.

The impact blast will be tremendous. Who knows what it would do to the climate? It could be like the KT event." Madeline paused. "We don't have good observational data. We need a good telescope." She hesitated. "You don't know where there's a good telescope, do you?" A quiet smile lit her face.

Taylor chuckled without mirth. He noticed she had perfect teeth, a rarity these days. "Madeline, I hate to tell you, but I don't. However, I do know someone who's good at finding things. When we get back to the Hill, God willing, I'll have Del Corso find one for you." Del Corso would rue the day he cast his lot in with Beach's boys.

A Horse Soldier arrived on a lathered horse. "Sir, Fed scouts coming this way."

"Disperse," Taylor yelled. "Move it."

The convoy went into the long grass on the edge of the road, stepping lightly to avoid making tracks. They hid behind the scrawny bushes scattered among the weeds and grasses of an abandoned field. The road now contained only the cart with a load of hay and an old farmer complaining to his nag.

The group of Fed guards pulled to a halt next to the wagon.

"Hey," one of the Fed guards called. "You see any Clan soldiers?" Each of the dozen men had a black powder rifle.

"Whoa, Archie, whoa," The old man on the cart yelled in a querulous voice. "Damn horse won't do a thing I tell it," he said in a querulous tone. "Now, what did you say?"

"Did you see any Clan soldiers?"

"Clan soldiers? I don't know who you're talking about." The cart driver took his hat off and rubbed his bald head. "There was some folk heading south, toward Holgate." He pointed in the direction from where he'd come. Holgate was south and east, away from Defiance.

"Were they armed?"

"Come to think of it, they did carry them funny looking bows." The cart driver waved his hands to describe the bows' shape. "An' they all wore brown clothes."

The guards looked at each other and nodded. "How many?"

"Don't rightly know. Maybe a dozen." He cleared his throat and spat in the ditch. "Got anything to wet my whistle? Y'know, something that's a real phlegm cutter?"

"Sorry, we're on duty." The guards' leader turned and nodded to his men. "Let's go." They cantered off in the direction the cart driver had pointed.

At the sound of the retreating hoof beats, Taylor peered out from the grass to see the Fed guards disappear over a low hill. He nodded to the farmer on the cart. "Nice job."

The farmer straightened, shedding twenty years. "They were easy to fool and practice makes perfect." It was the third time he had played the role of an old man.

"The Fed must've stepped up their patrols."

The Clan militia arrived at the rendezvous point by late afternoon at the site of the abandoned Girl Scout camp. It was a collection of derelict log cabins among dense forest near a creek that flowed into the Maumee River, about a mile east of Defiance's outer perimeter. The foundry was located just inside the perimeter fence. Under the canopy of tall trees, there was very little undergrowth, which provided room for the Clan forces to regroup.

Del Corso reminded the squad leaders to enforce discipline to keep the assembled force quiet and out of sight. The militia would need a day of rest after their march from Rocky River. The horse-mounted soldiers would arrive before first light the following day to complete their forces.

Van Minh's crew reassembled the catapults, mounting them sideways on the carts. Del Corso positioned the munitions carts ready for the move-out and distributed rifled guns to three platoons of Clan marksmen. His deputies banned campfires and reminded the Clan forces to stay under the cover of trees. Del Corso's staff provided charcoal for smokeless cooking. Lastly, he organized a perimeter guard around the camp.

All through the next day, as Clan soldiers arrived, Del Corso's deputies directed them to their assembly points where they fed and watered their horses. Platoon leaders reviewed plans and checked their weapons. By the end of the day, every unit knew its role.

At midnight, the Clan sappers left to infiltrate the outer perimeter of Defiance and place black powder bombs at the base of the barricade by the entrance near the foundry. The sappers timed the bombs' fuses to ignite at dawn. The assault would start with the sun at their backs. Two hours before dawn, the militia and the Horse Soldiers moved into position.

This time, Taylor thought. *It will be different.*

CHAPTER THIRTY-FOUR

A bright flash lit the sky, followed by a booming sound that echoed across the countryside. A dark mushroom cloud rose into the pink almost-dawn horizon. Another blast sounded, followed by several more, the opening chorus to a storm. Several columns of black smoke rose high in the brightening sky.

The sappers' bombs had shattered the gates on Defiance's east and south palisade.

As the echoes faded, four hundred clan soldiers rose as one from the long grass in the paddock east of the east gate. Screaming war cries, they charged through the smoking remnants of the east gate. In only moments, they overran the surviving Fed guards. Units of Horse Soldiers moved through the wrecked barricade until they reached the barbed wire fence, where they stopped.

A soldier pulled out a heavy copper cable attached to a metal stake. His grizzled companion drove the stake into the ground with a mallet. The soldier dropped the cable over the top wire of the fence.

Bzzatt! The copper cable burned through the tightly strung wire with a shower of brilliant blue-white sparks. The cable dropped onto the next wire and burned through in a similar fashion. Along a wide section of the wire fence, similar scenes were repeated.

Fence down, the clan soldiers advanced.

"Look," Stanek called. "Here come the Feds." He pointed to the wide line of men trotting toward the break in the fence. "Archers," he yelled. "At the ready."

Two hundred men in brown simultaneously drew their bows, arrows pointing to the sky. Silent, they watched the Fed guards approach, waiting.

At about one hundred yards range, Stanek yelled, "Fire."

Two hundred arrows shot into the air.

As one man, the Fed guards dropped to the ground. Bobbing heads and waving grass showed that the guards were crawling forward. In the distance, more guards appeared.

Chris Kuchinski rode up. Binoculars dangled from her neck. "Stanek," she said. "Deploy the catapults. Place bombs at ten-yard intervals along their line." She pointed at the prone Fed guards. "Get the Horse Soldiers ready."

"Yes, sir."

"When they break, drive them back to the city. Hold up at the outskirts. Wait for us to catch up. You'll need support for your advance into the city." Three explosive bombs dropped short of the Feds' position.

The catapults laid down a volley of bombs that blew guns and body parts high into the air. More orange flashes blossomed along the Fed line. Men rose from the ground and ran helter-skelter back toward the city.

Chris yelled and waved her hand. The Horse Soldiers thundered after them, yelling and shooting arrows.

"The bombs did the trick," Stanek said. "Look at 'em run."

"You would too," Chris said.

The Horse Soldiers almost caught up with the Fed guards when a rolling volley of gunfire came from their right. The leading edge of the Horse Soldiers collapsed raggedly. The following ranks halted and wheeled about, picking up fallen comrades. They formed up and galloped south, away from the buildings, and headed toward an old railroad line. They stopped short, about a quarter mile distant.

Once out of range of the Fed guns, the Horse Soldiers stopped and waited for the rest of the Clan forces to catch up. They were within a quarter mile of the old Fire Station and stared at the cluster of buildings that marked the outskirts of the city.

The Horse Soldiers watched the Fed guards move into buildings to the west. To the north, toward the Maumee River, was a complex of industrial buildings with a large grassy hill behind. Something hummed loudly within the complex.

"Move up a platoon of rifles and put them to work." Chris pointed at the buildings to the west.

The Clan rifle marksmen moved toward the now quiet city outskirts carrying black powder rifles. These guns had been salvaged from pre-Collapse times. They were much valued, for they had greater range and accuracy than the guns the Clan now made. The riflemen took up positions in a patch of woods two hundred yards south of old railroad tracks. The rail embankment had been a part of the city's defenses. They adjusted their sights and waited. Upon receiving a signal, they opened fire.

After several Fed guards fell, the remaining guards disappeared behind the buildings.

The Clan riflemen ran to the tracks with the catapults following close behind. As the Clan soldiers crossed the railroad tracks, gunfire erupted from the row of low, brick buildings on the road that paralleled the tracks. The Clan forces waited until the catapults arrived.

More Fed guards appeared among the warehouses and complex of industrial buildings to the north.

Horse Soldiers continued to advance west over the flat open fields south of the old railroad tracks, encountering no resistance. Soon, they joined up with the Clan militia who'd stopped at a south entrance to outer Defiance that was adjacent to the Auglaize River. The Clan forces now controlled the land south of Defiance all the way to the Auglaize River.

༺

Billy awoke to the sound of explosions. At first, he thought it was thunder, but at the start of the "crack-crack-crack" of gunfire, he jumped out of bed. He ran to the power station, his long gray coat flapping. He ran into his guard commander.

"Captain Kerr," he said, almost out of breath. "What is happening?"

"Attack on the east and south gates of the outer defenses. They've reached the electric fence. Three guard units are on the way to stop them. I'm mobilizing all the guards." Kerr's face was red with anger.

"They surprised us. How come your friends didn't see them coming?"

"I do not know."

"Now we'll have trouble getting reinforcements."

"You must keep them away from the power plant," Billy said. "I will go there and get the cannon started. Find out how many attackers and send me a report. Now go." His defense plan called for stopping the Clan soldiers from behind fixed positions while holding several command units in reserve.

"Right." Kerr hurried away.

Billy contacted the Bird-that-Soars. There were no current surveillance data images. *Something strange is going on*, he thought.

"Mata ChaLik BuMaru," he called over the comm-net. "The eastern savages are attacking the power station where the last parts wait for you. Come and pick them up."

"The Bird-that-Soars cannot appear before so many Earth people during daylight." Mata ChaLik said. "You know that we must keep our presence secret from these savages."

"If the power station is overrun, the Egg-that-Flies will not get its propulsion tube finished." Bilik's voice rose to a shout. "Do you not understand?"

"You have become too much like one of the Earth people," Mata ChaLik said. "You have taken on the manners of these mammalian savages." His words were profoundly insulting to a Qu'uda. "You should realize your place in the community and where you are."

"If you do not come and pick up the castings, I will call the Keepers-of-the Egg directly," Bilik said.

Even if Bilik were the furthest outsider in the community, he knew that would get results. He knew Mata ChaLik would lose this argument and possibly even his position as speaker for the Egg-that-Flies. Mata ChaLik's status was no protection from a reprimand.

"It will be there as soon as it is possible for the Bird-that-Soars to leave," Mata ChaLik said. "It will take one-eighth of a sleep cycle."

∂

Billy reached his power station office. "Kevin."

"Yes, sir." Kevin's eyes widened in surprise. "What can I do for you?"

"Get the castings out of their molds immediately. Break the mold frames if necessary. Get them ready for pickup as soon as possible." Billy said. "Send Chip Wilson to me."

"Those castings are still damn hot." Kevin frowned.

"Do not argue," Billy said. "Get them out of the mold and ready for pick up. Now."

"Yes, sir." Kevin had that faraway look of a person who was figuring out how to handle the problem. "We'll get it done, somehow." He ran from the office and almost bumped into Chip Wilson. "He wants you." He pointed at Billy.

"Take charge of the cannon," Billy said. "Use the leather bags filled with small pieces of iron scrap." He knew that combination would work best against massed troops. "When it's ready, I'll give you the targets."

Billy sent a message to Kerr for a battle report.

∂

"Damn." Todd crouched behind a dead horse. Every time he tried to take a look, someone fired a gun at him. "Sooner or later, I'm gonna get my damn head blown off." His battle group had tried to cross the main road that ran east-west into Defiance. They'd met deadly opposition.

"Well, don't stick your head out so far, you stupid shit." Maggie Doolittle had attached herself to him as soon as she joined his squad. She had a burly quickness that came from growing up on a farm with five sisters and no brothers. Hard work had made her stronger than most men. "Look from one side, not over the top." They were trapped behind Todd's dead horse. He was still dazed from a blow to his head. Maggie had dragged him here, losing her horse in the process.

"Those damn guns are better than bows for fighting among houses," Todd said. "I wish I had a gun right now." It was a wish echoed by the survivors in Todd's battle group. The Clan forces had regrouped after retreating to the railroad tracks, leaving a few survivors trapped along the road.

Taylor watched the battle from a distance. Even though the battle group had not crossed the main road, he was satisfied with Chris Kuchinski's performance. She didn't waste her troops' lives. She used bombs thrown by the catapults plus a lot of arrows, instead of using troops as cannon fodder. "Well, Chris," Taylor asked. "Are the Fed guards the same as those at Perrysburg?"

"A lot of similarities. These have more discipline and better fire control. They're good soldiers, they fight well, they're putting up a good defense—"

A loud *BOOM* came from the complex of industrial buildings. Half a dozen archers went down as though cut with an invisible knife.

"Son of a bitch." Taylor stood up in his stirrups. He peered through his binoculars. He saw a long metal tube pointing at the Clan lines. "They do have artillery. Chris, get your troops under cover." He pointed at the old industrial complex. "That's where the shot came from."

"Yeah, but what is it?"

"Think of it as a giant rifle."

Chris nodded. "Stanek, move the archers away. All soldiers not in active combat must take shelter in there." She pointed at a partially demolished building. "Like that."

BOOM! The weapon in the building complex spoke again. Its invisible hand reached out. This time it smote the group of Clan Elders who were clustered near the railroad tracks observing the battle. Several fell to the ground.

Oh, shit, Taylor thought. *There'll be hell to pay over this.* He spurred his horse across the tracks to get to them. It was worse than he'd feared; one was already dead. "Everyone behind those buildings." Taylor pointed to houses distant from the battle. He beckoned to several Clan soldiers to come and help the injured. "Move them to cover, now."

The soldiers slung the injured over their horses and trotted south, away from the front. Blood dripped steadily from Beach's head. His eyes were glazed and his mouth hung slackly open. White bone protruded from Ramsey's arm. Ramsey cursed in a rhythm matching the motion of the horse that carried him.

Taylor turned and spurred his horse back toward the front. "Van Minh, it's time to use your weapon."

"Yes, sir." Van Minh nodded.

Taylor pointed towards the complex of industrial buildings. "The cannon, over there." The remnant of a huge parking lot lay between the buildings. The cannon sat within mounds of dirt that might have been a part of long-abandoned landscaping.

"Yes, sir."

"Pick out your target carefully before you fire." Taylor pointed to a giant crossbow that fired explosive bolts. "Remember, if you stand still, you're a goner."

"Yes, sir." Van Minh nodded. The giant crossbow had come from Taylor's storage barn. It was left over from the days immediately after the Collapse. He'd spent two weeks refurbishing it.

"If you get hit by a round from that artillery piece, I'm never going to get to eat your father's food again." A trace of a smile crossed his face. "Now that'd be a real disaster."

"Yes, sir. Lemme take a look at it first." Van Minh climbed onto the roof of a dilapidated building. He lay down to observe the industrial buildings.

"Chris," Taylor called. "Van Minh is getting a fix on the artillery piece. Then he's going after it with a big crossbow."

"Good." Chris nodded. "As soon as he makes his move, I'll have a rifle platoon give him covering fire."

CHAPTER THIRTY-FIVE

"This gun sure shakes up those Clan bastards." Chip Wilson, who oversaw the steel cannon, had on his first shot, hit some archers. Later, he'd hit a group of men on horses watching the action. After each hit, he did a little victory dance.

Kevin was hot and sweaty. He cursed with a proficiency that came from a long acquaintance of working with laborers. He raised his voice and added curses while urging on the workers' efforts.

His team of workers, stripped to the waist, had removed all three castings from their molds and placed them on heavy timbers near the cannon. Waves of heat still rose from them. The only thing left to do was stand the castings upright on their sides, for which he needed a team of horses. They placed supports under the castings and rigged the block and tackle.

Kevin's men used the horses to get two castings upright. As they lashed the horses to hoist the last casting vertical, something flashed in between the cannon and the castings and exploded. The horses, wild-eyed, backed up, screaming, out of control, trampling workers and breaking bones. Blood splashed brightly red onto the dark ground. The partially elevated casting—a fourteen-foot diameter iron cylinder—slipped off its wood framework. It fell and landed hard.

Two of Chip's men screamed loudly. They had gaping wounds that spouted blood.

Chip stared at the Clan forces. Over two hundred yards away, a horse-drawn wagon carrying a mechanical contraption slowly traversed down the main road.

Puffs of gray smoke shot out from the ditch beside the road. Several of Chip's workers staggered and fell as the sound of a volley of gunfire reached them.

"Sir, sir," Chip yelled to Billy. "They're killing my men." He pointed at the distant marksmen.

Billy turned to a waiting messenger. "Tell Captain Kerr to come here."

Kevin joined Chip and the cannon's crew who had sought shelter among the buildings and behind the generators.

As Billy watched, something flew from the wagon. It struck the ground just short of the cannon and exploded violently.

"Use the empty molds to build a barrier," Billy said. "Get the cannon back into operation. Fire at that wagon." He pointed at the slow-moving vehicle that was firing at them. More puffs of smoke erupted from the ditch. Bullets thudded around them.

Chip started to shake.

"Yes," Billy said. "They have developed new tactics."

Kevin's men pushed an empty mold forward to make a barrier in front of the cannon. Before they finished, another line of smoke erupted from the ditch. Several more of Kevin's men fell to the ground bleeding. Kevin put his hands over his eyes, slumped to the ground, and began to cry.

"What's the Hell's going on?" asked an out-of-breath Kerr. "Why isn't the cannon firing?"

"Captain Kerr," Billy said. "The Clan has a device that throws explosives from the road to the power station. They also have guns with the same range. They have injured some of the cannon crew and Kevin's work party."

Kerr stared at the flat, open area in front of the power station that offered no cover for advancing men or horses and should have been a killing zone. No one had expected the attack would move in this direction. As he scanned the area with his binoculars, the wagon stopped. Something flew from it in a low, flat arc toward them. It hit the side of a turbine generator and exploded. The turbine began to screech.

"Shut the turbine unit down." Billy waved his arms, urging someone to act.

The turbine sighed into silence as Crosby and Joyce took it off-line.

The wagon started to move again. A horseman from the Clan line rode up to it and pointed toward them.

Kerr turned to Billy. "I'll send some rifles over here to get that wagon. That oughta discourage them."

Billy watched him trot away. There was not much for him to do. The Bird-that-Soars was long overdue.

ॐ

"Did you see where Van Minh's last shot went?" Taylor asked anxiously. "Did it hit a generator?"

"I think so," Chris said.

"Jesus Christ, that's one of the things we want to keep."

"Tell Van Minh to lay off the power generating units," Chris said. "Get that to him, now."

Stanek galloped away.

"Our soldiers have reached the Feds' defense line in the outer city," Chris said. "We're ready to drive toward the bridge that crosses the river into Defiance. The Fed will have to retreat."

Taylor nodded silently.

From the direction of the city came the steady drumbeat of exploding bombs thrown by the catapults.

ॐ

"Sir, the enemy has almost cut our forces in half." Cal Majewski was breathing hard as he gave his report. He was one of Kerr's veteran Fed guards from Perrysburg. "There's a risk of a break-through to the bridge. If that happens, we'll have no way to get back into the City."

"Shit," Kerr said to no one in particular. "Majewski," he said. "Organize a phased withdrawal. Move the units to the south perimeter along the railroad embankment and Preston Run. From the bridge over the Preston Run ravine, form a line along the main road to the power station. Get some men on the roof of the old hospital and the old Shuller factory. That'll force the Clan to cross the road under our guns. Leapfrog the units out of the pocket in the south, nice and easy-like. Got it?"

"Yes, sir." Majewski saluted and left.

Kerr grabbed a couple of messengers. "You, tell Dixon to bring his command unit up to the Preston Run Bridge. If we counterattack, he'll be the anvil. And you, tell the power station cannon to target Clan forces on the main road."

The retreat went smoothly.

~

The Clan soldiers advanced through the deserted southern section of the outer city. Each time they tried to cross the main road into the City they came under heavy rifle fire from marksmen on top of the hospital and the old industrial building.

The Clan advance stopped. They had left almost half of a battle group on the road.

It was a stalemate.

CHAPTER THIRTY-SIX

Todd Sinkton stared out across the wide boulevard. Waves of heat rose from the crumbling asphalt. On the other side of the road, just beyond the deserted parking lot, was a battered line of old stores. Within the ruins of the old shops, Todd knew there were Fed guards with guns. Earlier, those gunmen had cut to pieces a charge by Horse Soldiers who tried to cross the road.

"I could use a drink and something to eat," Todd said.

Maggie Doolittle sat next to Todd; her back pressed tightly against an old concrete planter. That and a dead horse was their cover. "Yeah, me, too. I got a feeling that we ain't gonna get any." Her blond hair was stringy. Sweat lined her forehead and her round face was red.

Todd could smell her. Even though she needed a bath, something about her reminded him he had not seen Naomi, his wife, in over a month. Maggie had made it obvious she wanted an intimate relationship.

Shit, it just isn't fair. *This is what makes a man break his marriage vows.*

Distantly, a gun cracked. Instinctively, he crouched closer to Maggie. *The longer this lasts, the more likely I'm gonna get killed.* He shivered in spite of the heat.

Smoke drifted across the road, the acrid smell of burning buildings mingled with the sewer-like smell of torn guts. Bodies of men and horses lay up and down the road. Some still moved, their blood draining into the gutter. Amid the cries and moans, came the steady thud of explosions from bombs thrown from the Clan's catapults.

A gun cracked. Something whined inches above their heads.

"Lordy." Maggie grabbed Todd's thigh. "If I survive the day, I'm going to need a good screwing to get unwound."

At that moment, her offer seemed more appealing than ever to Todd. "Let's just get through the day, okay?"

Forgive me, Naomi, for thinking of another woman. It was as though he had already committed adultery and done five years of service to the Clan, all in one day. There was no end in sight.

The Fed guards dug in on the other side made it suicidal to cross the road. Nearby, the stout masonry wall and gate guarding the bridge over the Preston Run ravine had guns sticking out of it like spines on a porcupine. In the other direction was a complex of industrial buildings. Something hurled missiles huge distances. Despite their earlier successes, the Clan's forces were at a standstill.

Maggie cleared her throat, spat, and glanced at the sky. The brassy sun was hot and high above. It was almost noon.

Van Minh aimed the large crossbow carefully. The last cannon blast was too close. Then a Fed marksman hit one of his men. *Son-of-bitch*, Van Minh thought. *This is getting more difficult.* He pushed his crew to move faster. Something seemed to have happened; the cannon fell silent and the rifle fire slowed. *It is only a matter of time now*, he thought, *before our clan Horse Soldiers sweep them away.*

The wind picked up, hot out of the southwest, adding moist air and haze to the smoke drifting over the generators. South of the foundry, grass fields rippled like waves in an ocean. Dust devils marched across the cracked and crumbling asphalt parking lot.

Chip's crew re-oriented the cannon to aim it down the main road leading to Defiance. The makeshift barricade of mold and other casting equipment provided a place to crawl into and away from the hot sun. Men crouched in holes and cursed the Clan. Each time an explosive projectile fell near them, they ducked and swore in unison.

"That's odd," Chip said to no one in particular. "No bombs are falling beyond the barricade."

Billy sat with his back to the abandoned casting mold. His long, gray cloak hung loosely about him while his wide-brimmed hat kept his face in shadow. "Mata ChaLik BuMaru." He spoke into the comm-net. "Where is the Bird-that-Soars? You said it would arrive in one-eighth sleep cycle. That time has long since passed. Our position grows precarious."

"We are holding a nearby position. Is it safe to land the Bird-that-Soars in the middle of battle?" Mata ChaLik's voice conveyed anger.

"Safe or not, you must send it," Bilik said. "You must get these castings to the Egg-that-Flies."

"I'll send the Bird-that-Soars," Mata ChaLik said. His tone of voice indicated his unwillingness. "Prepare your people."

Billy jumped up and beckoned a messenger. "Tell Captain Kerr the flying machine will soon arrive. He must prepare his people for its wind." He pushed at the messenger. "Hurry."

The messenger glanced south toward the Clan lines and took off running west toward Defiance.

"Chip," Billy said. "The flying machine comes. It will bring a strong wind. Get your men into the foundry."

"Flying machine?" Chip asked. "Wind?"

"Like Perrysburg?" Pete Cutler's ears perked up. He was a veteran of that battle. He had seen what the flying machine did to the Clan Horse Soldiers. "Man, we gotta get shelter. That sucker's wind will knock you silly."

"Warn them at the power station," said Billy.

In small groups, the Fed guards retreated into the foundry's rusty metal building. The power station was now deserted, except for Joyce who stayed next to the generators. Billy remained by the cannon, on the barricade, watching and waiting.

A huge, dark wedge-shaped apparition shrieked across the sky and disappeared. The sound faded, changed in tone, and again grew louder. A dark shape came out of the east. It was low and large and followed the main road into town, directly toward the generators. It screamed overhead toward Defiance. Before it reached the Auglaize River, it banked and turned south. The dark triangle swept in a circle over the assembled forces of the Clan and turned back toward the complex of industrial buildings.

All fighting stopped.

As the machine approached the buildings, its engines screamed even louder. Diverting ducts rotated thrust downward. Flaps on its wings rose like a set of shelves. Its forward velocity slowed. At the same time, its landing gear descended like the talons of a giant bird of prey. It slowed to a hover and descended with a gentleness that belied its overwhelming noise.

~

As the flying craft circled, Taylor realized it was bigger than he had imagined—it was as big as a 747 or even a C-5A.

"Oh, my God." He pointed at it as it flew toward Defiance. "That's not any aircraft from before the Collapse." It sort of looked like the Space Shuttle, except that it was longer, more streamlined, with stubby fins at the end of each wing. And much, much larger. It also had no markings.

Lordy, Taylor thought, *it's landing like a giant jump jet.* Slowly, ever so slowly, it settled to the ground behind the generators. Its engines faded into silence. Again, the sound from turbine generators could be heard, singing their monotonous refrain.

"Let's go." Taylor climbed on his horse. "We've got to get to that flying machine and see what it is."

Chris's eyebrows rose. "Isn't that kind of dangerous?"

"Maybe. It's an aircraft, not a tank. It's out of its element. It didn't use any weapons at Perrysburg."

Chris's left arm was still only marginally useful; a souvenir from that experience. "I hear you, Taylor." She swallowed hard and gestured to Stanek. "Move out."

Five platoons of Clan soldiers mounted. They followed Taylor in formation toward the flying machine. Closing upon the barricade, gunfire erupted from the buildings to the left.

"Platoons 'A,' 'B,' and 'C,' stop the gunfire from those buildings." Chris pointed.

The three platoons dressed their ranks and wheeled off at a trot. They reformed into a line with a cry that started at one end of the line. They filled the air with Clan battle cries. The horsemen thundered into the foundry. The Clan battle group, held in reserve all morning, was fresh and fought hard. The fight was short and vicious. The Fed guards soon surrendered.

Platoons "D" and "E" continued at a walking pace behind Taylor toward the generators, with Van Minh's wagon following. The crossbow men had spent a long hot morning shooting explosive bolts and were tired. They voiced frustration they hadn't damaged the artillery piece.

They got within thirty yards of the jumble of metal that surrounded the artillery piece when a sharp "*crack*" rang out. A Horse Soldier toppled from his saddle. A companion dismounted and slung him over his horse. Each time the crack rang out, another Horse Soldier fell.

"Whoa," Chris yelled. "About face and retreat on the double." The battle group wheeled and galloped out of range.

"Holy shit. Will you look at this?" Stanek said. Six Soldiers had been shot through the center of their foreheads.

Taylor stood in his stirrups. "Ten silver pieces to the first scout who spots the marksman."

Several scouts trotted forward, hugging close to their horses. They rode fast, parallel to the barricade. Even after several passes, nothing happened.

Taylor sketched a diagram in the dust. "Van Minh, take the big crossbow in closer to the barricade. We'll send in a platoon to draw the Feds' fire. Chris, use the catapults to drop a volley of shrapnel bombs above the barricade, near the generators, fuse 'em for aerial explosions.

When you see movement, Van Minh, let 'em have it with an explosive bolt." Taylor looked up from the sketch. "Remember, don't hit the generators. Got it?"

"'A' platoon, mount up and move out," Chris called out. "Parallel to that barrier. Give Van Minh cover. If anything moves, shoot it."

The catapults moved a hundred and fifty yards from the barricade. They threw aerial bombs, starting at the far end and working along the ramshackle barricade. A dark, shadowy figure moved behind the barricade away from the explosions.

"A" platoon wheeled about, moved closer, and dropped a volley of arrows into that part of the barricade. The catapults continued their methodical patter of bomb placement. Nothing moved and no shots were fired.

"Look," Van Minh called. "Something is moving on the flying machine."

The machine started to vibrate, and a wing flap wiggled.

"It's moving. Wing it. Don't let it get away." Van Minh's crew swiveled the crossbow and fired a bolt toward the silent, stationary flying machine.

As the bolt neared the flying machine, lightning lashed out, more brilliant than the noonday sun. A jagged blue-white coruscation met the bolt in mid-flight. As lightning flared again, a vibrating chord of thunderous volume rolled across the field. Another beam of blue-white light lashed out. The giant crossbow shattered into smoking shards.

The soldiers' horses screamed, reared, and fled.

Van Minh's moans broke the ensuing silence. He was on the ground, blackened and burned, with bright red blood streaming from his head. His companions had been torn to pieces and carbonized. All sounds of battle faded.

Over the sound of the turbines, in the direction of the generators, came a woman's high-pitched voice, keening a message of despair.

CHAPTER THIRTY-SEVEN

"Mata ChaLik BuMaru, the Bird-that-Soars has arrived. It is attaching clamps to the two castings. I will put lifting hooks on the casting that is stuck in the mud." Bilik relayed his intentions to Mata ChaLik as he dragged the clamping hooks on long polycarbon cables toward the mud-covered iron ring.

In the distance, Billy heard a crackle of gunfire from the foundry. He concentrated on attaching the lifting hooks.

"Savages approach," the defense system on the Bird-that-Soars said.

Billy tightened the last clamping hook and ran to the barricade. The Clan horsemen drew closer. He took out his personal defense weapon and opened fire. After several shots, the horsemen picked up their dead, executed an orderly turn, and rode out of range.

So well disciplined, Billy thought.

Under Billy's direction, the Bird-that-Soars slowly reeled in the polycarbon cables. The muddy iron ring twisted upright and rose to the craft's fuselage. Magnetic clamps lowered to the pre-positioned castings and locked onto them. Once Billy was sure the magnetic clamps were in place, he returned to the barricade.

BOOM! A shower of metal crashed near him.

Never underestimate one's foe. It was a message that came from his tactics biocomputer. *Keep moving. The pattern of the projectiles is obvious. Soon, it will reach you.*

Billy moved immediately after an aerial bomb exploded nearby. As he moved, he caught a glimpse of someone huddling between two generator units. It was Joyce! She had not gone to the foundry with the others. Billy ran toward the generators.

It is dangerous to move in that direction, came another message from his tactics biocomputer.

Billy ignored the biocomputer.

An aerial bomb exploded above him. Metal shards raked him, ricocheting off his armored hat and slicing into his body. The impossibly loud sound and shockwave arrived simultaneously, driving him to the ground. It was the last thing he remembered as a curtain of pain crashed down on him.

ॐ

Joyce saw Billy knocked off his feet by the explosion. As he lay on the muddy ground, dark blood welled out to glisten wetly on his clothing at multiple points.

"Billeee." Joyce ran toward him. "Omigod, Billy." She slipped in the mud and fell on him. "Billy, I'm sorry, Billy, I didn't mean to hurt you." She ran her hands over his body and caught her breath. He was limp.

Another aerial bomb exploded nearby, and metal screamed past. "No," she cried.

It was death to remain here. Joyce put her arms around Billy's torso and dragged him toward the generators, sobbing and swearing. Several times she slipped in the mud. Each time, Billy landed solidly on top of her. She pulled Billy between the generators and pushed him under the massive steel casing.

"Please, Billy, don't die on me." Joyce opened his clothes to look for his wounds. Blood was everywhere. It was purple. His body was misshapen, like it had been broken in many places. His breathing was shallow.

I must be going mad, she thought. *Everything about him looks unreal.*

The world lit up with a brilliant light. A thunderous chord vibrated her entire being. For a moment she was blinded and deaf. Just as her eyes began to recover, there was another brilliant flash. Her ears rang with the sound of a gong that never ended.

The world became a red haze. Joyce brought her hands to her face. She licked her lips and her tongue touched her hands, still wet with Billy's blood. It didn't taste like blood. It tasted coppery, metallic, unlike anything she knew. She closed her eyes, reached out until she felt Billy. She pulled him close and wrapped her arms around him.

"Billeee," she screamed. "Dear God, please don't let him die." His body lay limp in her arms. "Billy, please. No-No-No-No-No ..." Her world had gone mad.

ح

Dixon watched the fighting from his fortified position on the bridge over the creek called Preston Run. His command group of Fed guards hadn't fired a single shot all day but had just seen the Clan soldiers storm the foundry.

Now, he thought. *The Clan's next move will be against us. We have two hundred and fifty guns, all loaded and ready.*

"Pass the word," he said to Ray Papadopolous, his aide. "We're going to see some action, and soon."

ح

The engines of the flying machine howled and stirred a cloud of debris from the vicinity of the power plant.

"Seek cover, now," Chris bellowed at the top of her voice. "The wind from that machine kills." Without waiting to see if any followed, she spurred her horse to a gallop and headed toward the foundry.

"Run," Chris yelled as she passed by Taylor.

Taylor spurred his horse.

The flying machine slowly rose, its vectored-thrust engines screaming. It pivoted in place until it faced directly toward the fleeing soldiers. Its nose rose slightly, as it began to move toward the foundry.

It had three huge, black circular items suspended under the main part of its body.

Taylor realized he wouldn't reach cover in time. He reined in the horse and dismounted. He grabbed the bridle and dragged it down. Reluctantly, the horse lowered itself to the ground. Taylor crawled next to it, holding the bit tightly and waited. The blast of air was warm and powerful.

Chris was right, Taylor thought. *It doesn't have the odor of burnt hydrocarbons.* The downdraft ripped at his clothing, and then it was gone. He saw the flying machine pass over fleeing riders, scattering them as it turned before reaching the foundry.

The flying machine swung west and flew low over the main road, directly toward the city with a rooster tail of dust following. Both Clan soldiers and Fed guards stared.

Dixon's command group hadn't been at Perrysburg, but now they had a head-on view of the flying machine's approach. It looked like a giant bird of prey. Its two openings at the front seemed to glare directly at them like black, evil eyes. As its landing struts folded up, the flying machine seemed alive and malevolent. It came closer and closer, until it was almost on top of them.

"FIRE!" Ray Papadopolous's voice roared out.

"NO!" Dixon yelled.

He was too late.

Two hundred and fifty guns fired as one directly at the flying machine. A sheet of flame rose from the bridge with a sound like a giant avalanche of steel. The lead bullets, moving at fifteen hundred feet per second, struck the flying machine with a combined energy of almost four hundred thousand foot-pounds of energy.

Almost simultaneously a flash brighter than the sun and the sound of a giant banjo chord filled Dixon's world.

It was the last thing he ever heard.

As the flying machine passed over the bridge trailing dust and dropping fragments of metal, a huge greasy-black mushroom cloud rose from the bridge. The howl from the craft became a stutter and the craft lurched downward. A part of its wing with the iron castings beneath touched a tall pine, neatly clipping its top off. The flying machine belched and an unsteady howl resumed as it passed low over the City of Defiance. It increased speed and rose in the sky toward the sun, now making a warbling scream as though hurt.

Mata ChaLik was shaken. It was first time in many generations any Qu'uda craft had come under hostile fire.

The craft's defense system had used its particle beam weapons to sweep the cloud of lead projectiles from the air, but it was too late, for the savages' guns had been too close. The defense system's reaction time had been slower than the time of flight of the lead slugs. They had smashed through the skin and the heat resisting tiles that protected the nose of the Bird-that-Soars. Several lead slugs had found the engines.

The ship's particle beams had vaporized water and fat in the bodies of the savages and caused a huge explosion.

The deep energy demands from the weapon systems had discharged the Bird-that-Soars' reserve energy. Its engines were damaged and had come close to slowing to stalling speed from the lead slugs and ingested flying debris. There were numerous holes in its heat shield and body. Power leaked from the engines through numerous holes. The instruments revealed if he shut the engines down, they would never run again without a rebuild.

Savages. Mata ChaLik felt his head crest engorge and shake. *Dry land egg-sucking mammalian vermin. They're a menace to the entire universe. They must be exterminated.*

Taylor realized taking the complex of the industrial buildings and the destruction of the defenses on the bridge over the ravine had given him the keys to victory. It was time to move.

The Horse Soldiers bypassed the Fed guards along the main road. They drove through the wrecked defenses at Preston Creek and its hundreds of burned and smoking bodies. Skirting the carnage, they crossed over the bridge into the city.

Defiance had no reserves.

The Clan quickly took the city and trapped the majority of the Fed's forces north of the main road against the river, where they had no supplies, nor hope of reinforcement. After two hours of fierce house-to-house fighting, they surrendered.

The Clan lost almost an entire battle group when the flying machine passed over them. The final assault on the city cost more casualties. Of the two thousand that started out, almost six hundred were either dead or injured.

Taylor followed a group of soldiers to the idling turbine generators. It was time to see what made the electricity.

Close by to them, someone was crying. He wended his way to the generators, carefully picking his path through the debris. On the way, he encountered a woman sitting on the ground, covered in mud and blood. In her arms, she held a small man in dark clothing.

"Billy, please don't die." The woman's tears had washed away the grime on her face to form tiny rivulets, leaving streaks on her dirt-covered face. "Please, Billy, say something to me." She invoked Billy's name as if in a prayer of desperation, over and over again.

Holy Cow, Taylor thought. *That's him*. Her use of the name Billy and the description of Billy Potato matched the man in the woman's arms.

We've got their leader.

Billy Potato was motionless and covered in blood.

CHAPTER THIRTY-EIGHT

"I miss you, Mata ChaLik." Cha KinLaat DoMar's voice was distant through the static and hiss of the comm-net. "Take me back to the Egg-that-Flies. I'm lonely. I'm tired of this planet. It's too bright, the sky is the wrong color. It's too alien. Send the Bird-that-Soars for me, please."

"The Bird-that-Soars cannot return to the surface. The savages' projectile weapons damaged it. It cannot be repaired before we depart," Mata ChaLik said.

"Mata ChaLik, I want to come back, to you."

"You must become a guardian-of-the-eggs."

"I'm not trained to do that, I'm an analyst—"

"The Bird-that-Soars cannot return. It is damaged and there's no time left to repair it."

"When will you come back, for me and our egg?"

"You must guard the eight-squared plus four-times-eight eggs that are on the surface. You must nourish the wrigglers when they come forth in eight-squared times-two days. You must train them to be social and conforming Qu'uda." Mata ChaLik paused. "We shall return in eight-to-the-fourth days."

"Eight-to-the-fourth days." To Cha KinLaat those words were a ten-year sentence in Hell.

"Mata ChaLik, you must send the Bird-that-Soars back for me as soon as it is repaired. You can do it, I know you can. You're the spokesperson for the Keepers-of-the-Egg; you're at the center. For me, our egg, please."

"The Keepers-of-the-Egg chose you to be the guardian-of-the-eggs and trainer of the wrigglers. Someone must do it, and you are there. You have had some of the modifications, so you can survive that world. You must accept your role. It matters little, since you are not close to the center, anyway. Besides, the native species of this planet are too dangerous for us to risk further contact without war craft."

"Please," Cha KinLaat said, her voice reduced to a whimper. "Don't leave me here."

"When we return, it shall be with Birds-of-War. You must make do with the supplies on hand. There will be no more. You must adapt and learn what is useful. We will need your knowledge so that we may survive on this world."

"But, but—"

"Prepare your biocomputer to receive a data file. It is survival information Bilik Pudjata gathered. The Keepers-of-the-Egg are finished with him. He is cast out from our circle, gone forever. Cha KinLaat, this is the best I can do."

Mata ChaLik hesitated. "I shall miss you."

"Don't leave me, please."

"Good-bye." Mata ChaLik cut the comm-net link as soon as he downloaded the data file. *Even if I do miss Cha KinLaat, there are many more females on the Egg-that-Flies. I should not have any problem finding a new coupling partner.* He'd already received praise from the Keepers-of-the-Egg after he'd told them he had persuaded Cha KinLaat to stay on the surface as guardian-of-the-eggs. It was a move he needed to do to get back to the center.

ও

Dr. Encirlik peeled the clothing off the strangely shaped wounded man. She had given up trying to cut them off after her scissors and scalpel became dull from the effort. The man also had a padded inner vest and trousers made from a similar fabric. She'd discovered his hat was really a helmet, which probably had saved his life by deflecting the shrapnel away from his head.

As Dr. Encirlik examined him, the hair on the back of her neck rose. *Something is wrong, very wrong*, she thought.

Not only is his physical structure unfamiliar, his knee joints are backward, too. As she cleaned its wounds, she realized the blood was not red, but closer in color to purple. This was unlike anything she had ever seen. The patient continued to breathe slowly and shallowly, with a body temperature elevated to fever levels. He showed no signs of reviving.

"Taylor, I don't know what it is or where it's from. It isn't human. It may not even be a mammal. I wish I had an X-ray machine to check its skeletal structure. This is totally beyond anything I've ever seen, even in medical school. I'm afraid to use any medication on it." Dr. Encirlik sighed.

"Yes?" Taylor listened intently.

"If I suspended my grasp on reality, I'd guess this creature is a member of a reptile family. Look, the pupils in its eyes are slits, here's a vestigial tail and a skin flap covers its genitalia. I'm not even sure what gender it is, if gender is the right word. Look, there are scars on the sides of the fingers. I think it may have had the connecting skin flaps removed. This hair looks like a transplant. Its fever worries me most. I'm afraid to use a cold-water bath to bring its temperature down." Dr. Encirlik's voice pitched higher than normal and her pupils had dilated.

Taylor had to agree this was one strange creature. "Let me see if anyone can shed any light on his condition."

"Who, for example?"

"I'm going to start with the woman who was with it by the generators. I'll get back to you if I find anything out. I need it alive—it's the key to getting answers. Keep it warm and undisturbed and hope that it regains consciousness. If it does, first ask it what's required to treat it, and then send for me."

CHAPTER THIRTY-NINE

"Hello, I'm Taylor MacPherson." The long-faced man just seemed to appear in front of Joyce. "What's your name?"

Joyce lay on the bed and stared at the flaking paint on the ceiling. The stories she had heard about MacPherson, the war leader, made her want to keep her mouth closed.

"I need some information." Taylor paused, obviously choosing his words carefully. "There's a problem. There's no one to look after your friend."

"My friend?"

"Yes, the one we found with you."

"Billy's dead. Hell, I was there when he got killed."

"He's alive, just barely, unconscious and running a fever."

Joyce felt as though her world had just gone upside down. "Billy's not dead?" She sat upright, holding the sheet up to her neck.

Taylor nodded. A trace of sweat glistened on his tanned brow. "He's in the hospital."

"Omigod." Joyce put her hand to her mouth. The sheet slipped from her hands. "Can I see him? Please."

"Okay, but who are you? How do you know this Billy?" Taylor asked in the tone of voice that expected an answer, his eyes never leaving her face.

"Joyce Vargas." She thought about their relationship. "Billy's my friend. Well, I mean, I work for him on the generator and electrical equipment."

"Where's Billy from?" he asked.

"I'm not sure. I think he's a foreigner." She wasn't sure she should reveal what she had been told in confidence. They had put him in the hospital. That meant someone cared. "He comes from some place very far away, but he's going back—"

"Going back where?"

"I don't know. The last time we talked, he said something about going away." Concern for Billy made her speak. "Where is he? I want to see him."

"We'll go see him. But first, put some clothes on." Taylor turned toward the ill-fitting door. "I'll be back in five minutes." He glanced back before closing the door.

Joyce grabbed the sheet and pulled it up. *Mercy*, she thought. *How long have I been talking to him with my boobs hanging out?*

Her clothes were on a chair, neatly folded. As she slipped into them, she realized they had been washed.

"That Billy sure had a lot of clothes on," Taylor said as he directed Joyce toward a low, wooden building. A group of guards stood by its door. "Probably saved his life." The late afternoon was muggy. Heat lightning flickered on the horizon amid towering clouds that had a greenish-purple cast.

"Billy always wore a lot of clothing. It didn't matter whether it was hot or cold." *Dear God*, she thought, *I hope he's all right.* "He's a good man and he's done a lot for us. That explosion hit so hard, I was sure he was dead. When it happened, I really didn't feel like I had anything left to live for."

Billy's alive. Her heart sang. *I'm going to see him.*

"Dr. Encirlik, this is Joyce Vargas." Taylor pointed to a thin, wiry woman in white coat stained with blood. She had a gray pallor and bags under her eyes. She glanced up from washing her hands in a chipped enamel basin with the briefest trace of a nod.

Distantly, thunder rumbled.

"Do you know what Billy is?" Dr. Encirlik asked in an abrupt manner.

"What Billy is?" Joyce could smell disinfectant. "Why, he's the leader of the Midwest Federation ..."

"Don't get smart with me." Dr. Encirlik's voice had a harsh edge.

"Dr. Encirlik, please. I don't think Ms. Vargas understood your question," Taylor said. "Let me re-phrase that for you. Joyce, d'you know where Billy came from?"

"Billy never told me where he came from, 'cept that it was from far away. He spoke funny, like he didn't understand a lot of things. That's why I think he's a foreigner. He used to ask me what people meant when they said certain things. Like when the Clan delegation came to Defiance." Joyce recounted her conversation with Billy.

"That's all very interesting, but did you notice anything different about Billy? For example, was he physically different?" Taylor put out his hand to restrain Doctor Encirlik.

"Well, even though he's a small man, he's as quick as greased lightning and as strong as an ox. He must have been in a bad accident at one time because his bones seem to be out of place." Joyce remembered the moment they shared together. It seemed like such a long time ago.

"What did Billy look like to you without his clothes on?" Dr. Encirlik looked at her as though she were an object.

"I never saw him naked," Joyce said. *You bitch*, she thought. *I don't like this woman, this doctor.* "We were never intimate."

Dr. Encirlik ran her hand over her thin black hair and shook her head. "The elevated body temperature suggests it must have an infection. I've got too many of our own people to care for without worrying about ..." She paused. "This. There's nothing I can do for it, anyway."

"If we do nothing." Taylor furrowed his eyebrows. "Billy may die." His eyes never left Joyce.

"Please," Joyce said. "Do something."

"It's just I don't know what to do," Dr. Encirlik said. "And I don't have the time to ..."

"I'll take care of him." Tears came to Joyce's eyes. "Just tell me what to do. I'll sit with him. I'll do whatever has to be done. You see, Billy and I are ..." She stopped. *True, we never consummated our relationship, but* ... "Friends. I like him, a lot. There's never been anyone like him before. I'd do anything for him." Flickers of lightning momentarily brightened the dim room.

"Just keep Billy warm and hope for the best." Doctor Encirlik picked up several well-washed bandages and put them in her coat pocket. "I don't know what Billy is. I do know I've got too many other people who need help, casualties of this stupid war."

"You can't just let him die." Joyce wiped the tears that had begun to run down her cheeks. "It wouldn't be right."

"Maybe Dr. Encirlik can let you care for him, but first, you've got to know what you're getting into," Taylor said.

Dr. Encirlik drew back the covers and held a flickering oil lamp over the still and silent Billy.

Joyce stared. *It's Billy, all right, with that familiar deadpan expression on his face. Omigod, his body doesn't look right. He's not like any man I've ever seen. His rib cage is too long and has a raised central breastbone.* She glanced at his crotch. *Why, he doesn't have pubic hair or a pecker.* There was a bulging flap of skin where the penis should be. *Maybe Billy is a she. Have I been coming on to a dike and didn't realize it? His knee joints are wrong, too.*

Billy looked weak and helpless. Something made her stroke his forehead. "I don't care what he is, I'll look after him. When we started to like each other, he wanted me to know he was different before we went any further. I didn't realize what he meant." At that moment, she realized that he'd always been truthful. *I trust him even if the others don't,* she thought. "He's not from here, he's from somewhere else."

"It's your headache now. Dr. Encirlik, tell her what to do." Taylor turned to Joyce. "There'll be guards posted at all times. We can't let him escape. If he recovers, there are a lot of questions he has to answer. Do you understand?"

Thunder pealed nearby, and rain began to rattle on the roof.

"Yes." She sniffed. In a strange sort of way, she felt something like gratitude toward this gruff war leader.

ಌ

For several days, Cha KinLaat cried and begged into the comm-net, but its only reply was static. She tried to reach Bilik Pudjata but got no answer there, either.

Has he, she thought, *become insane and died from being expelled from the community?* She felt alone and abandoned. Her two female companions had received similar messages.

The unrelenting hostility of the creatures and insects of this overly bright world steadily wore her down.

Why? She thought, *why did I deserve to be cast beyond even the fringe, far from the center? Have I not done everything I could and more for our mission?* Insanity gnawed at the edge of her consciousness. *They just didn't care about me anymore.*

Now she began to understand what Bilik had experienced.

ಌ

Joyce bathed and cleaned the unconscious Billy for two days, watching over him day and night. She prayed for him, invoking the name of every saint she could remember. Billy's wounds rapidly knitted together without infection.

The scar tissue that formed on Billy's wounds was greenish-yellow.

CHAPTER FORTY

"Sir, sir," said a young boy with close-cropped blond hair. "Dr. Encirlik said to tell you the patient is awake."

"Good." Taylor turned and hurried to the hospital.

"It seems," Dr. Encirlik said, rinsing her hands. "All it needs is food and water. It's making a remarkable recovery."

"Let me see your, er, patient," Taylor said.

"This way." Dr. Encirlik pointed down the hall.

"Oh, Mr. MacPherson." Joyce rose from the side of Billy's bed.

Bright sunlight streamed through an open window. Outside, sparrows squabbled over squatting rights in a leafy maple.

"Hello. Can you excuse us?" Taylor steered Joyce toward the door before she could answer. "I must talk with Billy."

"When can I come back?" Joyce resisted his push. Deep lines made creases between her eyebrows.

"Later." Taylor raised his hand on her shoulder to guide her through the door.

"When will that be?" Joyce removed his hand.

"A couple of hours from now."

"Really?" Joyce's eyes narrowed.

"Really," Taylor said. "I promise." He nodded briefly.

Joyce left slowly.

After Taylor closed the door, he turned toward Billy, who was sitting up in bed. "I'm Taylor MacPherson, leader of the Clan. And you are?"

"Billy Potato. Leader of the Midwest Federation." He wore a loose-fitting robe that concealed his physique.

"Billy?" Taylor asked. "Is that really your name?"

Billy sighed. He had been unconscious for three days, sedated by his biocomputer while growth hormones speeded the healing of his wounds. He had been stripped of his clothing and examined closely.

They knew.

"I am called Billy Potato by the Midwest Federation people. It is the way they pronounce my name."

"Well, what is your name?" Taylor said.

"Bilik Pudjata of the Qu'uda." Billy used the deep grunting inflection used by his people.

"What?" Taylor asked. "I don't think I can pronounce that."

"Then call me Billy Potato."

"I see. Where are you from?"

"My home is so far away, if I tried to describe it, you would not understand." Billy did not want to antagonize this man who had been so ruthless in warfare.

"What was the flying machine that showed up at Perrysburg and Defiance? What makes it fly?"

"In your language, it is called the Bird-that-Soars."

"What powers it?" Taylor asked.

Billy thought about the question. *How do you explain advanced technology to a primitive savage?* "It is impossible to explain its power source to someone who does not understand nakru." He used the Qu'uda term for fusion technology.

"Try me," Taylor said. "I'm not ignorant."

"It works by combining matter, which, in their joining, destroys matter and releases energy...."

"What kind of matter?" Taylor asked.

"One is the type of matter that forms water."

Taylor took a breath. "Hydrogen? The lightest element?"

"Yes. That is one form of nakru." Billy paused. *This savage seems to understand.* "It uses a combination of magnetic and electric fields to start the reaction, which releases large amounts of energy."

"Your aircraft uses this as its propulsion source?"

"Yes," Billy said. "We use it for the drive system in our craft."

"It can't be fusion." Taylor took a deep breath. "Nobody figured out how to fuse matter, well, except for making bombs."

"Fusion?" Billy had caught only that part of his comment. "The controlled joining of matter? You have it?"

"No, we had fusion bombs," Taylor said with a bitter laugh. "And we used them to destroy our civilization."

"Ah." Billy sighed. "So, it was your fusion weapons?"

"Yes, it was our fusion weapons that did it. Enough of that," Taylor said. "Where do you come from?"

"Qu'uda."

"Cooter? Where's that?"

"It is a long way off," Billy said. "You would not know it."

"Try me. My computer has maps that show every city, town, village, road, and street that existed prior to the Collapse."

"Qu'uda is not on this planet. It is not in this star system. It is," Billy said. His biocomputer calculated the distance. "The distance light travels in ten of your years."

Taylor shook his head. "This getting to be too much."

"You have a computer?" Billy had heard Taylor mention a computer with retrieval capabilities. *This civilization may not be primitive at all.* "Is it in you now?"

Taylor stared at Billy. "What do you mean, have it in you?" he asked. "Do you have a computer in you?"

"Yes."

"You have a computer in your body? Now, at this moment?"

"I have two biocomputers in me," Billy said.

Taylor took a deep breath. "Where?"

"Here." Billy raised his hands and pointed to the bulges under his arms.

"How?" Taylor's eyes narrowed.

"Biocomputers are grown from neural tissue." Billy realized the

Clan war leader understood something about this topic. "I do not know that science well enough to say how."

Taylor stared at Billy, eyes wide, mouth open.

"Where is your computer?" Billy asked. "Is it in you now?"

"In me?" Taylor said slowly. "No, we don't use biological computers. Ours are electronic." He looked away before returning his gaze to Billy. "How did you get here?"

"In the Egg-that-Flies. It is a home that travels between star systems."

"Where is it?"

"It was damaged by a human weapon while in orbit around the Earth. That is the reason I am here. I came to make parts to repair its propulsion system. It must leave orbit very soon." Billy wondered what the crew of the ship was doing. On waking, he had started to check the messages stored in his biocomputer, but Joyce had distracted him.

"Prove to me you came from another star system," Taylor said. "Show me something that's totally different from anything on this planet. I know the distances between the stars. The time needed to travel between them has to be very long, or the velocity very high. Either way that requires one hell of a drive system."

"There is another type of fusion propulsion system from a damaged Bird-that-Soars in Defiance. It powers the electric generators." Billy paused. "Was hydrogen fusion technology on this planet only used for explosives?"

Taylor nodded. "That's right. Is the fusion system in the power plant dangerous?"

"Dangerous?" Billy asked. "How?"

"Well, can it be made into a bomb? What about radioactivity? Y'know, radiation?"

"No. In the Bird-that-Soars, there is a system that fuses matter without producing radioactive wastes. The system in the Egg-that-Flies uses a different type."

"Ah." Taylor said. "Aneutronic fusion." He stared at Billy for a moment. "Look, I know this is interesting, but it's going to have to wait until I check out the power plant."

"The fusion power source is a drive unit," Billy said. "It supplies a stream of heated atmosphere to the gas turbines. The fusion drive unit is about the same size as the gas turbine that powers the generators."

༈

Two of the three electric generators still hummed. Taylor carefully examined their power source. The more he looked, the less sense it made to him. The squat, cylindrical device, about twelve feet long and six feet in diameter, had no nameplate or any markings that he could read. Logic told him it was producing a steady stream of high temperature gas that fed through the turbines. There was no natural gas or fuel oil pipeline connection. It was, however, supplied with water, and apparently generated hydrogen and oxygen as a byproduct.

༈

"When're they returning for you?" Taylor asked.

"No one responds to my call," Billy said. He'd finally heard the message from Mata ChaLik, which told him what his crewmates thought of him. Their rejection triggered his depression, which began to paralyze his thought processes. He struggled to answer. "In about ten years. Not for me, only the others."

"Why so long?"

"They will go to the gas giant planet of this system and gather fuel," Billy hesitated. "They will also make weapons."

Taylor frowned. "Well, what about that flying machine, the Bird-that-Soars?"

"The Bird-that-Soars cannot return. It was damaged by gunfire at Defiance. They cannot risk their last shuttle. It would be too dangerous."

"Your own kind just up and left you for ten years?"

"If that were all, it would be nothing. Our species is very long-lived. We view time differently than you do. Unless there is a physical restraint, we can wait forever."

"Then what's really wrong?" Taylor said as he crossed his arms on his chest. His frown deepened.

"They will not communicate with me. Their last message was sent some time ago while I was unconscious. I just found it in my biocomputer." Billy felt lost and alone. It took effort to speak.

"The Qu'uda on the Egg-that-Flies will return and remove all traces of their technology left by my visit. Your people's war-like nature frightens them. They will make sure you will not have anything that could ever be used for interstellar travel."

"Why?"

"They are afraid you will get off your planet."

"I'm not sure I understand their fear. It's a damn big step to go from interplanetary to interstellar travel. We also live in a big universe. So, I really don't see a problem." Taylor said. "You mentioned the others, who're they?"

"Other Qu'uda who were left behind. They will guard the eggs, watch over them until they hatch," Billy sighed. "They will raise the young ones, the wrigglers."

"Eggs? What eggs?" Taylor asked. "What's this?"

"The attack by the orbital weapon was a great shock to the crew. That induced gender changes in many, who then mated and laid eggs. It is a survival trait of my race. There are about one hundred eggs in a hatching area on an island off the coast to the south. Three Qu'uda were left behind to guard the eggs.

"Soon, the Egg-that-Flies will send a near-light speed message pod back to Qu'uda to tell of their findings and your war-like nature. The Defenders will take every action to protect our species. Destroy you, if necessary."

"Why don't they just leave? There's no way we're a threat to them."

"Your war-like nature is the danger. That makes you a threat. After they eliminate you as a threat, they will use Earth as an outpost for other voyages of discovery in this sector of the star cluster. There are reasons to believe there may be other alien life forms beyond this star system."

"Oh, man." Taylor sighed. "I need to hear the whole story." He sat down in the chair next to the bed and put his head in his hands. "All right, let me hear the whole thing."

Billy told him about the Star Seeker's expedition and its encounter with the alien Hoo-Lii. He explained the reason for the iron foundry and how he made the castings to repair the Egg-that-Flies. He went on to explain that once the ship orbited one of the gas giant planets and refueled, its crew would gather materials from asteroids and rebuild the shuttles, and even create war craft.

"Taylor MacPherson," Billy said, struggling with his growing depression. "I am beyond the fringe of my community. My people on the Egg-that-Flies no longer want me. I am too different from them. I have become like an alien to them. I no longer belong. Therefore, I must die." His voice faded.

Taylor leaned forward to listen. "What d'you mean, they don't accept you?" he asked. "So what if you're different from them? Why must you die?"

"I must belong. Every Qu'uda must belong. If we do not belong, we become insane and die." Billy almost choked on the words. He did not want to face that reality.

"I sure don't understand," Taylor said. "You spent years away from your people making the parts to save their precious ship. Now they abandon you? Just like that? Why?" Taylor's voice rose. "Why're you letting yourself get into a funk because your people are ungrateful bastards?"

"They changed me to look like your people. That makes me different. Different is undesirable." Billy struggled to get the words out. "I have been here too long. I have taken on your mannerisms. Now I behave like you. To the Qu'uda on the Egg-that-Flies, I am an alien. I no longer conform. I do not belong, I have no community."

He turned away from Taylor and closed his eyes. Dark depression seized him. The fatal decline had started.

"Billy, you're here," Taylor said.

He felt a cool hand touch his hot skin.

"You can be one of us." Taylor's voice sounded distant. "Even if you don't look like us, or even act like us, you can still fit in here. Hells-bells, you fooled us."

CHAPTER FORTY-ONE

Taylor ran down the corridor and called, "Joyce." He spotted her. "Joyce, come here, now." He beckoned.

Joyce's head snapped up at the sound of his voice. "Me?" she said. "What's wrong?"

"Look, we've got a problem with Billy," Taylor said. "He's talking about dying. You've got to help him."

"Dying?" Joyce asked. "What've you done to him?"

"It's not us, it's his own people. They've disowned him, thrown him out. He needs a new home." Taylor paused. "That's where you come in."

"Me?" A frown filled Joyce's face. "What exactly have you got in mind?" She drew back from Taylor.

Taylor took a deep breath and began to speak slowly. "Look, Billy needs to belong, more than anything. He needs a friend, a home. His own people are aliens called the Qu'uda and they've disowned him. Thrown him out on the street, so to speak. It's driving him crazy. He's to the point he's given up on living." He shook his head.

"Aliens?"

"Yes, aliens. He's a being from another planet."

"Oh, wow. Now you say his people have disowned him? Are you sure it's not something I said? Or did you do something to him?"

"No, no, no." Taylor raised his hands, palms out. "Don't you understand? He needs someone to make him feel wanted. He needs to feel this is his home, here, on Earth, in Defiance. If you want to help him, prevent him from going crazy and dying, tell him how you feel about him."

"What do you want me to do?" Joyce chewed on her lower lip. "I'd like to help, but ..." Her voice trailed off. Her eyes narrowed. "What exactly do you have in mind?"

Taylor shook his head. "Please, I'm not asking you to do anything with him or to him." He took a deep breath. "I thought you cared about Billy. I guess I was mistaken." He looked away from her while watching her out of the corner of his eye. "If you won't help, he'll probably die."

"I do care." Lines between Joyce's eyebrows deepened. "Even if he's different, he's still special to me."

"All right," Taylor said. "Let's go see him. Now."

ᘒ

"Billy, it's me, Joyce."

Billy opened his eyes and stared. It was Joyce, the message-bearer. She was not his own kind. He closed his eyes.

"I'm so glad you're better." Joyce moved alongside the bed and slipped her hand beneath the covers to grasp his hand. "I was so worried while you were unconscious." She pulled his hand up to her lips.

"I know you're a Cooter from somewhere else. It doesn't matter, Billy, I still like you. Please don't go, stay. You belong here. The people need you, I need you." She put her hand on his shoulder.

"Joyce." Billy raised his hand and touched her face.

"Oh, Billy." Joyce leaned her head against him.

"I cannot leave. I am not wanted anymore."

"Oh, Billy, I'm so glad you're staying." She sighed. "I was afraid you'd leave. You're the only person who has made me feel like this. You belong here, with me."

"Joyce, we talk, but to what purpose?"

She squeezed his hand and kissed him on his forehead. "Oh, Billy, you mean a lot to me."

"I cannot join the Earth people. It is just not possible. How could you accept me? I am not the same species."

Taylor spoke from the doorway, "You can belong here."

Joyce nodded. "He's right."

"I am not the same as you. I am Qu'uda, which is alien to you."

"Our culture has a history of accepting strangers," Taylor said. "At one time, it was known as a nation of immigrants."

"How can your species be both violent and accepting?" Billy grew silent. "I have been away so long, it makes my memory of Qu'uda seem almost unreal."

"You're the best leader the Midwest Federation ever had," Joyce said. "You did more for us than any of our previous leaders. The people knew that and they died for you. Whether you realize it or not, you've belonged here ever since you became our leader. You were the center of our community."

Her words triggered a feeling within Billy reminding him of earlier times. It was like a great weight had been lifted from him and fear started to evaporate. "What will I do now?" It is strange how this Earth woman could say things that mean so much. It was like she had a special insight.

"Well." Taylor paused for a moment. "How would you like to be a teacher? An educator who brings us out of our primitive savagery."

"Perhaps," Billy said slowly. "I know much about Qu'uda technology. There is much information in my archives."

"You can belong here, we need you." Taylor spoke rapidly. "You see the Midwest Federation and the Clan will merge. Its representatives will become Clan Elders and your people will have the same rights they always had." He paused and frowned. "You won't be a leader. We've got more important things in mind for you. Teach us what you know. Get your computer talking to ours." He nodded.

"Yes," Billy said. "That role might be useful."

"We must spread fusion drive technology widely. When the Qu'uda come back, they'll never be able to remove it," Taylor said. "They'll also get one helluva surprise."

ॐ

"The motion reads as follows: Midwest Federation shall unite with the Clan with four new members to expand the Council of Elders up to a total of nine members. The new Elders shall be elected from the cities of Defiance, Napoleon, Bryan, and the western farming communities. The people from the Midwest Federation shall retain all lawfully acquired properties and enjoy the same rights and privileges as every Clan member. All those in favor signify by raising their hands," Taylor's voice rang out over the packed council chamber.

"Aye." The Elders approved the measure unanimously.

"The next item is the question of the establishment of a university. Mr. Billy Potato has agreed to be the first instructor at the University of High Technology to train people on the use of Qu'uda technology. Will the Clan approve the level of funding for the university in the budget package? All those in favor, signify by raising their hands." Taylor stared at audience in the chambers.

Many smiled. They already knew the outcome, for the Council had thoroughly discussed the issues over the past two weeks. The Council meeting was a formality.

"Aye." The Elders spoke in unison. Even though it was not stated, it was understood that Taylor would lead the new school after stepping down from the Council.

Taylor was tired. The campaign and the events of the past month had left him drained. He was determined to set the Clan on a course that would restore a technological civilization. He realized the next years would be as challenging as the first years of the formation of the Clan.

Perhaps the Qu'uda will come back and try to take away our keys to freedom and put us back in the prison of low technology and ignorance. Taylor was now sure the Clan would see the dawn that would take them out of the night brought on by the Collapse.

It would be time to work hard to build a critical mass and get the university established. Billy had already shown them how the fusion drive unit worked, for it was the essence of simplicity. However, it would require much effort before they could replicate it due to the materials required for its construction. Taylor had an objective to build a fusion power unit within five years.

Billy assured him the goal was achievable. There was an abundance of electrical power, and his biocomputers' archives had plans for a wide range of technologies. Billy had a nucleus of trained workers in Defiance and Taylor had technicians at his laboratory at Berea. Their joint resources would start the university. Joyce had already agreed to join Billy on its staff and teach electrical engineering.

৲

The fusion drive of the Egg-that-Flies drew a long, pencil-lead thin stream of blue-white fire across the night sky as it fled its orbit around the Earth. The fiery trace slowly moved north across the night sky to disappear over the horizon. The next night it reappeared as a tiny dot of light, only to grow smaller and smaller, eventually lost among the stars.

Its departure left Bilik Pudjata with mixed feelings. It meant his former identity had truly died. From now on, he would be Billy Potato, a man of Earth, belonging to a new community, with a new home and a new identity.

৲

Andros Island.

The sight of the departing Egg-that-Flies depressed Cha KinLaat DoMar.

She had just dropped her egg under primitive conditions amid a wealth of filth, with no pain deadeners or community support. She felt rejected, neglected, and on the edge of insanity. The smug, complacent Qu'uda community that had rejected Bilik Pudjata, had abandoned her, too.

As a guardian, she was a failure. Already, a long, low reptile with large, teeth-filled jaws had eaten several of the eggs. Her leg throbbed from the wound she'd gotten when she'd fought and killed it.

The tidal flats had a plethora of life, its many creatures swam swiftly and were difficult to catch. Flying creatures sought to feed on her eggs and tiny creatures sought to take her blood.

Life was harsh on this bizarre and brightly lit planet. Her skin itched from the ultraviolet radiation. When hunger had overcome her squeamishness, she'd killed a long, sinuous creature and eaten it. Now she felt sick to her stomach. She had changed. No longer did she value docility and the desire to conform; that was a thing of the past. When the Egg-that-Flies returned, Cha KinLaat knew she would find those who cast her aside in this desolate place.

The seed of hatred had germinated.

She vowed vengeance.

ABOUT THE AUTHOR

Malcolm Wood, born in England, came to the USA at age fourteen and graduated from Aurora, Ohio High School and Kent State University with a degree in chemistry while working full-time. Three years later, he fulfilled a self-made promise and spent two years traveling around the world. After resuming a career in chemistry, he obtained a MA in economics. About thirty years ago, he became a registered professional engineer in two disciplines (petroleum and environmental engineering), leading to a career in finance, and later, environmental consulting.

It was about this time he resumed writing fiction while working for a company that prepared economic analyzes on specific industry sectors. Since these publications contained a significant element of fiction, it motivated him to start writing fiction. He attended numerous writing workshops and joined the Cleveland Science Fiction Critiquing group (also known as the Cajun Sushi Hamsters from Hell), which had such writers as Geoff Landis, S. Andrew Swann, Charles Oberndorf and Maureen McHugh. Their critiques and comments pushed Malcolm hard to improve his craft. Almost twenty years ago, he formed the West Side Writers Fiction critiquing group, dedicated to writing at a professional level. During this time, he finished twelve novels and a biography of his travels.

His activities include obtaining a private pilot's license and a competition driver's license. In addition to writing, he has found time to ski, hunt, taste wine, and enjoy gourmet food.

IF YOU LIKED ...

If you liked Stranger, you might also enjoy:

Collapse

by M.B. Wood

Ignition

by Kevin J Anderson & Doug Beason

Alternitech

by Kevin J Anderson

OTHER WORDFIRE PRESS TITLES BY M.B. WOOD

Collapse

Coming Soon:

Blue Gem

New Star

Dawn

Our list of other WordFire Press authors and titles is always growing. To find out more and to see our selection of titles, visit us at:

wordfirepress.com

www.ingramcontent.com/pod-product-compliance
Lightning Source LLC
Chambersburg PA
CBHW050253110726
47898CB00007B/2395